ABOUT THE AUTHOR

John P Crangle was born in Ireland in 1941 and educated in Dublin where he met his wife Maeve and it is in this city that they have spent most of their lives together. After a spell in the legal department of a large banking organisation he commenced studying aviation, qualified as a pilot and quickly rose to the rank of Chief Flight Instructor.

In 1986 he was requested to set up a flight training organisation at Dublin Airport and for 15 years he trained over 43 pilots to commercial pilot level, 27 of whom became First Officers with airlines worldwide. Some of his students are now Captains in their own right. Numerous trophies were awarded to him over the years and in 1996 through his wife's studies into the problems surrounding the Fear of Flying, he became very interested in this area and now devotes much of his time to this work.

He officially retired in 2005 which actually means nothing as he is frequently asked to attend conferences worldwide connected with the Fear of Flying and on a regular basis he is requested to give seminars on the Theory of Flight. He has written four chapters in his wife's recent book, Conquering your Fear of Flying by Dr Maeve Byrne Crangle, which has been translated into six languages and is sold worldwide.

This small input into writing inspired him to pen his first fictional novel which he freely admits has given him great pleasure and much enjoyment. He travels extensively with Maeve and if one were to ask him to sum up his life in broad-spectrum, he would simply say that it has been one big party.

January 2009

DEDICATIONS

This book is dedicated to my loving wife Maeve who, having listened to this story for over twenty-five years, has finally seen it in print. I want to sincerely thank her for all her assistance but, most essentially I want to thank her for her eternal love and devotion for without her contribution this book would never have reached fruition.

I am also indebted to my good friend Alan Murphy for all his direction and guidance which he gave so freely when I was embarking on this journey.

I would especially like to thank my sister-in-law, Winnie, for being such a good and patient listener and also Gail Richards for all her very incisive editing.

And finally my heartfelt gratitude to my very good friend Marlou Norman of The Book Angels for bringing everything together in such a pleasant, amiable and professional manner.

McDonagh

14/5/2010

To my good friend and companion, Danny,

THE

TRANSATLANTIC

CONSPIRACY

with Best wishes

JOHN P CRANGLE

John

Published 2009 by arima publishing

www.arimapublishing.com

ISBN 978 1 84549 368 4

© John P Crangle 2009

Typeset in Garamond 13/16

Swirl is an imprint of arima publishing.

arima publishing
ASK House, Northgate Avenue
Bury St Edmunds, Suffolk IP32 6BB
t: (+44) 01284 700321
www.arimapublishing.com

CONTENTS

FOREWORD

In order to understand the powers and influence of the Catholic Church in Ireland we must return to the middle of the eighteenth century when Ireland was under British rule. This was not a pleasant time in this green and fertile land as the Irish people were uneducated, very poor and survived virtually solely on the potato. One of the most successful steps taken by the Catholic Church during its revivalist period in sixteenth century Europe had been the setting up of seminaries, which were special schools for training clergy. Most of these were destroyed during the French Revolution and when things settled down again only three were reopened: one in Paris, one in Rome and one in Salamanca. No such college was permitted for Catholics in Ireland.

In 1760, even though Ireland was a separate kingdom from Britain, with its own Parliament, it was still ruled directly by the King of England. With Britain at war again with France the Irish bishops, who literally controlled the Irish people, seized the opportunity and requested the Irish Parliament's permission to establish a seminary at the village of Maynooth on the outskirts of Dublin. Permission was granted immediately as Britain was afraid that the bishops might allow the French to infiltrate through Ireland, thus posing a serious threat to them.

In 1800, under the Act of Union, the Irish Parliament was abolished and this opened the door for Irish Members of Parliament to sit at Westminster. The same rule applies in Northern Ireland to this present day.

With the granting of the Act of Union, the Catholic bishops became even more uneasy as they thought they might lose control over the people. They need not have worried because the Irish potato crop failed in 1845 resulting in the Great Irish Famine which lasted until 1850. Over a million people emigrated and thousands died at the side of the road. It is ironic that Maynooth College rose to great grandeur and splendour during this disastrous period of history. The only person who died in the college during the famine was the Reverend President, and he died from natural causes.

However, in 1875 a well educated Irish gentleman called Charles Stewart Parnell was elected as MP for County Meath into the British House of Commons. At that time the Parnellite Party held the balance of power in Westminster and in 1886 it looked certain that Parnell would succeed in gaining Home Rule for Ireland which would give this small and impoverished country the same status as Canada or Australia. However, Parnell decided to marry his long-time lover, a divorcée called Kitty O'Shea. The controlling Catholic bishops condemned him from the pulpit as an adulterer for revealing this act of love and would not recognise his marriage. Parnell not only lost the Home Rule vote but also his Parnellite Party and died a broken man aged only forty-five. His biographer wrote:

"Parnell was a victim of the all powerful Catholic Church who preferred to see the man crushed than the people of Ireland attaining freedom."

In the general strike of 1913, much hardship was created and once again the Catholic Church was in the front line, openly condemning the striking workers. During the dispute priests physically prevented the children of striking families from being sent on holiday trips to trade union families in "godless" England, where at least these hungry children would have been willingly fed.

On Easter Monday in 1916 a group of revolutionaries and intellectuals pasted a Proclamation on the outside walls of the GPO in Dublin declaring Ireland a Republic. They then occupied the building. After much bloodshed they surrendered a week later but it was the beginning of major significant change as the signatories, as they were known, were all executed by the British. For the first time ever, popular opinion swung away from the Catholic Church and Ireland freely and openly entered into a guerrilla war of independence against the British. When peace talks were agreed and truces signed in 1921, the newly formed Irish Free State government and the weak Irish ruling classes fell back into the waiting arms of the Catholic Church.

After 800 years of British domination a new ruling body was standing in the wings about to take its place. In order to establish themselves the powers within the Catholic Church made arrangements to hold the thirty-first Eucharistic Congress in Ireland in 1932. According to a report from that time, the 1932 Congress was hugely significant in terms of asserting the identity of the Irish Free State as a leading Catholic nation. This Catholic enclave on the north western corner of Europe was totally untouched by revolution or reformation and, according to them, was to last forever. The article went on to say that this was to be one of the largest public spectacles of the twentieth century and Dublin was to become the very capital of the Catholic world. The *Irish Press* reported that:

"Hundreds of Bishops from all over the world marched slowly and pensively resembling a long red and white thread through thousands of priests who were wearing black cassocks with white surplices. It took over four hours for the procession to pass down O'Connell Street."

It has to be noted that since Ireland was such an impoverished nation, it took over twenty years to recover from the extreme costs and debts surrounding this event.

According to the *Official College Almanac*, in 1937 a meeting took place on the balcony of the prestigious Blackrock College between the headmaster, Rev Dr John Charles McQuaid, later to become Archbishop of Dublin, and Mr Eamon de Valera, later to become President of Ireland, and portions of the Irish Constitution were composed. Ireland remained neutral during World War Two and declared itself a republic in 1948. The constitution was then passed into law with bishops being consulted on every syllable. Among its articles was the following:

"The Republic of Ireland recognises the special position of the Holy Roman Catholic and Apostolic Church who will act as guardians of the faith professed by the majority of its citizens."

This article was not repealed until 1972.

In 1951, the bishops were instrumental in bringing down the Labour majority coalition government by likening it to a form of Socialism and invoking people's fears of totalitarian rule. According to an *Irish Independent* survey carried out in 1983 the Church in Dublin alone owned 234 churches, 713 schools, 473 private houses and over 100 community centres. The Church's fear of totalitarian aggression or communism is not surprising when you consider that its material base in Dublin at that time amounted to in excess of €170m.

During the 1950s and '60s – the period of time in which this story begins – hundreds of priests were ordained annually in Dublin. Every church had a parish priest with at least eight curates. Some had chaplainries in schools and convents which they regarded as full-time occupations. Every Irish mother of that time hoped that at least one of her sons would become a priest as it was looked upon not only as a blessing but as a very good career. Where are all those priests today? Statistics dictate that the majority of them have left the priesthood.

The Sunday Times of 11th September 2005 carried a review of John McGahern's autobiographical book *Memoir*. McGahern describes what it was like to be brought up in Ireland in the 1930s and '40s. According to McGahern, Ireland then was pretty much remote from what might be called European civilisation. The Roman Catholic Church controlled everything. It censored books, newspapers, magazines and films. It positively encouraged the corporal punishment of children. McGahern's first novel *The Dark* was published in 1965 and was denounced from the altar; he was sacked from his teaching job on the orders of the Archbishop of Dublin. He sought help from his union but unfortunately for McGahern the General Secretary sided with the archbishop.

By 1990 the child abuse scandals, which have been very well documented, were appearing every morning as banner headlines in our daily newspapers. In 1997 the "yes" vote in the divorce referendum was regarded as a great success for the free thinking people of Ireland. The bishops once again lectured their diminished flock from their pulpits but this time those within were not listening. This pious nation was breaking all the rules regarding Mass attendance, going to confession and the entertainment of impure thoughts. For years Irish Catholics had been kept in place more by fear of damnation than anything else, but those days were now over. The big loser in this referendum was the Catholic Church, as in their time they wielded great power, but they wielded it disgracefully. Despite their Christian rhetoric, they often failed to show an iota of compassion to those that really needed it.

This is the story of one episode from that era of domination.

J P CRANGLE – DUBLIN – 2009

PART ONE

IRELAND

CHAPTER 1

Approximately an hour and a half before dawn the captain made his initial radio call requesting clearance to descend into Irish airspace. It had just turned 5.45am Irish time as the Boeing 747 began to pass from night into day, and the brightness in the eastern sky heralded another sunrise.

"Shannon Control, good morning. Shamrock 104, Flight Level 330."

"Good morning 104, pass your message."

"104 inbound from New York, routing toward Achill. Request descent."

"Roger, 104; we have you identified; descent approved. Welcome home."

Brendan Duffy had slept most of the way across the Atlantic from JFK International and he was now being awakened for breakfast. After the service, the cabin crew in their immaculately groomed green uniforms started to distribute landing cards.

"Do you have an Irish passport, sir?" a bright young stewardess asked him.

"No, honey, I don't."

"If you are a foreigner, sir, you'll need a landing card," she replied.

"No, honey, I'm not a foreigner. I'm an American."

She smiled sweetly at him and offered him a card saying, "That's fine, sir, foreigners and Americans have to complete these cards anyway."

As the sun was rising in the eastern summer sky, the pilots lowered the 747 gracefully to make a perfect landing.

The terminal building at Shannon Airport was clammy and humid and swarmed with people. A westbound flight from London to Chicago had been diverted because of a bomb scare. The Irish Army were now searching the aircraft, which was parked in the centre of the airfield well away from the main building. All baggage from the diverted flight was being unloaded and searched separately and was then randomly delivered on any available carousel. In situations such as this, luggage can be delayed for hours, and Duffy was delighted that he had managed to secure his suitcase so quickly. As he walked out the exit gate he noticed the anxious looks on the faces of the stranded passengers, who were probably wondering if they would ever see their luggage again.

Outside, in the arrivals area, he found a drinks stand and asked for a black coffee and a Danish pastry. The waitress returned with the coffee and remarked,

"We have pastries all right, sir, but don't ask me where they came from."

He was a bit surprised by her remark and thought she was joking. He offered her a twenty dollar bill and as she wasn't smiling, he realised that her last remark was quite serious. As he shook his head to clear his brain she returned with his change in Irish punts. He examined the strange money that was now in his hand, with animals and harps on all its coins, and then she spoke again.

"You'd do well to change a few of those dollars before leaving the airport, sir, as they'll give you a lousy rate of exchange in all the tourist areas."

She went on to tell him that the mighty dollar would not stretch very far outside the boundaries of Shannon Airport and he started to ponder his situation. For the first time Duffy realised that the US dollar might not be as valuable as he first thought and, raising his hat, he gave the young woman a kindly smile. She looked up from what she was doing and with a cheery nod directed him towards a local bank. He thanked her once again, and this time he was pleased to notice that she was smiling back at him as she continued to arrange the cups and saucers on the counter in front of her.

As he sipped his coffee and picked at his pastry, he looked around and observed that the stranded passengers were mostly

French and British. They looked very nervous as they sat surrounded by numerous pieces of luggage. There was a distinctive difference between them and the happy outbound Irish and American passengers who were now checking in for the early morning departure to Boston.

On finishing his snack, he pulled his suitcase after him to the bank and at the cashier's hatch he offered ten twenty dollar bills for exchange. He was handed back £90.12 in Irish money. He checked again the rate of exchange notice board that was prominently displayed behind the counter of the bank as he was quite surprised to have received a lesser amount than he had tendered. However, he marvelled at the finger dexterity of the teller, so fluid of movement at such an early hour in the morning and he realised that he had been treated with courtesy and politeness. He also noticed that the entire procedure was completed without any hint of the stage Irish accent that he had heard so often in old Hollywood movies and on late night television chat shows. This indeed was a modern country.

He thanked the young man and made his way to the car-hire desks. He proceeded to rent a car from the company offering the best rates. After all the formalities were completed, he was given detailed instructions as to where the car was parked and informed about the keep left rule.

Then it suddenly dawned on him that he had crossed the Atlantic, there was a five hour time difference, he was not allowed to carry his weapon any more, the money was different, there were different rules for driving, and the only common link was the spoken language which, because of its lilting accent, sounded completely different anyway. Brendan Duffy PI had arrived in Ireland on Saturday 9th August 1975.

CHAPTER 2

Duffy was about five foot nine inches tall, with a ruddy complexion, balding grey hair, blue eyes, was overweight and dressed in a shabby double-breasted pinstriped blue suit, the jacket of which looked as if it was too big for him. He was trying hard to look respectable and every day his recovery was getting easier and better. He always wore a hat. As he sat behind the steering wheel of his rented car, he played with the gearshift. It was years since he had driven a car with a stick shift and now he also had to cope with all the new driving rules. In addition, he thought, he was driving on the wrong side of the road.

The car-hire agent's parting words were:

"You'll be grand, sir. Just don't stop for petrol for the first hundred miles, and – oh, yes – watch out for the roundabouts."

What in God's name were roundabouts, Duffy thought to himself, and also, what in God's name was petrol?

He studied the road map and left Shannon Airport in the direction of Ennis. He drove at a steady thirty miles per hour as he was not at all certain where he was going. As he drove along the road he admired the scenery and the green fields that reminded him of the patchwork-quilt landscapes he had so often seen when visiting New England. He was amazed at all the ancient ruins and stopped to admire the famous Bunratty Castle but overhearing one of his fellow countrymen remark: "Why did they build such a lovely castle so close to the main road?" he drove on very quickly.

At Ennis he turned left on to the N85 which took him all the way to Lahinch, the parental family home of Gavin O'Neill. It was mid afternoon when he arrived at this pleasant market town. He drove his car around the square and parked outside the local hotel that was situated on its south western corner. He carried his suitcase inside and proceeded to the reception area. This was a rural hotel, and everything moved at a very slow pace. Some people were registering in front of him so he sat down on a large sofa and comfortably observed what was going on. He found it hard to come to terms with the relaxed pace of life and was shocked when he saw that some of the waitresses carried only a single plate of food or a single glass of water at a time.

"This is a far cry from the hustle and bustle of Manhattan," he mused to himself, realising that there was no way that this would work back in New York. His daydreaming was interrupted by a cheerful greeting from the young receptionist.

"Good afternoon, sir; how can I help you over there?"

"How you doing? Are you doing OK?" he drawled back in his broad Brooklyn accent and she politely asked him if he was from the States.

"No way!" he replied in a jovial manner. "I'm from New York, New York."

She looked at him innocently as his joke failed to register with her and his face took on an embarrassed expression. He endeavoured to explain that he had just arrived at Shannon on the overnight flight from Kennedy Airport. She smiled pleasantly and advised him to take a rest and she would arrange a wake-up call so that he could come down for dinner about eight o'clock. This brought the grin back to his face.

"I could get used to this lifestyle," he thought again to himself, but dismissed the notion quickly when he realised that there was no elevator in the hotel. However, his worries were short-lived as he was informed that his room was only on the first floor. A young porter carried up his suitcase and, not knowing the correct value of his new money, Duffy gave him a handful of coins, much to the young man's surprise and delight.

"Thank you, sir. If there is anything else that you want, just ask for me, my name is Tom."

"Thank you, Tom," he said and when the door was closed he lay down on the bed fully dressed and fell sound asleep.

His telephone rang at 8.15pm. Startled, he took a fit of the shakes but quickly got himself under control with a series of deep breaths. The call was the reminder for dinner. He got up from the bed, and as he ran his hand across his face, he decided that he would shave before going downstairs. After all, it was Stateside since he last had a razor in his hands.

When he left his room and got to the bottom of the staircase, he headed directly into the bar. He knew this was not the place for him to be, but he was drawn within its doors like a moth to a flame. He looked in awe at the row of men, standing in tight formation along the counter, drinking large glasses of Guinness. Straight bourbon was his drink and he associated all beers as only fit for washing cars, but as he was now in Ireland, and as Ireland was the home of Guinness, he decided he was going to have one. One couldn't do him any harm.

He squeezed himself in to the counter as far as he could, and ordered a pint of Guinness, and qualifying his remark he pointed at the glass belonging to the man standing next to him.

"I'll have what he's having," he said, still pointing at the glass.

If this had been New York, that drink would have been back faster than he could have said Staten Island, but this was Lahinch on the west coast of Ireland, where there was a totally different speed for everything.

During the minutes that he waited, his eyes surveyed the entire room. He looked at the pictures dangling from hooks on the dark walls and noticed the cigarette smoke that hung like a grey haze around the mirrors behind the bar. As he adjusted his gaze, he suddenly blinked as he saw his full reflection looking back at him from one of these mirrors, and sobriety hit him full smack in the face.

"Jesus H Christ, what the fucking hell am I doing in here?" he muttered and in an act of panic he excused himself, pretending to the man standing beside him that the barman probably did not fully understand his accent anyway. By the time he reached the exit, a bewildered barman had returned with a perfect creamy pint of Guinness and was placing it on the counter, at the exact spot that Duffy had just vacated.

"Where did the Yank go?" the barman asked in a surprised tone, and almost immediately another customer spoke up,

"Don't worry, Michael, sure I'll have that one."

Duffy was now in the dining room panting and sweating profusely, thanking his lucky stars and all the saints in heaven for saving him. He got the shakes again when he realised that he had been so close to disaster. One sip and he would have thrown away everything that he had gained during the past six months following his rehabilitation in St Thomas' Psychiatric Hospital on Long Island. How stupid he felt and thought how many times in the past he had decided that 'just one wouldn't do any harm' and within days he was back in the detoxification ward again. This time he had made up his mind that he was never returning to an establishment like St Thomas'.

He stumbled to a table and sat down. He picked up the menu and as it was a set dinner, decided to have the full three course meal. Apart from being addicted to drink, he was also addicted to food, but that was alright. Following the soup, his main course arrived, and after moving the mountain of vegetables aside he was pleased to discover thick slices of roast beef.

The following morning he awoke late and had a light breakfast in his room. He called Tom and asked him if he knew where the Turlough O'Neill family residence was located. He was told that Mrs O'Neill lived on her own in a fine house about six miles out of the town on the Kilkee Road. Duffy got into his car and drove out to the farm where he saw a sizeable herd of cattle and a neatly kept farmhouse. He noticed three or four farmhands attending to their daily chores and everything seemed to be quite normal. This was enough to let him know that Gavin came from a good family background. In his mind he had never doubted this, but still he had wanted to inspect everything for himself. He thought about all that had happened in the family over the past few years, and he was unsure if tensions still persisted, so he left well enough alone and did not enter. He was content with what he saw and drove back into town.

Duffy was a keen golfer and followed the four Majors with great enthusiasm. He had never played a championship course but knew that Ireland had many such venues. He enquired at the hotel where the famous Lahinch golf course was located and was directed out on to the coast road. When he arrived, he got out of his car and just stood there. He removed his hat and, scratching his head, looked totally bewildered.

"How the hell could anyone in their right mind play golf on a place like that?" he mumbled. "It's all bloody sand dunes and bracken. Where the fuck are the fairways? I never saw anything like this in my life before."

He loved the game of golf but there was no way he was going to tackle such a course that did not compare to the manicured parkland courses of the United States. It was then that he remembered that Ireland was famous for its links courses which were totally different to the courses back home. In fact, the games could be described as two very different and distinctive sports. He just buttoned his jacket, got into the car and drove back to Lahinch. Once there, he made his way to the Catholic Church and asked a woman who was inside polishing the seats if she knew where the rector was.

"Wrong name, mister," she informed him as she kept polishing the wooden pews. "He's the parish priest and he's a canon, but we all just call him Father. Sometimes he can be terrible cranky and when he gets into one of his moods he acts just like a misplaced Pope."

"Do you think I could see him?" asked Duffy with a smile on his face and she showed him the way to the parochial house.

"Thank you, ma'am," he said, respectfully touching his hat as usual, and the woman nodded politely and continued with her polishing.

He walked up the steps of the parochial house, knocked on the large mahogany door of this very impressive building and realised that he must be encountering a very important member of the community. He was shown into a sitting room by a thin frail-looking woman in a very prim suit. A few minutes later a rather rounded priestly gentleman appeared. Duffy introduced himself and enquired after a Father Joseph Slattery. He was informed that Father Slattery had retired and was now living in a nursing home in the West Cork town of Clonakilty. He asked the Canon if he knew of a Father Fagan and was informed that he had never heard of the man. After exchanging a few more pleasantries, they shook hands and Duffy raised his hat again and returned to his car.

He had made a definite start on his many enquiries and it was crucial that he tracked down Father Slattery, as Duffy always believed that the only place to start investigations was at the source. He realised however that he was still jet-lagged from his transatlantic flight so he drove back to the hotel, requested a wake-up call for dinner and went to bed. Never did a bed feel so comfortable and he was asleep in seconds. After dinner that evening he went directly back to bed again, and slept right through the night without interruption.

The following morning he made his way to the dining room and was served a full Irish breakfast, which in the States would have sufficed as an evening meal. He paid his bill, thanked everyone for their hospitality and set off in the direction of Clonakilty.

He drove down the road to Killimer and took the car ferry to Tarbert. The hour long trip across the mouth of the Shannon river gave him plenty of time for reflection. He thought of all the unsavoury places he had frequented in his career and all the rogues and vagabonds that he had been associated with throughout his working life. Now at the age of fifty-six he hoped that there still might be a slim chance of him finding happiness in this vast and wonderful world. He was aching to meet someone special, and since he had stopped drinking he knew he would be a faithful companion and a dedicated friend. Chucking the booze was one thing, but he also needed a reason for living in order to stay stopped. All these thoughts whisked through his mind as the car ferry ploughed its way across the Shannon Estuary.

CHAPTER 3

As the Ennis bus rolled into Lahinch, Gavin O'Neill looked out through its misted windows at the arrays of Christmas lights that adorned the shop windows in its long main street. It was 1952, he was just twelve years old, and he was returning home for his Christmas holidays, having completed his first term in a Dublin boarding school. He could hardly believe that he was actually in Lahinch again. During the last three and a half months he had thought of nothing else; only what this moment was going to be like.

At the beginning of term in September, his home-made calendar, pasted to the inside flap of his desk, had totalled 104 days to the Christmas break. The desks in this austere study hall were only a few feet apart and at the top of the hall was a large pulpit-shaped lectern desk, with steps on either side, which gave the supervising cleric a perfect view of every student. On the walls were paintings of various saints and venerable people looking down at him with what he imagined to be disapproving stares, but today Gavin hadn't cared. Today was 17th December and his list calendar read zero. The long-awaited date had arrived. He was going home.

The journey from Dublin to Ennis by train was long and tedious. The train shunted along through winter fields and small towns, but Gavin didn't mind as he felt so happy. Even though he was only a few hours out of Oakwood College, he felt as if it was now a distant memory. He transferred to a bus at Ennis, and he knew that his parents would be waiting for him at the Lahinch depot.

When the bus came to a halt in the town square, Gavin eagerly made his way to the passenger door, which was located at the back. As he moved down the aisle between the seats, he looked through the windows to see if his parents were waiting for him. Suddenly his heart jumped with joy, for not only did he see them standing in the depot, but he also saw his old grand uncle Kevin who had braved the cold weather to welcome him home. This man was the most important person in his life. He was the *magic man* who willingly created so many toys from bits and pieces that other people had discarded, turning them into all sorts of things, such as river boats, model aeroplanes and even a pram-wheeled soapbox go-kart which Gavin proudly decorated with bottle tops. On certain occasions, he would darken the small hallway of his two-storey cottage with heavy curtains, turning the small area into a miniature cinema. On many Saturday afternoons during wintertime, Gavin would project still pictures of Donald Duck, Pluto and Johnny Appleseed onto a white sheet from a single frame camera projector that his mother had received from her cousin in America. Only a very special group of selected friends were allowed to view these "movies", and they would sit silently on kitchen chairs, watching everything attentively, as if they were sitting in the famous Metropole cinema in Dublin or the Savoy cinema in Cork City. This old man made everything possible for this little boy whose imagination was one of his greatest possessions.

"Heavens, how you have grown!" exclaimed Gavin's mother. "Nothing seems to fit you any more." His father was a man of deep feeling but he was unable to express it. He approached Gavin in his usual bashful way, and touching him on the shoulder, welcomed him home. This simple gesture in itself took a great deal of effort, yet Gavin knew that it was sincere. Finally, his uncle Kevin was next in line, and he lifted the boy up high in his arms and told him that there might be snow overnight, so he had made him a wooden toboggan that tomorrow would skim across the ground. On hearing this, Gavin beamed from ear to ear and gave the old man a big hug. Now he definitely knew that he had arrived home safely. He was the happiest boy in the world.

On Christmas Eve, nearly all the town's people went to Midnight Mass, which finished about 1.15am. As Gavin was now at boarding school, he was considered old enough to go to Midnight Mass this year. When they returned home he was given a hot drink and a slice of toast and tucked up in bed to await the arrival of Santa Claus. Gavin, like so many of the other children in the town, did not believe in Father Christmas any more, but it was better to pretend to believe, just in case. Tired from Midnight Mass, he was asleep within seconds.

After breakfast the following morning, all the presents were opened and then the day really got under way. He visited other houses, showing his friends what he had received, and in turn his friends showed him their gifts. In Gavin's mind, Christmas dinner was a long and boring affair that was mainly for adults, but he always stayed at the table knowing that afterwards he could amuse himself for hours with all his various presents. Yes, these holidays were very special times indeed.

Unfortunately, in times of great joy, there can also be great sorrow and quite suddenly in the middle of January, tragedy struck. Grand uncle Kevin died aged seventy-seven. Gone were Gavin's happy days that were meticulously planned for the summer months ahead. Gone were the soapbox guiders, the toboggans, and the cinema. On a cold and wet winter's morning, grand uncle Kevin was laid to rest.

The approaching date of his return to boarding school took the edge off his grief, as he felt that nothing could be worse than returning to Oakwood, but return he did. He was a diligent student and he came top of his class that year in spite of everything.

Gavin hated being at Oakwood College but he could never express these feelings to his parents. He just managed to get through the following years by utilising his gift of imagination that had been so brilliantly impressed on his mind by his grand uncle. He possessed the ability to transpose himself to any place in the world where he wanted to be, and this was what he did during those very tough early years.

As he approached adolescence his hormones were going in every direction, but unfortunately they were also trapped within the body that was trapped within the walls of Oakwood College. The strict rules of the Catholic religion were so engraved on his mind that every morning when he awoke he wondered if he would ever escape the fires of hell for another day.

One Sunday morning at general assembly all the boarders were informed that a certain priest was gone.

"Gone where?" was the general question. Gone to the Mother House was the only answer given. His name was never mentioned again but it was rumoured that some of the senior boarders had reported him for molesting a young junior boarder. The boy's name was not disclosed either and the matter was never referred to again.

It was when Gavin was fourteen that he secretly heard that his uncle Kevin had always disapproved of his parents' decision to send him to a boarding school. This kindly old gentleman had already raised an orphaned nephew and stated that he would have willingly looked after Gavin rather than *have him in that place*. These remarks were kept well away from his mother's ears.

Mrs O'Neill was a very strong-willed woman. She was quite overweight and spoke with a broad West of Ireland accent. There is no doubt that she would have been very upset if she had thought that any of her decisions regarding the schooling of her son were in question. In a small rural community it would have been a terrible reflection against her if the local population had ever thought that her only child had been sent away just because she couldn't look after him. The secret was kept safe, and Gavin never mentioned it, but he realised that his mother did hold great power and authority over all those who came in contact with her. He reconciled himself because he knew that his parents had sent him to boarding school only because they thought that the standard of education was higher than that of any local school. In giving him this fine education they believed they were giving him the best start in life and thereby doing the very best that any parents could do for their son.

During the summer term of 1955 Gavin took three golf clubs back to the college with him. Once again he transported himself in his mind and imagined that he was driving the best courses of the world, shooting lovely broad fairways and putting on the finest greens. He hit balls from every conceivable angle between and over the uprights of the football poles. He was becoming a very good golfer.

Gavin successfully passed his Intermediate State Examination, which was the first rung up the ladder of success towards university. As a reward he was allowed to go on the school summer tour to Rome, where he visited the Vatican and saw all the treasures that belonged to the Catholic Church. He marvelled at the Dome of St Peter's, the paintings by Michelangelo on the ceiling of the Sistine chapel, and the marble sculpture known as the Pietà.

The Swiss Guards looked very elegant in their colourful uniforms, contrasting completely with the ushers who were dressed in short black buttoned-up jackets, black hose, black knee breeches and black patent leather shoes with large silver buckles. These men preceded the cardinals and bishops and rang hand bells and banged the floor with long staffs in order that the people would part and make way for the Princes of the Church, who were dressed in red and scarlet robes. As these eminent Churchmen swished past in their long flowing red capes with scarlet buttons and matching threads, Gavin reflected that he was very far removed from their world and this left him feeling completely confused about religion in general and the Catholic Church in particular.

He thought that this couldn't have been the Church that Jesus gave to St Peter and this trip left many doubts in his mind. Instead of clarifying what the Church really represented, the more worldly goods and splendour he saw the more bewildered he became about the spirituality therein. As he stood in the centre of St Peter's Basilica, he thought of the parable which states that "it is easier for a camel to pass through the eye of a needle than for a rich man to get into heaven". Thinking of this, he found it difficult to understand how the Pope, the caretaker of all this wealth within the Vatican and the Catholic Church, was ever going to get into Heaven. These powerful and provoking thoughts challenged the preconceptions of his mind, but realistic answers were not forthcoming. A trip that was meant to enlighten him left him terribly confused.

He returned to boarding school the next September mindful that he had only two more full years to complete, so he set himself a task. He decided that he was going to spend the maximum time outside the walls of Oakwood that was legally possible. He commenced working on a master plan immediately.

The school was run by an order of missionary religious priests who spent most of their time teaching. Corporal punishment was still used for reprimanding students found breaking any rules, particularly the rule of absent without leave or *bunking off* as it was generally known. Getting outside the walls for a few hours of freedom was every boarder's dream, as some of these young boys were often prisoners from the start to the end of every term.

His strategy meant that he had to examine every possibility, and he was surprised when he discovered that academic achievement was not rewarded with *days outside*. Even the players on the elite football teams did not merit this privilege. His investigations revealed that the least likely but most beneficial of all was to join the Legion of Mary. The St Vincent de Paul Society came a close runner-up.

He discovered that all the members of the Legion of Mary got out of college every Sunday to sell Catholic newspapers from a stand outside the local church. Furthermore, the secretary of the college Legion of Mary was entitled to attend a presidium meeting every second Sunday in a church hall in Dublin. First things first, however: he had to make plans to get himself accepted into the college Legion.

Gavin commenced using religion to his best advantage. He deliberately became a model student. He sat in the front row of every class, did his work diligently, and became completely engrossed in all things "good and holy." He even became an altar boy. Eventually when the time was right, he got an excellent reference from the vice-president of the college, who was a friend of his father's. Gavin did not feel one bit guilty about doing this, as he remembered his uncle Kevin's words, "It's not what you know that gets you places, it's who you know."

On Sunday 2nd October 1956 he was duly elected a member of the college Legion of Mary. This was the first step completed, and the next move was to get himself elected as an officer. Early in the new year during the spring term, the secretary was taken suddenly ill with appendicitis, and Gavin volunteered to take his place – on a temporary basis, of course. Due to ongoing illness the secretary never returned and as Gavin was considered a suitable replacement he was automatically elected to the position permanently. This was the second step accomplished. He was in. Gavin attended his first presidium meeting in Dublin the following Sunday week.

He had cracked the system.

CHAPTER 4

Gavin had now commenced his last year at Oakwood College and he was determined to work hard at all his studies and pass his exams with honours. With his officership well established and secured within the Legion of Mary, he was able to spend as much time as he wanted outside the college walls.

In keeping with college tradition, the sixth year students had their own rooms in a special building that was also shared with some of the clergy. This separated them from the open dormitory floors where sexual abuse did occur from time to time. On a November morning in 1957, another priest was accused of *interfering* with some young boys in one of these dormitories and, instead of the police being notified, the matter was hushed up and the priest was quickly relocated. In those days no one criticised the clergy and this was the second such case during Gavin's time in Oakwood. Of course there must have been others, but these were the only two that gained any notoriety. He was disgusted by these revelations.

Notwithstanding this, Gavin was delighted when the Vice President of the college, the Rev James Gallagher, better known as *Jemmie* because of the copious amounts of Jameson whiskey he consumed, asked him if he would light the fire in his study each evening during the winter months and also serve his Mass on a Sunday morning. Even though the College was awash with priests, most of them had chaplainry duties in various convents on Sundays, so there were very few of them around for priestly duties after 10.00am. *Jemmie* was also the chaplain to the local battalion of army reservists. Lighting his fire was not looked upon as a chore but as an opportunity to better things, and Gavin jumped at the offer.

He soon discovered that this scholarly gentleman usually got boozed out of his skull every Saturday night, and was still too hung over to say his official Mass in the college chapel on a Sunday morning. This meant that on Sunday mornings Gavin was allowed to attend Mass in Donnybrook village. On many Sunday afternoons, *Jemmie* was seen sneaking back to his room, wearing his tight army bomber jacket over his clerical collar, and invariably looking the worse for wear after a skin full of drink. However, it also has to be said that he had a kind heart and every Friday night Gavin would find a packet of cigarettes and five single shillings on the table in his study. This he regarded this as his wages and he was using the system to his best advantage. Now, at last, he was running his own show.

Though he did attend some meetings on behalf of the Legion of Mary, most of his free time was spent in cafés. He met many people at the meetings, including girls – yes girls – which was a forbidden word at Oakwood. He had his first date following one of these meetings and this made him feel very important indeed. Gavin was now learning more about love and the fair sex than about Mary and the Virgin Madonna. This was a far cry from the timid little boy who entered this dreary establishment five years before.

Despite all his new adventures, Gavin always kept a very close eye on his studies as the Leaving Certificate examinations were coming up the following June and these were to be his ticket to university.

It's an unwritten law that the sun always shines brilliantly when sitting examinations, and the year of 1958 was no exception. Gavin had just turned eighteen. It was one of the hottest summers on record and sitting in the examination hall the heat was almost unbearable. The students who were not sitting state examinations had been sent home two weeks early so that they would not be a distraction to those who were revising and studying. As a result, there was a relaxation of all college rules and regulations.

Every evening Gavin would go for a walk along the banks of the River Dodder and return via the seafront. He would gaze at the familiar red lighthouse, situated out in the middle of Dublin Bay, which had become an everyday part of his life over the past six years. Dun Laoghaire harbour could be seen clearly in the distance, and as he walked along the water's edge at Sandymount strand he thought of Buck Mulligan, a character from James Joyce's forbidden book, *Ulysses*, that he had secretly tried to read on many occasions but always failed.

The evening sun danced its reflections against the top of the water, creating a gentle movement of light. Over the past six years he had never appreciated these simple views and now it was nearly too late, as it was almost time for him to leave the college and become a man. As he turned to stroll back to Oakwood, he heard the horn of the mail boat sounding farewell to Ireland once again as it left Dun Laoghaire harbour on its nightly pilgrimage to Holyhead. It brought instantly to his mind the thought of many thousands of Irish men and women who had had no option but to take that route, seeking out a new existence and a new life in England. These were serious times and none as serious as what might lie ahead, as a brand new beginning was awaiting him. Gavin was planning to enter the tourist industry.

On his way back along the Coast Road one evening he took a short cut that brought him to the side entrance of the college. It was there that he met some day-pupils from his own class and they were conducting post mortems on how they had performed in various examinations. Gavin never did this, as he reckoned that once the exam was finished there was nothing anyone could do to change the outcome. He simply worked out approximately how he had done by marking himself harder and stricter than any examiner could possibly do, and if he made it over forty percent he felt he was safe.

"Are you going to the dance on Friday night?" one of them asked him.

"I didn't know there was one on," he replied.

"Yes, we are going into Dublin and meeting under Clerys clock in O'Connell Street at 7.30."

"OK," replied Gavin. "I'd love to join you, thanks very much, and thanks for asking me."

"No problem," came the reply. "Great you can make it. See you on Friday night at 7.30pm. By the way, have you any more exams?"

"Yes, French tomorrow and Art on Friday and that's the lot."

He got on better with the day-boys than he did with the boarders, mainly because the escape mechanisms that he had put in place over the last two years meant that he could relate better to them. These were a great bunch of guys, so he was looking forward to Friday night. It wasn't the dance that really attracted him, it was the sociable company of his peers he was looking forward to.

On Thursday he entered the examination hall and sat at his small table. He had a pencil, a sharpener, an eraser, a ruler and his fountain pen. He sat and waited until the superintendent announced on the stroke of 10.00am that they could turn over their papers and begin. They had until 1.00pm to finish. The superintendent always finished the same way, by wishing everyone "good luck" in Gaelige, but on this occasion as it was the French paper he said "bonne chance". Gavin read the paper from start to finish, and found that he could answer five of the eight questions without any difficulty; he realised that even by his own high standard of self-marking, he had passed. He relaxed and completed a very comprehensive examination.

The following day he had Art and this was his last exam. He enjoyed Art very much and as he felt that he would do quite well, all pressure was off. He was constantly thinking about the dance on Friday night with his friends, and decided it was time to arrange his departure from the college.

It was 6.00pm on Thursday evening when he made his way up to the Dean's quarters which overlooked the quadrangle. He knocked on his study door.

"Come in," was the response and Gavin entered.

"Good evening, Father," he said and the priest acknowledged his presence by asking how the exams were going.

"Very well, Father," he replied. "I've my last one tomorrow. Er, I want to make arrangements about leaving college on Saturday morning, Father, so that I can phone my parents later this evening."

"Sorry, Gavin," came the immediate reply. "That's not possible. You have to be packed and gone by 2.00pm on Friday. You have to be out tomorrow."

"Eh, Father but I want to stay another night and leave early on Saturday morning."

"Sorry, did you not hear me correctly the first time?" came the response. "You must be out of the college immediately after your last exam tomorrow."

A long pause developed.

"Is that all?" enquired the Dean.

"Eh, yes, yes," stuttered Gavin.

"Well, good luck now, and close the door after you on your way out."

Gavin left the Dean's study very disappointed and terribly upset.

This was such a cold and harsh way to treat any young man who had been sheltered and practically reared within the bosom of this confraternity for such a long period of time. The clergy were simply not interested in him any more, and he asked himself if they had ever been interested in him in the first place. Gavin mulled over this dichotomy. Ironically he had spent six years mentally transporting himself away and physically working the system to get beyond the walls of Oakwood and now, on his final day, all he wanted to do was to voluntarily stay one extra night in order to meet his friends, and this was flatly refused. He couldn't understand their reasoning, but he had learnt long ago that there was no point in arguing with the Deans, as they were a law unto themselves. All things considered, he realised that they were not a caring community nor was Oakwood College a good place to linger any longer than necessary.

He was completely deflated and, as he had nowhere to stay on Friday night, he could not go to the dance. He did not know the day-boys' parents at all so he could not ask them for overnight accommodation and he hadn't enough money for a hotel bedroom. As he did not want to be wandering the streets of Dublin in the hours of darkness, the following morning he sat his Art exam and immediately afterwards packed his suitcase; then without a backward glance he got on a bus to Kingsbridge railway station and boarded the afternoon train for Ennis. He never saw those day-boys again.

CHAPTER 5

In that same year, Gabriella de Leon chatted with her classmates before rushing off to board the large green double-decker bus which stopped outside St Brigid's Convent School in Killiney. This bus also stopped at the bottom of Aylesbury Road, where she would get off and walk the short distance to the Georgian residence that had a large flag hanging from its tall white flagpole in the front garden. It was the Spanish flag and Gabriella de Leon was the daughter of the Spanish Ambassador to Ireland. She had been born in Spain but had lived in Dublin for nearly four years and she had just completed her Intermediate State Examination. Because of her origins, she was exempt from taking Irish as a compulsory subject, but she loved Irish history and Irish culture. She spoke English with a slight Castilian accent.

She could have had a private car collecting her every day, but she preferred the view from the top of the double-decker bus and just wanted to be like the rest of the girls in her class. During the short journey from Killiney to Aylesbury Road, the bus passed through Dun Laoghaire and she loved looking at the mail boat and the beaches, and admiring the red lighthouse out in the middle of Dublin Bay. She also liked the parks she passed and on occasion she was delighted to see the steam train puffing along the coast as it made its way from Westland Row Station in Dublin to the seaside town of Bray.

In her spare time she played tennis and was an avid reader. Apart from this she loved going into Dublin city and sitting in places like Bewley's Oriental Tea Rooms or the Rainbow Café where she would listen to Pat Boone records on the jukebox. She also enjoyed going into the large department stores such as Brown Thomas and Switzers in the fashionable Grafton Street area, and Clerys and Arnotts in downtown Dublin. For ages she would stare at the shelves of make-up and longed for the day that she would be allowed to wear some herself. She was delighted when her mother gave her an extra few shillings in her weekly pocket money, so that she could buy her favourite magazines.

She knew that in time she would possibly return to Madrid or live in some other capital city, but at the moment she was in Dublin and she liked being there very much. She was a very independent self-assured young lady and excelled in all her studies. She had just turned fifteen and was much too young to think any further into the future. Little did she know what an exciting future lay in store for her.

CHAPTER 6

The new sound of rock'n'roll had reached the West Coast of Ireland and had even made it to Lahinch. Bill Haley and the Comets were the first major breakthrough but Elvis was the man. He was hated by some and loved by others, but his music brought a new dimension to everyone, young and old. Every jukebox in every town was crammed full of these records and at the Strand cinema in Lahinch Cliff Richard was "Going on a summer holiday". Music was everywhere and Paul Anka had just written a song called *Diana* which was on everyone's lips. Buddy Holly and the Big Bopper were killed in a plane crash, but they left their legacy to others. A new generation of music had just been born.

America was still Ireland's nearest and dearest friend, and families were still going to Shannon Airport to catch the Constellations and Stratocrusiers to New York's Idlewild Airport. Many families looking for a better lifestyle left sobbing loved ones behind, never expecting to see them again. Tears were shed in every corner of Ireland as mass emigration was rampant throughout the country. Successive governments tried to stem the flow but it was all to no avail as there was virtually no employment in the rural areas. Dublin, which had a weekly moving population, was the country's hub. The workers would arrive into the city on Sunday evenings, stay in lodgings during the week, which was an industry in itself, and return to their home towns every Friday evening. It was once remarked by a Dublin wit, as he spent about thirty minutes pondering his pint of Guinness in a pub after Mass one Sunday morning, "Jaysus, isn't it great to get the city back to ourselves at weekends."

It was also at this time that the European Economic Community came into existence and Ireland voted to become a member state. Eamon de Valera, or Dev as he was known, was one of the leaders of the 1916 Easter Rebellion and the only one to escape death by firing squad, and now he was the duly elected President of Ireland.

During the rebellion, he had been the commander of a garrison at Bolands Mills on the south side of Dublin City and was sentenced to be executed with the other leaders. However since he was an American citizen by birth such an action could have affected the delicate Anglo-American relationships that existed. His death sentence was commuted to life imprisonment by the occupying British authorities at that time.

Religious oppression was still very widespread in Ireland and the Catholic Church still tried to rule with an iron fist. There was no doubt whatsoever that Church and State walked hand in hand on many occasions, depending which party was in Government. The Church opposed certain bills, brought down various government ministers, and even tried to stop Catholics attending Trinity College, which was originally a Protestant university. A dispensation had to be obtained from the Archbishop's Palace in order for a Catholic to attend this university. The Church's policies were dictated by John Charles McQuaid, Archbishop of Dublin, who was a defender of rigorous orthodoxy and strict conservatism and one of the most influential figures in mid twentieth century Ireland. As a Catholic by birth, Gavin made a formal application and was granted permission to attend Trinity. He did this more to appease his mother's feelings than his own conscience and the following October he entered Trinity College as a junior freshman.

The university of Trinity College is situated in the middle of Dublin and is bordered on one side by Nassau Street with College Street on the other. In front of its main gates are statues of Burke and Goldsmith, who appear to be overlooking the financial district of College Green and Dame Street. Due to the Archbishop's strict ruling, very few Catholics had ever put foot inside these noble walls. On his first day, Gavin walked slowly through the main gate and thought to himself that he was going to be very happy and contented for the next four years in this very dignified place.

Small tables littered the passageways as second- and third-year students tried to entice the newcomers to join clubs and societies. Voices echoed from every portal encouraging the new students to join organisations such as the Debating Society, the Art Group, the Camera Club, the Rugby Club and the Student Union. There was even a representative from the local bank offering student loans. These were essentially given to students on their parents' personal guarantees and the representative was only short of a notice hanging around his neck saying *poor students need not apply*.

The entrance fee to the various societies was only a couple of Irish punts, but even so, with limited resources, Gavin had to be selective. He knew that he had to join one or two of them, as this was the only way he was going to make new friends. As he walked across the cobbled stones, past the university chapel on the left, under the Campanile on the right and towards the Old Library, which housed the famous Book of Kells, he thought to himself that he had never seen so many happy young people in his entire life. Everyone seemed to be laughing and talking together with a definite purpose in mind and once again he felt that this college was the right place for him to be. It resembled an oasis, right in the heart of Dublin.

By answering various advertisements in the evening newspapers he managed to get a small room to rent in Ranelagh, the student quarter of Dublin. This area had everything to suit his needs, as it was near shops and was on a direct bus route to the city centre. He could cycle to Trinity in fifteen minutes and walk to the top of Grafton Street in slightly over half an hour. The room contained a bed, a cooker, a large sofa, and a wardrobe. A desk and chair were situated in the bay window area which overlooked a small garden. Little did he realise at this stage of his life that as the seasons changed and the years passed he would gradually get to know every inch of that ever-changing view.

The following morning was his first day in a lecture theatre. It was an overwhelming experience. He positioned himself about the sixth row back, close to the middle and noticed that others appeared to be as self-conscious as he was. He also noticed that some knew each other, while others sat motionless, seemingly afraid to speak. The lecturer entered the theatre and without looking at the class walked directly to the blackboard and wrote in very large print:

TAKE RESPONSIBILITY FOR YOUR OWN LEARNING

The lecturer then walked to the podium. He told the class that this was the greatest lesson they could ever learn. He went on to say that some would be very successful during their university days and go on to do great things, while others would drop out and fall by the wayside. He advised all to keep a journal during their first year, and write it up at the end of every week, particularly those who were taking psychology, as they would be obliged to write an essay on how they had grown throughout the terms. Gavin made a particular note of this as, apart from taking economics as his major subject, he had to couple this with another subject and had chosen psychology.

The lecturer spoke at length about the rigours of learning and studying, and ended by saying that the road to hell was paved with good intentions and that it was up to everyone here to decide which road to take. He left no one in any doubt of what was expected from them and Gavin thought that with all the distractions of university life he could easily be left behind if he didn't concentrate. He made an immediate decision to be as hardworking and industrious as possible without completely missing out on the social opportunities offered by university life.

Gone were the school bells that called him to compulsory study. Gone were the lurking priests who enforced the daily routines. Gone forever were his boarding school days. This was the start of an entirely new way of life which only he could control. After the lecture he met a couple of people, shook hands, enquired where they came from and asked if they were interested in any sports.

"Drinking and screwing, if you can call that a sport," came one reply, which brought smiles to those present.

"Seriously," one of them said, "I was a good hurler at the Roscommon Christian Brothers, so I changed my grip from left over right, to right over left and it worked, so I'm at the golf now."

"Great," said Gavin. "I play golf as well. What's your handicap?"

"The golf clubs," interjected a third party, and once again they all burst out laughing.

"We must have a round sometime," suggested Gavin. "There's a municipal course out at Howth, which you can play without having to be a member of a Club, and it doesn't cost an arm and a leg."

"Do you know something?" came a reply. "This conversation could be better handled with a pint in our hands, over in Davy Byrne's."

Gavin had made his first friends at Trinity College.

He spent many enjoyable hours debating various subjects and topics in Trinity's Buttery restaurant, Davy Byrne's pub, and Bewley's café. These were his main haunts and even though Gavin was not a regular drinker he really enjoyed listening to stories from others. Harry, one of his new friends, was studying medicine, and during the long summer break between secondary school and university had joined a circus as a general factotum. His major claim to fame was that he had shovelled all kinds of shit, from snake shit to elephant shit, and even got £5 a week extra for sharing his caravan with the dwarf.

"Do you know something?" he would say. "You see, my Ma was very friendly with the wife of the man who owned the circus, as some of the time they had a house in our street. They didn't always live in a tent. When I joined the circus, I had to go up to her caravan every night to let her know that I was OK as she took a special interest in me, and I would ring the bell and Peter would let me in.

"The lady would then contact my Ma and everything would be hunky dory, so I went up night after night and when I rang the bell, there was Peter to let me in.

"One night I had a few drinks on board, and when Peter answered the door I asked him if his mammy was in. Jaysus, it was so funny."

"What's so funny about that?" came a frustrated question. "Wasn't Peter their son?"

"No way! He was their fucking chimp."

"A chimp!" yelled Gavin, laughing.

"Yea, a fucking chimp let me in every night. He was the family pet; the same way as you would have a cat or a dog. If you think that's funny wait till I tell you about Sylvester the knife thrower, especially when he'd a few jars on him, and blindfolded as well. You see, he used to throw the knives to certain beats of popular tunes that the organ player would thump out on the organ. Once these loud pre-rehearsed notes were heard, Sylvester would let fly with his knives and, when done correctly, it was fairly safe."

"Bloody hell," came the amazed responses. "Fairly safe? That sounds fairly dangerous."

."Only for the girl," came Harry's boozy reply, "and you won't shagging believe what I am going to tell you next, because this particular night the fucking organ player and Sylvester were both pissed out of their minds. There was Sylvester blindfolded and trying to stand upright with six blades in his hand. The girl was in a one piece costume as usual, blindfolded and strapped to a revolving wheel and when the organ player fumbled the first loud note, Sylvester let fly and the first knife just missed the poor thing by a fucking whisker.

"The Ring Master had to cut the act short immediately and a couple of bollixes in the audience were actually shouting for their money back. I had to be held back as I was nearly going to deck one of them. To tell you the truth, the girl didn't react at all until her blindfold was removed and when she realised how close she'd been to death she got wild hysterical. Jaysus, we had an awful job calming her down and it nearly ruined the entire night."

Gavin's life was not only full of hard work, it was also full of lively happy laughter.

CHAPTER 7

As the year progressed, Harry, Patrick and Gavin became good pals and soon they were hatching plans for the long summer holidays that lay ahead.

"Firstly, let's get our shagging exams out of the way," said Patrick. "We don't want any re-sits in the autumn. That would really fuck things up."

This they all agreed and while there was a lot of companionship between them they kept everything evenly balanced with their studies. Some macho guys at university openly bragged about the things that they did with girls, and how they could always get their knickers down on the first date, but the lads knew this didn't happen. If any young women had actually made a pass at any of these so called macho studs, they would have run a hundred miles.

Gavin and his friends went to dances and hops, as they were called locally, and met different girls on a regular basis. Gavin didn't tie himself down to anyone steady but, like all young people of his age, he engaged in some lingering French kissing and heavy petting. In one voice, they all agreed that getting into a serious relationship at that time of their lives was not on. After all, the world was just sitting out there, waiting for them to arrive.

On occasions, Gavin had to go to University College Dublin, or UCD as it was known, in order to borrow certain books from its extensive library. On this particular Wednesday, as he was cycling up Grafton Street towards St Stephen's Green, he nearly fell off his bicycle when he recognised a face from the past. It was William Doyle.

William and Gavin were at Oakwood College together and had met in the dormitory on their very first night. Their respective parents were tucking them into bed before saying goodbye to them for more than a three month period. The place was swilling with tears.

One could say that this pair grew up together, as their beds in the dormitory were only a foot apart. After shaking hands and exchanging heartfelt greetings, they went to a local café in Baggot Street and, over large mugs of coffee, recalled what was happening in their lives at the moment. Gavin told William that he was going into the tourist industry and he was studying for a B.Com at Trinity with psychology as the second subject. William said that he was reading Law at UCD and they suggested that from now on they would meet regularly. It fascinated Gavin how two people from different parts of Ireland could bump into each other so unexpectedly.

"William," asked Gavin. "Can I ask you a personal question that puzzled me for years?"

"Yes, sure," retorted Willie. "Go on ahead."

"Do you remember in second year, when we were thirteen, we got that God fearing sermon about touching ourselves with our fingers and hands? It was all about impurity and the receiving of Holy Communion without Confession and all that stuff, and how it was a mortal sin and if you died you would go to hell. I don't know about you, but it really scared the shit out of me."

"Yes, vaguely," acknowledged William, with a smile on his face.

"Well," continued Gavin. "At that time I heard you in the bed, night after night, week after week, even month after month moaning and groaning, and I knew exactly what you were doing, but every morning you always went to Holy Communion as if nothing had happened."

"Heavens above, I remember that now," replied William, laughing out quite loudly. "Semantics is a wonderful thing, Gavin, and the Catholic Church has been using it as an excuse for hundreds of years.

"You see, Gavin, at that time I had absolutely no sense whatsoever. I was as green as grass and I simply took everything that the clergy said as utter truth and the literal word of God, so I just banged my penis against the mattress every night until it blew. I never touched myself with my fingers nor my hands, so as far as I was concerned, I wasn't committing any sin and I was OK for Holy Communion the following morning. You could call it a *no-hands job*, if you know what I mean."

They roared with laughter.

"Not that it ever was a sin," they agreed. They also agreed that the Church looked on any sort of pleasure as lust, and the concept of mortal sin grew from that phenomenon; and they concurred that if the truth be known the clergy were probably fornicating behind closed doors anyway.

"Now that I am studying law," continued William, "I realise that back in those days we knew absolutely nothing about life, and upon reflection I am fully convinced that we were the last of the gobshites."

CHAPTER 8

The summer vacations came around much faster than expected. The university terms were much shorter than those at secondary school and in 1959 plans were in place for their first trip to France and Spain. Gavin and Patrick wanted to expand their language skills and Harry just wanted to come for the ride. He enjoyed studying medicine but needed some leisure time away from its all-consuming schedule. To spend time with Gavin and Patrick was the perfect tonic. They were very happy and excited at the prospect of taking a flight.

None of them had ever been up in an aeroplane before, and the feeling of anticipation among them was exhilarating. Travelling in an aeroplane was part of the holiday, and they had bored lots of people with their plans, but always managed to get a laugh. While sitting in the lecture theatre, Patrick asked one of his friends, who was sitting between a couple of girls,

"What's the difference between being up on an aeroplane and being up on a woman?"

They all shook their heads from side to side indicating that they did not know.

"Go on, tell us, what's the difference then?" the friend asked, completely ignoring the two females.

"Don't know," smirked Patrick, "I was never up on an aeroplane."

This brought broad smiles and a few playful punches from the girls.

They were flying out on an Aer Lingus flight from Dublin to Cherbourg, with plans to hitch-hike down the west coast of France as far as Biarritz and then cross the border into Spain. As they boarded the DC3 at Dublin Airport for the two-hour twenty-minute flight to Europe, the first part of their adventure was under way.

After landing at Cherbourg, they made their way down the

peninsula until they came to a sight that really stunned them completely. They had seen posters of it many times but to see the real thing was something sensational. It was simply breathtaking. They hadn't known that it was on their route, and when they saw the shadowy shape in the distance, they just thought that it was a ship on a distant horizon. It wasn't until they arrived in the small coastal town of Ponterson they realised that the ship they thought they had seen was in fact a majestic monastery with fairytale features rising up out of the sand. It was of course Mont St Michel. They spent two days exploring every nook and cranny of that ancient Abbey before moving on to St Malo.

They managed to get many lifts by various means and designs, and never refused any form of transportation. They adapted the Phileas Fogg theory that it was better to keep moving forward than to stay standing still. However, when they found themselves creaking along slowly on the back of a hayrick in western France, they felt that it was time to move on. Fortunately, they had the entire summer to complete this thrilling adventure. They eventually reached Bordeaux and headed south again to the French Atlantic resort of Biarritz. It was there that they crossed the Spanish border at the town of Irun. Chatting to locals, they discovered that the roads over the Sierras were of very poor quality and, as vehicles did not frequently travel these roads, lifts of any description would be very scarce. Their destination was Barcelona so it was decided to take the night train over the mountains from San Sebastian and arrive some time the following day.

This journey was quite an experience, as pulling the train was an old Spanish steam locomotive resembling something that should have been in a museum. As they stood on the veranda deck of the last carriage, hot cinders from the firebox of the engine spilled out onto the sides of the tracks and lit the gorse for many miles behind. Eventually these cinders extinguished themselves in the darkness of night. Slowly but surely the train snaked upwards and onwards, puffing and panting as it stopped at various small isolated stations.

It was 3.00pm the following afternoon when they arrived at the Mediterranean city of Barcelona in brilliant sunshine and humid conditions. They boarded a local bus that took them to the seaside town of Blanes and when they got there, they immediately went for a swim. Much to their surprise the sea was warm and this phenomenon amused them considerably as the seas around Ireland were always freezing cold. They pitched their tent at the end of a beach, adjacent to the town and stayed there for the next three weeks.

One particular evening Patrick and Harry decided to go to Barcelona for an overnight and, as they were staying at the city's youth hostel, it was essential that they took their sleeping bags with them. Gavin didn't mind at all as he had made friends with an Irish girl who was camping at the other end of the beach. Both of them were studying economics so this gave him the perfect opportunity to invite her out for a few drinks and discuss their future ambitions. On the way back to camp she asked if she could see his tent and after inspecting it, she slipped into the one remaining sleeping bag.

"I'm staying the night," she quipped. "I don't know where you're sleeping."

"I do," responded Gavin and getting into the same bag he zipped it up immediately. That was the night he lost his virginity.

It was coming near the end of July and as money was slowly running out, they all decided to head north again and spend the last part of their vacation in Paris. Gavin was pleased with this, as he loved the thought of going to Paris. He returned to Ireland in the middle of September, with just enough time to go home to Lahinch for a long weekend before returning to Dublin. In early October he was back again in his *home from home* in Ranelagh. He was living life to the fullest.

CHAPTER 9

Gavin sat in the Rainbow Café on O'Connell Street in Dublin, listening to the jukebox playing the number-one Beatles hit *She loves you.* He was waiting for his new girlfriend to arrive, as he was taking her to see *Some like it Hot* which was showing in the Savoy Cinema. He had known her for about two months and seen her about once every week. Her name was Geraldine and he had been introduced to her when he last visited Kilkee at the end of the summer holidays. As it happened her mother knew Gavin's mother in Lahinch and this was the link between them. At the moment Geraldine was in Dublin for a few weeks staying with some friends and he found her pretty and vivacious.

Geraldine was slightly older than Gavin and she had just qualified with an Arts Degree from UCD. Unfortunately this was not sufficient to get her a decent job in Ireland or in England. Because of this, she decided that it would be better to return home to Kilkee and become her father's full-time secretary. Her father was the local doctor.

He was glad that they were from the same county, and the fact that she played golf really attracted him to her. It was now early November and even though the days were getting shorter and colder, they still managed to play a couple of rounds. He was completely infatuated with her, much to Harry's and Patrick's disgust.

When she arrived at the café, he ordered a fresh pot of tea and they started to chat. From the window they could see Nelson's Pillar and they talked about their plans for Christmas. Eventually they went to the movies. Her visit to Dublin was all too short and she returned to Kilkee at the end of the following week. Life for Gavin settled into its mundane routine again. This was his second year at Trinity and now he had to study much harder.

He was breaking all the rules and regulations regarding serious relationships that he had previously discussed with his friends and he was becoming more and more besotted with Geraldine. He could not explain why his inner self kept telling him that he was too young and still not qualified, while his outer self found her so fascinating. This did not seem to deter him from committing to this serious relationship. He simply did not want to lose her. He phoned her at least twice every week and finally made up his mind that he was going to see her as often as he could. Generally on Friday evenings he commenced what seemed *the impossible journey*, as he joined the throngs of people vacating Dublin for the weekend.

It took the train nearly three hours to get to Limerick Junction, a further two hours to get to Ennis, and then he connected with the late bus to Kilkee, which could easily take another hour. Sometimes he did not arrive in Kilkee until after 10.30pm. The following Sunday afternoon he was back on the train again at Ennis, fighting his way to get a vacant seat. Most of the time he had to stand all the way to Dublin. This was a tiresome trip and even though Lahinch was only twenty-five miles from Kilkee there was no direct bus service connecting the two places. This meant that he could not stay at home at weekends, and instead had to spend two nights in a local hotel in Kilkee. This was a major drain on his allowance.

That Christmas, he invited Geraldine to Lahinch for dinner on St Stephen's Day. This pleased his mother very much as she thought that Geraldine was a lovely girl, but she was also impressed that her son had fallen for the doctor's daughter. Inwardly Gavin was also feeling very pleased with himself.

This was one of those long-distance romances and Gavin was doing all the running. When Patrick and Harry suggested that the sex must be good, Gavin replied that he was not sleeping with her at all. They couldn't believe this and teased him regularly on that subject. Whatever it was, something within Gavin drew him to Geraldine and he became so obsessed with her that he now travelled down to Kilkee every weekend without fail. It was during late spring that he began to show signs of fatigue, but he lived for the weekends and became a recluse during the week. His two friends became very concerned about him but he continued in spite of their disapproval and every time he phoned home his mother encouraged him further into the relationship. He had now been dating her very seriously for over six months.

It was approaching Easter and Gavin was cramming for his exams. On this particular day he was having lunch in the Buttery restaurant at Trinity when a young woman in her mid-thirties walked up to him.

"Hello, are you Gavin O'Neill?"

"Yes, yes," he responded, looking up from his plate of Irish stew.

"Eh, you don't know me." she went on. "My name is Sheila Maguire."

"Hi, Sheila," he replied. "No, I don't know you. How can I help you?"

"Are you still going out with Geraldine Murphy from Kilkee?" she enquired very directly.

"Yes, yes I am," retorted Gavin. "Is there a problem with that?"

"Well, I have to tell you something that you might not like to hear," she continued. "Do you know a guy called Joseph Hughes?"

"Yes, yes I do," commented Gavin. "He also lives in Kilkee and, as a matter of fact, I was speaking to him only last weekend when I was down there. How do you know him?"

"Well, it's like this," said Sheila. "I am not here to cause you any trouble but I am also from Kilkee, and you were a very good friend to my younger brother Paul when he was a boarder at Oakwood. Paul is working on the farm now with the father, but you looked after him very well especially when he was being bullied."

Gavin tried in vain to search his memory but couldn't dredge anything up. There followed a long pause and then he looked up at her and nodded.

"I'm glad I was of some assistance to him."

"Well," she repeated, "it's like this. There's no easy way to say it so I will tell you out straight. Joseph Hughes is stepping out with Geraldine Murphy behind your back, and has been doing so for the past two months."

Gavin dropped his knife and fork. He looked at her and she just stared back at him. He shook his head and asked her to repeat what she had just said, just in case there might be another Geraldine Murphy. In order to establish facts, he asked her what Geraldine's father did for a living.

"He's the local doctor," came the reply and she continued, "It's just that I don't want to see a fine young man like you getting hurt by that two-timing bitch. I'm up in Dublin at the moment doing some shopping in the sales so I decided to find you and put the record straight. You were very easy to find. I knew you were at Trinity College so I enquired at the front office and they told me that at this time of day you're usually in the Buttery. Apparently over the past few months you have become a person of very regular habits."

Gavin didn't know what to say. He didn't know whether to thank her or to scream at her and while he was making up his mind what to do, she slowly walked away. He just sat there alone silently staring into space wondering what the hell had happened in the last ten minutes. Did he imagine that a young woman had been sitting opposite him, telling him something that he didn't want to hear? Was he hallucinating? Had he heard correctly? Who the hell was Sheila Maguire? He decided that he had better check the story out anyway, so he phoned Kilkee immediately.

It seemed as if the phone was going to ring forever. Eventually when Geraldine answered it, he confronted her instantly with the details he had just heard from Miss Maguire. She went completely silent, which was enough proof for Gavin. She had betrayed him and there was no point in him yelling down the phone at her, but he still wanted to challenge her about what he had just heard.

"Do you realise that I travelled from Dublin to Kilkee to see you every weekend, and you were…"

Before he could finish his sentence the phone went dead. She had hung up on him without saying a word and there and then he made up his mind that he never wanted to see her again.

This indeed was an eventful afternoon and if Sheila Maguire had not found him that day the deceit could have continued indefinitely. Suddenly he felt completely lost in a "peculiar" sort of way. It wasn't easy to get the thought of her out of his mind and move on as he had put so much effort into this relationship. He didn't even know how he was going to spend his weekends without her. When he told his mother what had happened, instead of sympathizing, she implied that he must have done something drastically wrong to hurt the young lady's feelings, and stated that he would never find such a nice girl again.

It reminded him of the Dean's attitude at Oakwood and Gavin once again felt totally devastated and completely humiliated.

CHAPTER 10

That year the summer vacations abroad were put on hold as Harry had to re-sit some of his exams and this suited Gavin down to the ground. The following year however, with all exams passed, Patrick and Harry were heading off to Europe again, but Gavin decided not to join them. Instead, he split the summer between his uncle's house in Drogheda and his home in Lahinch. While he was in Drogheda he played golf at Bettystown and Baltray and through various contacts he managed to get himself a summer job in Butlin's holiday camp at Mosney in County Meath. He had a wonderful time at the holiday camp, mainly because he was a redcoat. He organised games, played with the kids, helped the elderly, and attracted a different girlfriend nearly every week. When the girls were leaving, most of them were in tears, promises were made that they would stay in contact forever, but they never did. His turnover in women was incredible.

As the weeks in Butlin's passed, he worried that it was quite possible that he could have made any one of these young women pregnant. Condoms were not readily available in the Ireland of the sixties and he had never realised that some girls, particularly those on vacation, could get so horny. On occasions he would go in to a local chemist shop to buy a packet of condoms but much to his horror, when he saw that the person serving behind the counter was a woman, he predictably walked out with another tube of toothpaste.

He didn't go *all the way* every time, but at certain times he had no option. For this very reason, he was determined not to wear his name badge and any time a girl asked him his name, he always responded with a fictitious one. He innocently thought that this would make him more inconspicuous and harder to find in case some father or big brother tried to track him down.

However, no one ever came looking for him and this caused him further concerns as now he started to wonder if everything was working and functioning properly, in the department directly below the buckle of his belt.

This was a long hot summer and, together with the staff from the holiday camp, many evenings were spent enjoying barbecues on beaches such as Laytown and Mornington Strand. Before returning to university for his final year, after which he had to do a practical, he revisited Lahinch and travelled to Kilkee. After discreet enquiries he was delighted when he was informed that his ex-girlfriend no longer lived there and had gone to England. Ireland was well rid of her, he thought.

During the first two terms of this final year Gavin fully revised all the major functions of economics. He knew that it was the study of production, distribution and consumption of goods and services but discovered that it was also concerned with the division of labour, finance, taxation, supply and demand. He also read various papers and learnt that economic theories had a long history, beginning in ancient times and developing throughout history. He was fascinated that, in the middle ages, feudalism was the economic system and, due to expansion in Europe between the sixteenth and eighteenth centuries, it led to mercantilism. It was the Industrial Revolution in the eighteenth century that brought capitalism and socialism to the forefront. He was looking forward to his work experience when he could put some of these theories into practice.

It was during the last term of his final year that he devoted all his energies entirely to psychology and, as a behaviour modification experiment towards his final examinations, he had to train a rat to run through a complicated maze. This was something similar to Pavlov's dog experiment. At first glance, this task seemed totally impossible.

It was late in the afternoon when he went down to the animal room which was located in the basement of the building. He was one of the last students to arrive to collect his rat and Colm, the laboratory manager, smiled and pointed to the corner shelf where the cages were stored.

"That's your rat over there," Colm instructed, pointing to the corner. "Introduce yourself to it, pick it up and weigh it; that's the first step."

"Holy God," yelled Gavin, happily surprised that it was a white fluffy creature with pink eyes and not the brown sewer rat that he had been expecting.

It had previously been explained that these animals had to be trained to do a number of tasks and, because they were baby rats, they had to be fed and looked after exclusively by that student for the six-week training duration. As the rats completed each task, they were rewarded with food pellets. The task consisted of four procedures, each one taking a lot of time and effort. Everything had to be done in reverse order and as the rat accomplished one specific task, another task was introduced. Gavin thought that this would never work, but little by little he became quite attached to the small creature that he named Snowball. He always wore the same clothes during his training sessions so that the rat got used to his smell, and he noticed that Snowball's nose and whiskers twitched immediately after it was lifted out of its cage. Six weeks later, Snowball completed its tasks successfully.

Firstly, it walked on a treadmill causing one full rotation, then it rushed to the other side of the box and pressed down a lever, which released a marble. With its nose it pushed this marble down a track and eventually got it out through a hole at the end and finally it pushed another lever to get its food, which was its reward. This entire procedure took the little creature less than four seconds to complete. Gavin learnt from this experiment how important it was to use patience in order to achieve desired results. He was awarded top marks for this study and he also learnt from this experiment that nothing was unachievable if one puts their mind to it, which was to benefit him greatly throughout his entire working life.

The day he handed Snowball back to Colm, he gave her an extra helping of food and he was assured that she would be very well treated. As he looked back at her from the door, the little creature had already eaten her fill and was snuggling down for a well deserved sleep.

During that year Gavin was not able to spend as much time with Harry and Patrick as he would have liked. His life pointed him in a different direction, but they still remained good friends and met every month.

For some, university life was coming to an end but for others it was just beginning. Gabriella de Leon had just celebrated her eighteen birthday and was studiously recapping for her Leaving Certificate examination at St Brigid's Convent school. Even at this early stage, her father had already placed her name on the registers at Trinity College Dublin and the Sorbonne in Paris.

CHAPTER 11

Like all young people, Gavin imagined that life was passing him by. In order to qualify with his final degree at University he had to complete ten months' work experience in a tourist office. He had all his exams secured and this was only a formality but it had to be accomplished. His uncle Peter from Drogheda managed to get him a position in the Louth Meath Tourist Board, based in the provincial town of Dundalk.

This town was very close to the boundary with the *Six Counties*, as it was known, and the town of Newry was only five miles on the other side of the border. Gavin had never crossed this frontier before and in order to do so he had to obtain a document called a *Triptique*, issued by the Irish Customs. This legally permitted the temporary exportation and importation of his car and this had to be stamped every time he crossed the border.

When he decided to make this journey, he drove very carefully up to the Irish Customs post, stopped his car and walked inside the building.

"How long are you going North?" he was asked.

"Oh, only for a few hours," he replied and his form was stamped and handed back to him.

He then proceeded down the road about a quarter of mile and stopped outside the British Customs post and again he was asked practically the same question. When he answered that he was only going into Northern Ireland for a few hours, he was asked: "Have you anything to declare?"

"No sir," he replied, but he was still requested to open the boot of his car for examination before he was allowed to go any further. He found all this very strange within the small country of Ireland but legally speaking he was now in part of the United Kingdom.

He drove through Newry, towards Rostrevor and over the Mourne Mountains to Newcastle. The scenery was breathtaking and apart from the occasional Union Jack flag, everything looked exactly the same as it did in the Republic of Ireland. The fields were still green. The cows and sheep looked exactly the same. The roads were not any different, but the atmosphere didn't seem quite right. There was an ominous feeling everywhere, as if something was going to happen, and he was quite happy when he was heading up the Dublin Road out of Newry towards Dundalk. He breathed a sigh of relief when he crossed the border back into the Republic.

With his uncle's help he secured lodgings on the Avenue Road in Dundalk, which he shared with a bank official called Ronan Cleary and an Irish Customs Officer called Dermot Hennessy. Both men were his own age and he enjoyed their company very much. They went out periodically to various pubs and during the first few months he was introduced to the practice of dancing in large marquees or carnivals, as they were locally known. These marquees had polished wooden floors on which to dance and everyone moved in an anticlockwise direction. He danced to all the new songs of the sixties and the hits of the late fifties and always attracted the attention of many teenage girls. He was really enjoying country life in this particular corner of Ireland.

On one beautiful spring evening Gavin was sitting in the Bayview Hotel, situated a few miles outside Dundalk. Dermot was there also and they were waiting for Ronan to arrive.

"I wonder what the hell's keeping him," asked Dermot, looking at his watch. "He's over half an hour late."

"I don't know," replied Gavin. "Maybe he's been asked to work late."

"Work, my arse," commented Dermot. "That guy wouldn't work in a fit."

At that moment, in strolled Ronan with a cocky grin on his face. He was stationed at the local branch of the Connaught & District Bank in Dundalk, but he was a native of Dublin City and a natural wit. Little did Gavin know that this young man was going to become one of his greatest friends.

Ronan had a very pronounced Dublin accent and spoke on most subjects with great authority, even though he hadn't a notion what he was talking about most of the time. He was a very amusing character and told many stories of certain activities that took place within the hallowed halls of banking.

"What kept you, Cleary?" asked Dermot. "O'Neill here is on his second fucking pint, so it's your round."

"Well," explained Ronan, "since I was sent to that godforsaken town last year on temporary duty, I swore that I would never be on time for anything again in my entire life."

"What do you mean?" enquired Gavin.

"Your life will be cut very short if you don't get the fucking drinks in," commented Dermot.

"Well, it's like this," continued Ronan. "Last year I was sent to a three-handed office. That's a branch where there are only three staff, the Manager, the Assistant Manager – who is usually a bollix because he probably blotted his copy book somewhere along the way and got shunted – and a junior clerk. You see, when the Manager goes on holidays, the Assistant Manager takes over the branch and, with the junior's help, they both just keep things ticking over. On this occasion, while the Manager was on holidays, the junior took sick, so I was sent over on relief duty. To tell you the truth, there was hardly enough fucking work for one, never mind two, but I wasn't complaining as I got six shillings and eight pence a day for temporary duty expenses, so I was on the pig's back."

"Go on," encouraged Gavin. "What's all this got to do with arriving so late this evening?"

"Well, it's like this," continued Ronan in his usual fashion. "The first week was all right. The Assistant Manager was an eccentric sort of a guy, about fifty-six years of age and he didn't give a shagging toss, which suited me down to the ground. In a way it was great, as every day we used to pull the door after us about 4.00pm and I would be into my first pint five minutes later. At the weekends I went home to Dublin on the motor-bike and returned early on Monday mornings. This particular Monday morning, I left Dublin at about 7.15am to avoid the heavy traffic and got into the town about 9.00am. As it happened, I was about half an hour early for work."

"Jaysus," commented Dermot in his broad Cork accent, "you're making a fucking meal out of this story. Will you finish it, for Christ's sake?"

"I will if you give me half a shagging chance," replied Ronan. "You see, I had the key to the hall door of the bank so I let myself in and there I was sitting at my desk getting all my dockets ready for the day's work when I heard a noise. I'll tell you lads, being inside a bank when the doors are closed is like being inside an empty church or inside a fucking pub after closing time when everyone has gone home. It's a terrible creepy place and you could hear a fucking pin drop. Bloody goose pimples came out all over me when I heard the noise again and I knew it was too loud to be a fucking mouse. I hadn't a clue what it was, but it definitely came from the Manager's office.

"Do you know something, I must have been bloody mad, because I made my way down to the door of the Manager's office and listened. I distinctly heard more noises. It could have been a fucking robber waiting for me with a gun or something, but curiosity got the better of me so I opened the door, took one look into the Manager's office and closed the door again immediately."

"What did you see?" asked Gavin and Dermot almost simultaneously.

"Do you really want to know?" asked Ronan in an inquisitive sort of way.

"Go on, for fuck's sake, before we thump you," they both yelled at him together.

"Well," he continued, "there was the Assistant Manager screwing the charwoman on the Manager's desk. Him with his trousers down around his ankles and her on her back on the desk with her legs in the air and her knickers hanging off her left foot."

"Fucking hell," exclaimed Dermot. "What a sight! What happened next?"

Gavin nearly fell out of his chair with laughter and the tears were running down his face.

"What did you do?" he managed to ask eventually.

"Nothing, absolutely nothing, sure what the fuck could I do? There he was, hard at it, so I closed the door quietly, returned to my desk and stamped some more shagging forms. I would say I had enough stamped for the next two weeks. Ten minutes later the Assistant Manager appeared and walked past me to his desk as if nothing had happened. A few minutes later, the charwoman appeared on the outside of the counter, and just carried on washing the floor with her mop and bucket. The subject was never mentioned."

"Never mentioned!" exclaimed Gavin.

"No," came the concluding remark. "It was as if it never happened, so from that day on I decided never to be on time for any appointments ever again."

CHAPTER 12

Dermot worked as a junior officer in the Customs House on the outskirts of Dundalk. He fully realised that this was one of the better duties in the Customs Service, as one of his colleagues, who had joined the service on exactly the same day as he did, had been posted to Dublin Port. His colleague's duty was to search the boilers of coal-boats that had just arrived from foreign parts. Dermot decided that he wanted to keep his plum job in Dundalk so he always addressed the public as sir or madam, as the case may be. This evening he arrived back at the lodgings with a broad smile on his face.

"Did you see the paper, lads? Kennedy is coming to Dublin next week. Do you think we could nip down there and maybe sneak a quick look at him?"

In 1960, John Fitzgerald Kennedy, a second-generation Irishman and also a Catholic, had been elected President of the United States. Gavin was very proud of this and for the first time in many ages Irish people throughout the world had a new hero to look up to.

June 26th until June 29th in the year 1963 was a historic era, as that was the time that President John Fitzgerald Kennedy, the thirty-fifth President of the United States of America, became the first US President to visit Ireland. It looked as if many changes might be on the way.

"I tell you what," said Ronan. "I'll finish early in the bank next Wednesday and Gavin, if you could arrange the car, that would be bloody great. Maybe Dermot, you could get your hands on some of those Customs passes, and you never know, we might all get to shaking hands with JFK yet."

"If pigs could fly," retorted Dermot. "There's no bloody chance of me getting you lot shagging Customs passes. You must be joking."

"Do you want us all to get arrested and jailed?" commented Gavin.

"Only joking, O'Neill," confirmed Ronan. "I'm only winding you up."

Nevertheless, a plan was hatched immediately, as this was a once-in-a-lifetime experience and too great a chance to miss. On Tuesday night it was decided unanimously that on the day in question, they would all act as local pressmen. They concurred that even if queried by the authorities, they could say that they were only masquerading as freelance journalists, trying to get a scoop for the local newspaper. However, it would be better if they looked the part so they decided to make themselves identity badges. A cheap shirt was bought solely for the purpose of obtaining the specially laminated paper in which it was wrapped.

It was also agreed that all cameras, no matter what size or shape, were to be placed on the back window shelf of their borrowed car and Dermot was asked to obtain the large wooden tripod from the local camera club.

Using the bank's paper guillotine, the special laminated paper from the shirt was cut into three very neat rectangular shapes about four inches long and one inch wide. Gavin was a very good artist and with special black ink and a broad-nibbed pen, he inscribed the word "official" across each one, as diligently as any calligrapher. These were their official badges. It was decided not to inscribe the word "press" as that might cause suspicion.

Ronan then took the three laminated pieces and carefully inserted each one into the bank's official seal, which meant absolutely nothing, but the indentation gave the badges a very official look. Large safety pins were secured to the back of each badge with the special strong adhesive tape that the branch used when sealing certain documents. Finally for the event Gavin borrowed his aunt Mary's Morris Minor, which was washed and polished until it gleamed. If his uncle Peter had known what they were planning, he would surely have had a stroke.

Waiting until 3.00pm on Wednesday June 26th 1963 seemed the

longest few hours of their lives. Eventually they met in Hanrahan's public house on Park Street, all dressed in their Sunday best and, looking very serious and very nervous, they walked up to the bar. The barman approached them with a sour look on his face.

"Well, what can I get you lot?"

"Three half ones for the road," called Ronan. "We're all off to Dublin to see Kennedy,"

"So is fucking Ireland," came the curt reply.

"Jaysus, there's no shagging answer to that," commented Dermot in his broad Cork accent and, downing their whiskeys in one gulp and with the barman's remarks still ringing in their ears, they marched out of the bar.

"Fucking bollix," commented Ronan, who was sitting in the front beside Gavin. "I'll never drink in that whoring pub again."

"Me neither," remarked Dermot, who was sitting in the back of the car surrounded by bits and pieces of photographic equipment. Straightening their shoulders and clearing their throats, they all tried once again to look confident and poised as they headed south from Dundalk towards the City of Dublin.

As Gavin eased the car into top gear, they drove through the small towns of Castlebellingham and Dunleer, crossed the River Boyne at Drogheda and made their way on towards Balbriggan. It was here that the traffic started to get heavy. It was just 5.30pm and Kennedy's plane was expected at 6.15pm.

They joined the long line of traffic that was now slowly winding its way towards Dublin Airport and eventually they reached the village of Swords about 6.10pm, but they were still five miles from the airport. They were now beginning to panic. Once again they checked the cameras and pinned the "official" badges to the lapels of their jackets. They all looked the part.

"For Christ's sake, would this fucking traffic ever move a bit faster," shouted Ronan. "We'll miss him if we don't do something fast."

"There's nothing I can do," replied Gavin. "Do you want me to sprout wings and fly?"

"Jaysus, O'Neill. That would be a great trick," commented Ronan. "Anything would be better than sitting here like fucking idiots."

"I think I can see the plane," shouted Dermot, looking out through the back window. "Look at the size of it! The fucking thing is coming straight for us."

The flight path approach to the main runway at Dublin Airport crossed the Dublin Swords Road almost diagonally and very close to a pub called the Coachman's Inn. It is at that spot that many drivers imagined at one time or another that a plane they saw coming in to land at Dublin was going to land right on top of them. So convincing was this illusion that, when it occurred, some drivers accidentally ended up in the ditch.

As it happened this evening, all the cars in front of them came to an abrupt stop, as their occupants wound down their windows to get a better look at Air Force One, as it passed so closely overhead.

"Right," said Ronan. "Let's go for it."

Slapping Gavin on the back he told Dermot to wind down his back window and stick his arm out, indicating that they were turning right.

Gavin didn't need any further encouragement and, switching on his headlights, slipped the gear stick into second, released the clutch and pulled out into the oncoming lane. They prayed that nothing would be coming from the opposite direction and as it happened nothing appeared in front of them.

"Keep on going, you good thing," roared Ronan excitedly, as if he was shouting on a horse at the Galway Races. They passed all the line of cars and within five minutes they were at the Collinstown Gate, which was the entrance to the Airport Road. They soon realised why there was no traffic heading north, as a policeman – a Garda Siochana – was standing in the middle of the road diverting all traffic away from the Airport. When he saw the Morris Minor approaching, he raised his white-gloved hand for them to stop immediately.

"Run the bastard over," commented Dermot from the back, but Gavin brought the car to a gentle stop beside the Garda.

Winding down his window, and before the policeman could open his mouth Gavin spoke to him in a very polished accent: "Good evening, Garda, we're official staff from Dundalk, down here to cover President Kennedy's arrival at Dublin. We have just seen his plane passing overhead and I think we are going to be late if we don't get up there immediately."

Gavin spoke every word as if his life depended on it. The Garda looked carefully at them all, cautiously glancing from one to the other, and he observed how well they were dressed. He also noticed the cameras, the camera bags and tripod in the back of the car and assumed that they were genuine reporters. He then moved a few steps backwards, held up his white-gloved hand again and stopped all oncoming traffic at the intersection.

"Turn right, lads," he said, indicating with a wave of his hand, "and straight up the Airport Road. The official car park is second on the left."

"Thank you, Garda," said Gavin courteously, and the three of them with serious faces, nodded their appreciation as the car turned right. They could hardly believe what had just happened. They were in a state of semi-shock.

"I don't fucking believe this and as soon as I get out of this shagging car I want you to give me a good hard kick up the arse just to make sure I am not dreaming," exploded Ronan, as the grin widened across his face.

"I would be delighted to oblige," responded Gavin.

"We've made it, we fucking made it," exclaimed Ronan.

Gavin drove up the road at a steady twenty-five miles per hour.

"It would be disastrous if we were caught for speeding at this point," he said and as they approached the car park, a steward signalled them into an appropriate parking space.

"I noticed you didn't mention any newspaper, O'Neill, that was great thinking; you'll certainly go far in your career," said Ronan, as he got out of the car.

"I'm not taking this whoring tripod with me," remarked Dermot.

"Jaysus, Hennessy," retorted Ronan, looking at Dermot, "you were so bleeding quiet back there, for a minute I thought you were shagging dead."

They got out, made sure their badges were straight, checked each other's suits and, taking the cameras and the camera bags with them, made their way towards the terminal building. There must have been 30,000 people within the official area to greet President Kennedy and on their way across the car park, they overheard from someone's portable radio that the road between the airport and the city was completely closed off and lined three-deep with people.

Now that they were in the cordoned off area, the next thing to do was to worm their way in as far as they could to the official barrier. They decided to split up, and to meet at the car later. They reckoned that by doing this they stood a better chance of seeing Kennedy, as three of them trying to get to the barrier at the same time would be totally impossible.

After a few unsuccessful attempts Gavin eventually got as far as the barrier. A red carpet had been rolled out from the terminal building and he watched as various army personnel arrived to take up their official positions. It was all very exciting.

Everyone was waiting patiently and then it happened; that famous announcement that was heard so often on radio reports and cinema newsreels.

"Ladies and gentlemen, the President of the United States of America."

As the Army Number One Band under the command of Commandant Jack O'Hara struck up *Hail to the Chief*, this tanned medium-built gentleman, immaculately groomed in a petrol-blue suit, appeared in the doorway of the terminal building. Gavin had seen this image many times in photographs but now he was seeing him in reality. Kennedy was only about fifty feet away from where Gavin was standing and as he paused he automatically went through that very familiar routine of straightening his tie with his right hand and fixing the middle button of his jacket with his left. His stylish quiff only enhanced his boyish features and as a microphone was placed in front of him, he simply drawled in his broad Boston accent.

"Thank you, Mr President, for inviting me to your country."

That was enough. The entire crowd erupted in cheers. Maybe it was because no one had ever heard Eamon de Valera being referred to as 'Mr President' before, but the roar of that crowd was heard in downtown Dublin. Nobody made any more speeches and Kennedy looked very pleased to get such a rapturous reception.

Then he raised his hand, waved to the crowds and as he made his way down the red carpet, he repeatedly fixed his tie and jacket again. He looked at everyone in a special way and gently waved to them as if they were the only ones he was looking at. He had that very special charisma. John Fitzgerald Kennedy had arrived in Ireland and everyone was very proud of him. In rural cottages dotted along Ireland's Atlantic seaboard, two pictures hung on the walls of most houses; one was of the Pope and the other was of JFK.

When he reached the end of the red carpet, an open-top Lincoln Continental, especially imported for the occasion, was waiting for him. John Kennedy stood up for the entire journey to Dublin's O'Connell Street, while President de Valera sat proudly beside him. No one in their wildest dreams could have imagined what was going to happen a few short months later in Dallas, but Gavin and the others felt privileged to have been there in Dublin Airport on that occasion to see history in the making.

**See author's footnote

CHAPTER 13

Gavin graduated with flying colours and in October was interviewed by the Irish International Tourist Association for a position as Assistant Head of the Western Region Tourism Authority, based in Limerick. He was delighted at being selected for this initial interview as this was an important posting. He knew that if he was successful, it would be a major achievement that could lead to greater things in the future.

One week later, an official envelope embossed with the government harp dropped through the letterbox of his family home in Lahinch. He had secured the job.

At the same time an ambitious American clerical student was one of a group of young seminarians being ordained to the priesthood in Rome.

Gavin moved to Limerick and found an apartment in the Raheen area of the City. He was only seven miles from his office and could drive this distance in less than twenty minutes. There were seven other employees. This was the first time that Gavin had been in charge of staff, so he decided to take things easy for the first few weeks. He rang most of his friends and was advised by Ronan to at least sweep the floor as a symbolic gesture which if nothing else would give them all something to talk about. It also let everyone know that a new broom had arrived.

His main task was overseeing the Limerick and Shannon Tourism District and finding ways of attracting more visitors to the region. He decided that one of the major benefits in the area was the proximity of Shannon Airport and he strongly felt that the American market was just waiting to be tapped. This was his first project. He drew up budget plans, worked long days and late nights and enjoyed every minute of it. He was happy and dedicated to his work. Gavin was a great communicator and had an excellent way with people.

It was approximately 7.30pm on a Thursday evening. He had

just finished working late trying to catch up on a few things before Christmas when suddenly his phone rang. As he lifted the receiver with his left hand he slipped his right arm into the sleeve of his overcoat.

"Good evening, Western Region Tourist Authority."

"Hello, Gavin," came the reply. "This is Henry Murphy, how are you keeping? Do you remember me? I'm Geraldine's brother. She heard you were back in the area and she asked me to give you a call."

Gavin didn't answer.

"I know she treated you fairly badly in the past," the caller continued, "but she hasn't been well lately. She has just returned from London and hearing from you would really do her the world of good."

Gavin was still frozen to the spot. He couldn't believe what he was hearing. He also noticed that with only one arm in his overcoat sleeve the rest of it hung across his shoulders like a cape. He just stood dumbfounded.

"Are you still there?" came the voice from down the phone again.

"Yes, I am," replied Gavin. "What's your name again?"

"Henry Murphy, Geraldine's brother. Don't you remember me?"

"Oh yeah, yes," he stuttered, but he was otherwise speechless.

"Well, I told her I would ring you," came the voice again, "and I know she would be delighted to hear from you. The number is Kilkee 874 in case you have forgotten. You should give her a buzz."

He hadn't forgotten the number, which was permanently imprinted in his brain having dialled it so many times in the past.

"Thanks, Henry, thanks for letting me know," and with that they said their polite goodbyes and hung up.

Gavin flopped down in the chair. The one vivid memory that

flashed into his mind was that of Sheila Maguire in the Buttery in Trinity College relating the entire two-timing saga to him and how devastated he had felt by Geraldine's disloyalty.

He kept asking himself why Geraldine had come back to haunt him at this stage of his life. He closed his eyes and thought long and deep. What possessed her to try and contact him again after such an act of unfaithfulness? Why was she looking for him? He couldn't find any answers to these questions, but yet he felt strangely flattered that she was now looking for him instead of the other way around. He often thought of her and had suffered many sleepless nights after their split-up and if it hadn't been for his friendship with Ronan and Dermot over the years, he didn't know what he would have done. They were not around any more and he knew if he had asked for Ronan's advice, he would have simply been told,

"Tell her to fuck off."

He made up his mind not to ring her, as deep down he knew he could never trust her again. Bottling it all up, he drove home to Lahinch for the weekend. He reckoned that a game of golf might clear his head and he would be in a better state of mind to deal with everything later. He survived through the Saturday without much bother but at Sunday dinner his mother noticed that he was unusually quiet. When she asked him if there was anything wrong with him, with mixed emotions he casually mentioned the telephone call he had received from Geraldine's brother.

"Heavens, that's great news," replied his mother delightedly, "and have you phoned her yet?"

"No," he said. "I haven't, and I don't think I will."

"Now, Gavin, that would be a big mistake. She is indeed a lovely girl."

He was not entirely surprised by his mother's reaction and he felt that she was dictating to him again, exactly the same way as she had when he was at boarding school.

"Mother," he said. "I am a grown man now and I can make my own decisions."

"Well, try and act like one," came the curt response. "I think Geraldine Murphy is a lovely person and you'll travel the length and breadth of Ireland before you'll find anyone better than her."

He should have known better than to mention the phone call to his mother as he knew he was not going to get any comfort from her. However, throughout the following week he couldn't get Geraldine out of his mind. He thought long and hard about what he was going to do. Eventually he rationalised that with Christmas coming up, it might be useful to have someone on hand to escort him to the black-tie functions that he would have to attend over the holiday season. She could be his accessory. He would use her the same way she used him. That weekend he decided to give her a quick call. He kept reassuring himself that he had no intention of dating her on a short-term or a long-term basis, but he was still very curious to see what she looked like and if she had changed much over the past three years. On Saturday evening he went out into the hallway of his home and, lifting the receiver, dialled her number.

"Hello, Geraldine, Gavin here."

"Hello, Gavin," she answered in an excited tone.

"Your brother rang me and told me that you have been ill. I hope it's nothing serious. How are you feeling now?"

"Oh, I am improving," came the pleasant reply. "I don't know what came over me when I was working in London. I found myself getting dizzy spells, so my father told me to get home as fast as possible."

"Wise decision," commented Gavin. "That's the beauty of having a doctor in the family."

There followed an awkward pause, but suddenly she broke the silence by saying,

"Thank you for calling me and how are you keeping yourself?"

"Not a bother," came the reply. "Pulling the devil by the tail and cleaning my nails on his horns."

"I see you're still as witty as ever," she giggled, and then they both laughed together.

"How is your mother? She's a lovely lady," Geraldine continued.

"She's great. Fussing over Christmas as usual," he responded.

Gavin suggested that perhaps during the coming week they could meet for lunch in Cruises Hotel in Limerick and she immediately jumped at the idea, saying that she would really look forward to it. At least, he thought to himself, lunch is in the middle of the day and quite safe. Had it been dinner, he might have had to make small talk for most of the evening and he wasn't sure if he could do that.

"Would Tuesday at 1.00pm be OK?"

"Great," she replied. "I'll be there."

As they hadn't much to say to each other, they exchanged no further conversation. They said their goodbyes until Tuesday. When Gavin replaced the receiver he returned to the dinner table with a smug look upon his face. For the first time he felt that he was controlling Geraldine, instead of her controlling him.

CHAPTER 14

They met in Cruises Hotel in Limerick as arranged and Gavin was very surprised to see how much she had changed in such a short space of time. Geraldine was no longer the girl he knew and she looked quite mature for her age. Her strawberry blonde hair had been cut and was now permed in tight curls. She wore a long dark three-quarter length coat that was buttoned up to her neck. When she took her coat off she was very simply dressed in a pink twin set, a navy skirt to her knees, stockings to match, and medium high heels. She wore a single string of pearls.

This was not the picture of the girl that he had secretly kept hidden in one of the many cabinets of his mind. This was not the picture that he would sometimes recollect, look at and scrutinise and put away again. This was a totally different person, attractive in a semi-sophisticated sort of a way, and this made him even more confused.

They didn't talk much when they met but she seemed happy to see him. Gavin, on the other hand, felt very uneasy. Lunch was ordered and after an hour of seemingly endless small talk, he told her that he had to get back to the office. She stood up while he politely held her coat for her and then she sat down again. He thanked her for coming, said goodbye and gave her a kiss on the cheek. As he paid the bill at the cashier's box he looked back at her and raised his hand in a gentle wave. He walked calmly out through the main door of the hotel and then like a dog released from a trap at a greyhound meeting, raced across the street directly into Timmon's public house and ordered a large whiskey. He stood there and reflected that maybe she had been seriously ill and maybe that was the reason she was not looking her best. Maybe he wasn't giving her a proper chance, but while he stood there pondering the previous hour, he downed the whiskey in two gulps. He wasn't sure what he was going to do next.

Christmas Day was on a Thursday that year, so everyone was

breaking up at lunchtime on Wednesday. Some staff from his office with long distances to travel left on Tuesday evening and on Christmas Eve the city was bursting at the seams with last-minute shoppers. It was about 7.30pm when he arrived home in Lahinch.

After Midnight Mass, they all sat around the fire drinking mulled wine and eating slices of spiced beef, which was the traditional custom.

"Have you been in touch with Geraldine?" his mother eventually asked.

"Yes," he replied.

"Well, how is she?"

"She's fine."

"Why don't you invite her over for dinner on St Stephen's evening?" his mother continued. "You know we would all love to see her."

He had a feeling of *déjà vu* but, rather than offend his mother at such a special time of year, he said he would call her shortly. They all retired to bed at 4.30 in the morning.

Uncle Peter and aunt Mary had driven down from Drogheda, and uncle Mick, his father's bachelor brother, made up the party of six that were staying in the house over the festive season. They were all invited for Christmas and as *Santa* had left various presents under the tree, these were officially opened after the huge dinner on Christmas Day. During the evening many neighbours called to wish one and all a Happy Christmas and, with a drink always at the ready, everybody was in great form. At about 8.00pm, when most had dozed off from the heat of the log fire, Gavin decided to ring Geraldine. The following day was St Stephen's Day, which in Ireland is nearly a repeat of Christmas Day but without the presents.

"Merry Christmas," he said as soon as she answered the phone.

"Gosh, I never thought I would ever hear you saying those words again," she replied. "I'm so delighted."

"Ma wants you to come over for dinner tomorrow evening. Do

you think you could make it?" he enquired.

"Is it your mother that wants me or is it you that wants me?" she asked inquisitively.

"Both of us," retorted Gavin. "You can always stay the night. It's a big house."

"I'd love to. At what time?"

"Come over about 6.00pm," replied Gavin and telling her that he was looking forward to seeing her, he put down the phone. Before returning to the warmth of the large sitting room he looked at his reflection in the mirror in the hallway and asked himself whether he was right in the head or not.

A couple of hours later his mother awoke apologising to everyone for being asleep for so long. As she got up out of the chair, cries of "don't worry yourself" came from around the room but she suggested that some cold turkey and salad might be a tasty bite before starting the game of cards. They all agreed and aunt Mary got up as well, and the two women made their way into the kitchen.

It was during supper that Gavin whispered to his mother that Geraldine was coming over for dinner the following evening and she would probably stay the night.

"That's great, son. I'm delighted. You've made my Christmas," enthused the mother and added that she would make up the bed in the *maid's room,* as it was known.

On St Stephen's night, Geraldine arrived on schedule and after a very satisfying dinner, the women started to talk among themselves. The four men decided to go down to O'Leary's Pub for a few drinks. There was no doubt that Gavin's mother was thrilled with Geraldine's presence. This reunion was something which she had prayed for, and now she was hoping that an engagement might quickly follow.

It was early January and everything was getting back to normal after the holiday season. Gavin had met Geraldine at least three times since Christmas. They had been to two formal dinner dances and each time she looked very elegant in her long black halter neck gown. Gavin looked quite distinguished in his tuxedo and many people told them that they looked very attractive together. Geraldine's health was improving rapidly and she definitely looked much better than she had eight weeks ago when they met in Cruises Hotel. His mother also mentioned that they made a lovely couple and he would be a fool if he let such a good girl slip through his fingers once again. One evening his mother surprised him by suggesting that it might be a good idea if he considered getting engaged shortly.

Strange as it may seem, Gavin was still attracted to Geraldine, despite what had happened in the past. Her beauty was still there even though her high-spiritedness was more subdued. These new characteristics really appealed to his mother, as she took them as a sign that Geraldine had finished all her gallivanting and wanted to settle down.

However, there was still a lingering gnawing feeling of unease deep within Gavin and no matter how much he tried he couldn't get rid of. He still found it very hard to trust her. Numerous '*what ifs*' flooded his mind and he tried to block them out by trying to convince himself that possibly his mother was correct and he was just being over-anxious. He was even going to ask Geraldine if she had seen Joseph Hughes recently, but decided against it.

He knew that in his mother's eyes Geraldine was a good catch, the best he was likely to find. Furthermore, she was a good-looking girl, came from a good family background, played golf and maybe if he put an engagement ring on her finger all the hidden fears that haunted him would evaporate.

The eventual outcome was that they dated seriously for three months and then, amid lavish joint celebrations by both families in the St Gregory Hotel and Country Club, Gavin and Geraldine got engaged. The year passed in a frenzy of activity and Gavin travelled home to Lahinch once every three weeks. The weekends that he had to stay in Limerick, Geraldine travelled there to be with him and he liked going to her family home in Kilkee, mostly because he always enjoyed a great round of golf with Doctor Murphy.

The wedding date was set for February 1965, and the wedding list was duly compiled. The plans seemed to take on a life of their own and Gavin was the last to be informed of any major arrangements. He felt like an outsider in the entire situation. His mother wanted her friends and relatives to be there and naturally the Murphy family wanted theirs also, but no one had asked Gavin who he wanted to invite. In spite of all this, he decided that he was going to invite William Doyle, his first school friend from Oakwood College. He also wanted to invite Patrick and Harry, his two pals from his university days, and of course Ronan and Dermot. These were the special people in his life and he insisted on Ronan being his best man.

CHAPTER 15

Gavin travelled up to Dublin about a week before the wedding and met his uncle Peter for lunch in Wynn's Hotel on Abbey Street. After chatting about football and rugby, Peter looked at him very seriously.

"I am very fond of you, Gavin, and I know your mother can be a bit forceful at times, but she means well. I know that she has taken a big shine to Geraldine but she's not marrying Geraldine. You're the one that's doing that, so are you absolutely sure you know what you're doing? It's just not on the rebound, is it?"

Sweat broke out on Gavin's face. How did his uncle know what he was thinking? Had he absentmindedly mentioned something to somebody that he shouldn't have mentioned? Once again he asked himself how his uncle Peter could have read his thoughts, or was it written all over his face? Composing himself as best as he could, he answered very assertively.

"I'm sure, Peter, I'm quite sure," he replied. But deep down he wasn't that sure. Last week his father had given him two hundred Irish punts as a wedding present and he had serious doubts whether to use the money to abscond or to buy a new car. These were not the rational thoughts of someone contemplating marriage. To mention anything to his mother at this late stage or even to broach the subject that he might be having second thoughts would be enough to cause her to have a heart attack. Anyway, his mother had already made up her mind that her Gavin was going to marry Geraldine Murphy, the doctor's daughter from Kilkee, and she was hoping to become a grandmother before the end of the following year. The invitations had been sent out, the presents were arriving, the date was fixed, so everything was *full steam ahead* as far as she was concerned

As Gavin drove back to Limerick city, he contemplated his uncle's words, but there was nothing he could do. He was looking for love and happiness and, putting all other notions completely out of his mind, he now really believed that he would find both ingredients within the marriage, and much more with the arrival of children.

Mainly for the convenience of the guests, the wedding was taking place in Limerick instead of Kilkee and all were pleased when the parish priest from Lahinch, Father Joseph Slattery, agreed to perform the ceremony. He was in his seventy-third year and Mrs Murphy and Mrs O'Neill were only too delighted to fuss over him.

Gavin's stag night was planned for the night before the wedding at Whelan's Pub in Limerick and afterwards he was booked into Cruises Hotel. Earlier on in the day Willie Doyle and his partner had flown into Shannon Airport from London's Heathrow. William was working in the Old Bailey court as a Junior Barrister and there was no doubt in Gavin's mind that he would make QC before the age of forty. Patrick also arrived from Germany, where he was working as a houseman in a hospital in Frankfurt. Harry flew into Dublin from Toronto where he was lecturing at a university. Dermot was still in the Customs and Excise in Dundalk, but had recently been promoted to Station Manager. Much to his surprise, Ronan had been promoted early in his career to the rank of Assistant Bank Manager and had been transferred to Dublin.

Dermot agreed to pick Ronan up on the way through Dublin and they drove down to Limerick together. All his friends were determined to attend his stag night and his wedding day regardless of distance or circumstances and this really pleased Gavin. They all met in Whelan's about 8.30pm.

"Since I'm the best man," commented Ronan after he had a few whiskeys inside him, "It's my job to screw the chief bridesmaid."

"She's a girl called Sally Rooney and she's a two-bag job," retorted Dermot.

"What do you mean she's a two-bag job?" slurred Ronan.

"A bag for her head and a bag for your head, just in case her bag falls off."

"Fuck me," came the slurry reply

"And do you know something else," pontificated Dermot, who was now trying to stand straight with a pint swaying in his hand. "They say she's still a virgin at 35 and she's so tight you could do yourself a serious injury if you were not careful."

"Jaysus, that's a desperate thing to say about the poor woman," slurred Ronan again. "She's not as bad as all that."

"She's bad enough," mumbled Dermot.

"Right," Ronan garbled on, "I'll do the second bridesmaid instead."

"She's just as bad looking," came the drunken reply, "and anyway, I thought I was getting her."

"Fucking hell. Then we'll have to toss for them," muttered Ronan as he downed another whiskey.

"Where in God's name did you meet those pair?" asked Patrick and Harry almost at the same time, but Gavin was still sober enough to honestly say that had it not been for this pair of likeable rogues he might not have coped so successfully after the initial break-up with Geraldine. He never talked much about that event in his life but his mind always kept returning to it. Even though he was so close to marrying her, he was still having serious doubts about what he was undertaking. He kept reassuring himself that after the ceremony, everything was going to be all right.

It has to be stated that William Doyle's girlfriend was a stunner, and she was very much admired by everyone she met, much to Willie's delight.

As the drink was starting to take control, Ronan was getting bawdier by the minute, and even suggested, much to Gavin's disgust and annoyance, that he should have asked Joseph Hughes to be his best man and Sheila Maguire to be the chief bridesmaid.

"Now that would give your mother something to talk about," he slurred.

However, the following morning Ronan was a different person

completely. He took his duties as best man very seriously and was all business, making sure that the bouquets of flowers had been delivered to Mrs Murphy and to Mrs O'Neill in accordance with tradition. He checked again to make sure that the bridal car and taxis were on time. He also checked the St Gregory Hotel and was assured that the piper was ready to welcome the wedding party. He doubled-checked that the sherry reception was laid out and the champagne was on ice. He looked very stylish in his morning suit with claw-hammer tails and as Dermot, Harry, Patrick, William and Henry were ushers and groomsmen, all were all dressed identically and everyone looked immaculate. As Ronan adjusted the pin in Gavin's cravat, he quietly whispered in his ear.

"I could always arrange a fast fucking jet out off Shannon within the hour. It's not too late yet."

"Fuck off, Ronan," replied Gavin. "Just you make sure you haven't forgotten the bloody ring."

With that Ronan summoned all his troops together like a sergeant major in the Irish army and gave them their final instructions.

"Action stations, everybody," he shouted. "Henry Murphy. Jaysus, where the fuck is Henry Murphy?"

"Eh, out here, Ronan," replied Henry from the corridor.

"Henry, what the hell are you doing out there? For Christ's sake get yourself in here immediately. Now, you look after the Murphy clan and try to remember that they sit on the left hand side of the church. OK?"

"Yes, Ronan."

"Dermot, you look after the O'Neills and for fuck's sake get it right."

"Patrick and Harry," he shouted again, "the both of you better be the best groomsmen that God has ever breathed on, or I will personally have you castrated."

They all had smiles on their faces, but they still took him very seriously.

"Dermot, have you got the envelopes for Father Slattery and the six altar boys?"

"Yes," replied Dermot.

"On second thoughts," he continued, "give the altar boys' envelopes to Willie Doyle just in case you get them fucking mixed up. I don't want Father Slattery having a shagging stroke from the shock of only getting a ten-shilling note in his envelope. Jaysus, I can cope with most things today, but a stroke is something I could do well without."

With that he sent them all on their way and William was detailed to personally look after Father Slattery.

The Church of the Holy Rosary was on the Ennis Road on the outskirts of Limerick and it was totally packed with local people. Everyone wanted to see the bride and everything looked exquisite. All the pews had been decorated with flowers the evening before.

The bride eventually arrived well over the customary four minutes late rule and even Gavin had started to wonder if she was going to turn up at all. Suddenly the wedding march sounded on the organ and, with her father walking beside her, Geraldine was gracefully escorted into the church. She was wearing the traditional long white dress and veil, which was greatly admired by the whispering onlookers as she walked past each row of seats. She looked fabulous.

The wedding service passed off without a hitch. After the ceremony Gavin and Geraldine got into the bridal car, followed by the other two cars containing both sets of parents, bridesmaids and the best man. They arrived at the hotel shortly before mid-day and after the sherry reception and the photographs, the meal was served in the main banqueting hall.

William called for silence as Father Slattery said Grace, and during the dessert course of the meal, Ronan called upon Gavin's and Geraldine's fathers to say a few words. Mr O'Neill just stood up, thanked everyone for coming and sat down again immediately. He was such a timid man that he was on his feet for less than thirty seconds and was quite embarrassed at having to stand up at all. On the other hand, Doctor Murphy delivered a very elegant speech and welcomed Gavin into the bosom of his family.

Ronan then called on Gavin to say a few words and to thank the bridesmaids for looking so charming. Gavin remarked that he would not say anything derogatory about the best man as his speech had yet to come, but he sincerely thanked him for his very special contribution in making the day such a wonderful success. This was met with a loud round of applause from all the guests.

Eventually Ronan stood up. Gavin buried his head in his hands and secretly said a prayer that he wouldn't say anything that was going to cause serious embarrassment.

"Reverend Father, respective parents, Geraldine and Gavin, what can I say that has never been said before? I won't keep you long," and then he proceeded to take eighteen sheets of paper out of his inside pocket. This was met with much laughter.

"I have been doing a bit of research into the O'Neill family background," he continued, "and I have found out that when Gavin was born he was so ugly the midwife slapped his mother's face instead of the baby's bottom."

This was met with slightly muted laughter and he continued.

"They used to take Gavin swimming every weekend but somehow he always managed to get out of the plastic bag and kept following them home."

This time, the remark was met with some raised eyebrows, but when he announced that Gavin's father always maintained that there was a hole in the condom, the glares he received from both sets of parents, particularly Mrs O'Neill, and the open-mouthed stare from Father Slattery, were sufficient for him to call it a day.

Ronan decided that he had got away with enough and changed his tone immediately.

"Seriously," he continued, "Gavin is a very lucky man to be getting such a lovely girl. Mr and Mrs O'Neill and Doctor and Mrs Murphy are lovely people, who I was delighted and honoured to meet last evening, and I can only say that they must be very proud of them both. I wish Gavin and Geraldine many long years of happiness together and may they live to see their children's children."

Knowing that he was in front again having resorted to the old traditional prose, he finally thanked everyone for coming and proposed the toast to the bride and groom. Much to his surprise, his speech was greeted with warm applause, led by Gavin, who was delighted that it was all over.

"Thanks a bundle," Gavin whispered to Ronan after he had sat down.

"You're very welcome," came the reply, "and I suppose it was a good job that I didn't thank Willie the Wanker for personally looking after Father Slattery."

Gavin just shook his head from side to side and Ronan's face broke into its usual broad grin as he soaked up all the acclaim he was receiving from everybody. Dancing followed the meal and then very shortly afterwards the bridesmaids hurried the bride away to a changing room. Ronan escorted Gavin to a bedroom and they gave each other a big hug, as everything had passed off so well.

"Get your ass out of here fast, O'Neill," he quipped. "You're wasting valuable drinking time."

At 6.30pm Ronan had a taxi organised to take the bride and groom to Shannon Airport, where they boarded a plane to London and onwards to Las Palmas, Grand Canaria, where they were to spend their honeymoon.

CHAPTER 16

The ferry churned into Tarbert and, after saying goodbye to some of the passengers he had met on board, Duffy was back in his car again heading towards Killarney. He decided that he was going to stay the night there in the Great Southern Hotel before attempting the drive over the mountain pass to Bantry, which is known as Molls Gap. He was informed that after Bantry the road improved considerably all the way to Clonakilty. One of his other reasons for staying in Killarney was to check out its famous golf course that he had read so much about in various golfing magazines. He remembered reading that it nestled between the lakes and the mountains and was one of the most scenic courses in Europe. Since he was so close to it, it would be a serious offence not to pay it a visit.

On his way to Killarney he passed through the large provincial town of Listowel and decided to stop for lunch. Once again it was served in a pub but as long as he sat in a corner where he could not see the bar he felt safe.

After lunch he had some time to spare so he wandered into the local court house to see what was going on. He had never been in a court outside America, so he didn't know what to expect.

At first sight he considered it a most unusual building and the courtroom looked quite small. At the farthest point from where he was standing at the door there was a large high dais where the judge was already seated in his black robes and black pepper coloured wig. This lofty podium had stairs at either side and to the left was the long jury box and to the right was the witness stand. The accused stood alone in a raised section directly in front of the judge and this was called the dock. Seated on benches at the front were wigged gentlemen, and Duffy assumed that these must be the barristers that he had read about in various foreign crime reports. The public sat in tiered seating and a row of steps at the entrance door to the chamber granted access to these seats. As proceedings were getting under way he sat down very quietly.

The first case was called and two itinerant traders, or travelling people as they are referred to in Ireland, climbed into the dock together. There was hardly enough room for both of them and they didn't seem to have anyone representing them.

"Superintendent," bellowed the Judge to a senior uniformed Garda who was prosecuting on behalf of the State. "What are they charged with?"

"Breaking and entering, your Honour," replied the senior police officer.

"Have you anything to say for yourselves before I pass sentence?" asked the judge, casually looking across at the two hopeless cases.

"Gosh, that was quick," Duffy thought to himself. "Sure is fast justice in this part of the country."

The two itinerants looked at each other and then one of them spoke,

"What did he say? What did the judge say?" the slightly deafer one asked repeatedly.

"He wants to know if we have any excuses for being in that man's house."

"Tell him we were only sheltering from the rain," came the audible response.

"Your Honour, sir, me and Tom were only sheltering from the rain," replied the younger one, looking innocently at the judge.

The judge nearly exploded and lambasted both of them, telling them that they had no right to be inside anyone's house and a home was a place where good people lived, not reprobates. "Six months each," he yelled at them.

"What did he say? What did he say?" echoed the deafer one again.

"He has given us six months each," came his friend's reply.

"Jaysus, that's not too bad at all. Sure we'll do that on our ear and we will be in out of the cold for the winter."

"I heard that," roared the judge. "Now you can have six months for the other ears as well and that will keep the both of you inside until the end of next summer. That's a year each in case you can't count or have you any more smart remarks for me? Take them down."

Suddenly Duffy realised that this was quite serious stuff and not really a jovial matter at all. He thought that New York was fast but this case was over in a matter of minutes. It was clear that the judge was quite familiar with the accused as in order to reach such a speedy decision they must have been up before him on many previous occasions.

With that Duffy left the court for fear that he might burst out laughing and get arrested for contempt. It was only when he was outside that he chuckled out loud.

Today the District Court of Ireland was sitting in the town of Listowel and during the coming weeks it would move to other towns within the County of Kerry. It was the judge's duty to travel around his District and he was regarded by all as a very respectable, fair minded and honourable gentleman. However, Duffy had never seen or heard anything quite like this before in his lifetime and it was going to be a great story to talk about when he got back to Brooklyn.

CHAPTER 17

By 1972 Gavin and Geraldine's family had expanded by two girls: Deirdre was born in 1966 and then Fiona. There was only fifteen months between them. There were no additional children mainly because twin beds were now installed in the master bedroom. Whatever love and affection had existed between Geraldine and Gavin in the early years had faded. They were only staying together for the sake of the children.

Gavin was still in Limerick and had made tremendous inroads into the tourism industry in that region. He was still a keen golfer and maintained his membership at Lahinch Golf Club, but also played the links courses of Listowel and Ballybunion. He found himself entertaining clients at least once a week and he had to make official trips to Dublin approximately every month. He saw his daughters every night, usually when they were tucked up in bed but he insisted on making time for them, mostly at weekends.

Geraldine had joined the local golf club and played every Tuesday and Saturday. She was also a member of the Lisfoy Bridge Club and that occupied most of her other free time. Her week was well planned. She was always at home on Sundays as they usually visited one or other of the grandparents for Sunday lunch, but unfortunately Geraldine was no longer *flavour of the month* with Mrs O'Neill. Indeed, she was no longer that wonderful girl who had married her son. On many occasions Gavin had to listen while his mother ranted and raved down the phone about the amount of time his wife was spending on golf courses and at bridge clubs, instead of being at home looking after the children.

"Those children are rearing themselves," she would say. "You'll have to put your foot down."

But what could he do? He knew that he had not the same warmth for Geraldine any more and the reverse equally applied. Whatever was in store, he just had to make the most of it. The present arrangement was probably the best as they very seldom came into direct contact with each other for long periods of time. The ironic thing was that he didn't play golf with her any more, although that had been one of the passions that originally attracted him to her, and he had never played bridge. He consoled himself by saying that he enjoyed his own company in the evenings and liked watching television without interruptions.

They argued and shouted at each other on many occasions and both of them threatened to leave from time to time, but they never did. They had parted company a few times, but only for a couple days at the most. They stayed together, knowing that what they had was better than nothing at all. The girls were only six and five years of age and despite everything Gavin and Geraldine did not want to break up the family while they were so young. But it was becoming a marriage of convenience.

That October, Gavin got a letter inviting him to dinner with the board of directors at headquarters in Dublin. Everyone was excited, including Geraldine, and for a short time things seemed to change for the better. He phoned his parents, and his mother was delighted that he was mixing in such distinguished company. When Geraldine rang her parents with the news, they were equally pleased. To celebrate the arrival of this letter, even though he hadn't a clue what it proposed, they decided to get a babysitter for the evening, and Gavin booked a table for two in the St. Gregory.

"We should do this more often," he said, looking across the dinner table at his wife, and she agreed with a nod.

"Brings back memories," he went on. "I can still see Ronan standing at the bar with a whiskey in his hand and you looking so lovely on the day."

This brought a faint smile to her lips but she lowered her head and looked sideways as if he had said something wrong.

It reminded him of the way a shy and embarrassed schoolgirl might respond. He had to remind himself that this was his wife he was talking to, and he wondered if he really knew her at all.

"You look lovely tonight as well," he added, trying to compliment her but she pretended she hadn't heard. Every time he tried to get close to her, or say something nice, she immediately put up a barrier. He wondered why they had ever got married, and considered that both of them had found the wrong partner. At times like this, Sheila Maguire's words always came back to haunt him. Gavin envied the couples at other tables who were laughing and smiling happily at each other and wished that he and his wife could be more like them.

The following morning he set out for Dublin. On the way up, he drove through the towns of Roscrea, Portlaoise and Kildare and onwards through Newbridge and into Naas. He arrived in Dublin by mid-afternoon and checked into the Gresham Hotel on O'Connell Street. After showering and shaving, he changed into his tuxedo and at 6.30pm the taxi he had arranged picked him up.

The taxi drove up O'Connell Street, passed the front of Trinity College that he knew so well and into Kildare Street. It then made its way around St. Stephen's Green and joined Morehampton Road. It finally turned left into Waterloo Road and stopped just beyond Baggot Street Bridge. This was the neighbourhood most frequented by the poet James Kavanagh and the writer Brendan Behan and Gavin was very familiar with this part of the city. When he entered the foyer of the Irish International Tourism Association's Headquarters on Pembroke Road, he was immediately shown into the Raglan suite. Within a few minutes Oliver Farrell, the Chief Executive, walked into the room.

"Hello, Gavin," he said, greeting him with a firm handshake. "It's good to see you."

"Thanks, Oliver," he replied. "It's certainly good to be here."

"We are having dinner this evening in the Liffey Room with Jack McConville, my deputy, who as you know is totally in charge of Regional Affairs, and Owen Hynes, who is the Company Secretary."

"I'm delighted to be in such esteemed company," smiled Gavin, and then the others entered the room and more greetings and handshakes were exchanged.

"This is a working dinner," commented Oliver, "so I think we should get started right away." With that they all made their way across the corridor and into the Liffey Suite.

The room was panelled in mahogany veneer that matched the table and the chairs. The long dining table was covered with a pure white Irish Linen tablecloth and the silver cutlery gleamed, as did the various crystal glasses and tumblers that were meticulously positioned at every place setting. The centrepiece on the table was an extremely large green wax candle with four separate wicks, each representing one of the four Provinces of Ireland. This room was part of the old house and dated back more than 200 years.

After a short speech by way of introduction, the Chief Executive looked at Gavin. "I suppose you're wondering why you've been called here tonight and why everything is so secretive?"

Gavin nodded by way of acknowledgement, and the CEO continued.

"I'll come straight to the point. We want you to take over the New York Office with the title of Senior Executive Vice President."

Gavin nearly choked on his beef Wellington and reached for a glass of water.

"We had to keep this appointment completely secret as it is an internal one and not a political one," continued Oliver. "The contracts are to run for a five-year period, with the usual *out clauses* in the event of extenuating circumstances. Your starting salary will be $75,000 per year, with expenses and annual reviews of course. If you accept this offer, you will take up the position on 23rd January next year, and you can stay at the New York Hilton on 6th Avenue for the first three months until you find suitable accommodation for your wife and family."

Gavin was completely astonished as he wiped the corner of his mouth with his white linen napkin.

Jack McConville jokingly interjected that the appointment was not essentially because of Gavin's good looks, which of course were a vital ingredient in the tourism industry, but mainly because he was a hard working individual who had injected fresh life into the Limerick and Shannon Regional Area. He added that after consulting with other members of the board they all agreed that Gavin was definitely the best man for the job.

"We only have one problem," continued the Chief Executive. "We need the contracts signed tonight so that we can release a press statement in the morning, and that's the reason why Owen is sitting beside you with his briefcase open and documents to hand."

"There is no problem whatsoever," commented Gavin assertively. "I can tell you right now that I am absolutely delighted and honoured to accept this promotion."

He stuttered on some words but he didn't care as he was beaming from ear to ear. He almost pinched his leg to make sure he wasn't dreaming. The documents were duly signed, witnessed and stamped with the official seal of the company and Gavin became a Senior Executive Vice President with immediate effect.

CHAPTER 18

It was decided that the family would go to a hotel for Christmas 1972, mainly because Geraldine said she didn't feel like cooking on Christmas Day. This decision was met with deep disgust from Mrs O'Neill, and Mrs Murphy wasn't too happy about it either. They both pointed out, in different ways, that the girls would be missing something by not having Christmas at home, but Geraldine was adamant. Gavin had no say in the matter and just followed on in blind obedience.

"What sort of a man are you? You're always dancing to her tune," his mother hissed down the phone. "Do you think that you can waltz in and out of this house when you feel like it on St Stephen's Day, because you can't. Your father and I will not put up with it."

"Don't worry, mother," he replied. "I won't be troubling you, as we're going up to Galway on Christmas Eve and not returning until after St Stephen's Day."

"Mother of God," she yelled. "What's got into you?" but he refrained from replying to her laments, as he knew it would only be heaping hot coals on already heated cinders.

"OK, OK, mother, I'll bring the children up on Christmas Eve about lunch time if that's all right."

"All right?" came the indignant reply, as Mrs. O'Neill seemed to forget what she had said a few seconds earlier and was now starting to contradict herself. "What a thing to say. All right? Sure the children are always welcome here at any time, and you should know that without me telling you."

"Yes, mother, I know," Gavin replied calmly.

With that he decided to stop talking and, letting her know that he was looking forward to seeing her, he replaced the phone with a deep sigh.

On Christmas Eve morning the children were thrilled as they drove along the road to Lahinch, as they were looking forward to seeing their granny and grandad. Gavin knew that he was adding more than two hours' driving time to the journey to Galway, but he also knew that it was well worth it, as it kept his mother's anger at bay.

They arrived in Lahinch at about 12.30pm and Mrs O'Neill was really pleased to see her grandchildren. She gave Gavin a kiss on the cheek but instead of following this with a kiss to Geraldine, she only offered her hand. Had it been any other time of the year, Geraldine might not have got out of the car at all. However, as it was Christmas, she grudgingly took Mrs O'Neill's hand and planted a small kiss on her mother-in-law's left cheek. This was followed with a slight nod. She knew there was no fondness left between them. Mrs O'Neill was all over her grandchildren, and was showing very spontaneous signs of love and affection.

Very few words were exchanged during lunch but the children were having such great fun opening their presents that they were oblivious to the tense atmosphere among the adults. Mr O'Neill was a man of very few words and simply remarked, "Sure Christmas is only a time for children."

They arrived at the hotel in Galway at 5.30pm and went to their room to relax and freshen up before going down for dinner.

Santa Claus arrived the following morning and breakfast was served until 11.00am. This was followed by Mass which was celebrated in the main ballroom. Lunch was served between 1.30pm and 3.00pm, which left some space before the Gala Dinner Dance at 8.00pm. All children under fourteen had their own dinner at 6.00pm and were then chaperoned to the television room while their parents dressed formally for the gala occasion. Dancing went on into the small hours and Gavin noticed that Geraldine seemed more willing to dance with the other men at the table, who were complete strangers to her, than dance with him. Eventually he just gave up, and spent most of his time at the bar.

St Stephen's Day was welcomed by the *Wren Boys*, which is a tradition in the Galway region. These small groups of people wander from village to village singing songs about the wren, the King of all Birds, and accept coins and small change, which are converted into Guinness and whiskey at a later stage in the evening.

After lunch a treasure hunt was arranged that covered half of County Galway and prizes were distributed at the dinner later that evening. Before dinner a snooker competition took place but this only attracted a few. Gavin did not participate either. The evening entertainment was practically a carbon copy of the night before and after breakfast the following morning they left for the long journey back to Limerick via Kilkee.

It was 3.00pm before they arrived in Kilkee and the Murphys were delighted to see them. The doctor had a very sincere handshake for Gavin and congratulated him on his recent promotion. He pushed a glass of whiskey into his hand and suggested that they try and arrange a round of golf before his departure for America. The girls enjoyed opening more presents and expressed their delight at having Santa Claus visit three times that year. At 8.00pm, after they had said their last goodbyes, Gavin pointed his car towards Limerick and, as he drove slowly out of the town, he knew that the Christmas times he had loved and enjoyed so much in his youth would never be the same again.

CHAPTER 19

On the morning of 23rd January 1973 they all piled into the car for the thirty minute drive to Shannon Airport. Gavin was saddened at leaving his family for the first time, but he knew that this was a wonderful opportunity to do all that he wanted to do with his life and to give the girls the best education that he could possibly afford.

The loving embraces from the children totally contrasted with a brush of the cheek from Geraldine. However, no matter what, he would remain faithful to her as long as he could, as he saw no real future without her.

He walked up to the check-in desk and presented his ticket and passport. A smiling Aer Lingus ground hostess greeted him and the formalities were completed in a few minutes. As he turned around and waved back to his family, another hostess appeared and ushered him into the VIP lounge. Inside he was offered a glass of champagne and his choice of newspapers.

"Irish Independent," he replied, and settling down in a large armchair he relaxed as he waited for his flight to be called.

About forty-five minutes later he was escorted out onto the apron at Shannon Airport, and then up the front steps of the aircraft where he was greeted at the door by the Cabin Manager. Before entering, he glanced back hopefully to see if there was any chance of seeing his children again. There wasn't.

"Good morning, Mr O'Neill. Welcome on board. Your seat is window 1A. I will be with you in a few minutes."

He was hardly in his seat when a younger hostess presented him with another glass of champagne and a selection of canapés.

"Maybe you would just prefer a glass of orange juice, sir?" she asked.

"No, no," replied Gavin. "This is just fine."

From where he sat, he admired the décor: the horseshoe bar, the fruit bowl, the flower arrangements and the spiral staircase that led upstairs to the private lounge. Just after take-off, when the aircraft started its slow climb to cruise level, the Cabin Manager returned and asked him how he was and if everything was to his satisfaction. He nodded his agreement and she then presented him with the menu and wine list. For dinner he had caviar and smoked salmon as a starter, followed by lobster thermidor and baked Alaska for dessert.

He was very much at ease in the spacious seat and watched the latest Hollywood movie on the wide screen that was rolled down from the ceiling of the aircraft. When the movie was over, curiosity got the better of him, and he made his way up the spiral staircase to the upper lounge, which is also known as the bubble, and sat on the leather wall seating that practically surrounded the entire area. As he looked through the window, he could see the snowy wastelands of Northern Labrador far below.

He arrived in New York about six and a half hours after leaving Shannon and he felt well fed, content and very refreshed. As this was his very first transatlantic crossing, it was difficult for him to realise that he had crossed the mighty ocean in such comfort and also experienced a five hour time shift. It was 9.00pm in Ireland but only 4.00pm on the east coast of America.

After passing through Immigration and Customs he made his way outside the terminal building, hailed a yellow taxi, and asked the driver to take him to the Hilton Hotel on 6th Avenue. The cab made its way down the Van Wyck Expressway, past the rows of wooden houses that lined the roadway on either side, before turning off onto the notoriously busy Long Island Expressway. As Gavin passed the many cemeteries visible on the way into the city, he wondered how many Irish people were buried there. Eventually the taxi entered the Queens Midtown Tunnel that connects to Manhattan Island at East 37th Street. The driver continued along this street, crossing Park and 5th Avenues until he reached 6th. Here he turned right and drove all the way up the Avenue of the

Americas until they reached the New York Hilton Hotel.

Gavin checked in and went to his room. He was quite tired. It was now 6.00pm local time, but his body clock was still on Irish time. As he sat and rested, he reflected again on the distance he had travelled in such a short space of time. He contacted the hotel operator and placed a call to Ireland. It was after 11.00pm there, and Geraldine would have had the children in bed long ago. It took twenty minutes for the phone to ring back and he was surprised that he could hear Geraldine's voice so clearly.

"Hello, how are you?" he asked. "I had a great flight and I am now in my bedroom."

"Isn't it well for some?" came the quirky reply, and then silence.

"I am going downstairs for something to eat shortly and then I'll turn in for the night."

"OK," came the reply in the same tone as before.

"Tell me," he continued, "how are the children?"

"Sure, they're great. Why wouldn't they be after seeing their Daddy going off in a big aeroplane today."

He never knew which way to take her. Was she trying to be funny? Was she being serious? Was she being sarcastic?

"Give them my love in the morning," he replied. They said goodbye to each other and hung up at the same time. He felt rejected and deflated when he should have been feeling on top of the world. He then went downstairs for his snack and when he returned to the room he was so tired that he was asleep before his head hit the pillow.

The following morning he made contact with the outgoing representative of the New York Office. He knew that he was replacing Paul Dunlop, who was returning to Ireland and he also knew that Paul was taking up his old job in Limerick, which definitely wasn't a promotion. Gavin liked Paul and, knowing that it wasn't his fault that Paul was being demoted, decided to take him out for dinner. He invited him to the Rotary Room of the Waldorf

Astoria Hotel and listened to his side of the story, pretending to be interested. The next day Gavin decided that it would be better policy to wait until Paul had time to empty his desk before moving in. Paul Dunlop departed for Ireland that same evening on flight EI 104.

The branch of the Irish International Tourism Association was on Park Avenue, just across the road from the New York branch of the Bank of Chicago. It was also situated quite close to the new branch of Allied Irish Banks which had recently opened and was now expanding well outside Ireland. The Association's suite was on the 34th floor of the McKenzie Building, and was of the open plan design that was now being introduced in major office buildings all over the United States. Gavin's private office was positioned in a corner of the main office and had two glass walls that were fitted with Venetian blinds. These could easily be closed when privacy was required. It was quite roomy and contained a large mahogany desk and matching bookcases and, as he was leaving that first evening, the engraver was already inscribing his name on the door. The wording, Mr Gavin O'Neill, Senior Executive Vice President, in gold lettering looked very impressive on the glass panel. "One thing for sure about the States," he thought to himself, "they don't waste much time in getting things done."

There were eight staff in the main office – two Irish and six Americans – and in order to win them over Gavin arranged dinner for everyone in the very fashionable Metropolitan Club in midtown Manhattan.

After dinner, he made an informal speech and pointed out to them that he was their new boss and as the New York Office was the *jewel in the crown,* he expected hard work and loyalty from them all. He went on to say that he would not tolerate gossip about anyone, past or present, and if there were any complaints about staff procedures they should arrive on his desk first. He didn't want to be the last to know. He informed them that most things could be solved without union intervention and also he had heard they were all very willing workers. He finally told them that he would be a very just and practical boss, that he was delighted to be associated with them and honoured to be in their company. Dinner was a success. They were all behind him.

The premier task he set himself over the next nine months was to meet all the general managers and heads of major airlines operating out of La Guardia and Kennedy Airports. He wanted to meet all the local tourist board managers and the chairpersons of the various chambers of commerce. He also decided that it would be good kudos to speak with those in charge of Irish social clubs in the New York region, as these were his grass roots. He immediately invited to lunch the presidents and vice presidents of all the major international banking organisations that had branches in New York. Later in the month he decided to dine with the head of the Port Authority Office, which is situated just off West 42nd Street. Finally he made it his business to meet the Mayor of New York and the Chief of Police, who was of Irish parentage.

He decided to return to Ireland in early March but he had to be back in New York again for the St Patrick's Day Parade, which is the largest of its kind in the world. He was certainly on top of his job and felt that 1973 was going to be a very hectic and a very productive year for him.

CHAPTER 20

Gavin's flight to Ireland on 3rd March was very relaxing. The aeroplane touched down at Shannon Airport on time at 6.30am GMT. It was still dark. After clearing customs he hurriedly got into a waiting taxi. During the forty minute drive to Limerick he thought of how lonely he was for the children and how little he missed Geraldine. His mind was in turmoil as he contemplated over and over again what had gone wrong between them. In the beginning both of them had had certain feelings for each other, but now there was no emotion linking them at all. Once again that conversation he had had with Sheila Maguire entered his head and he knew that he had married for all the wrong reasons. But there was no such thing as divorce in Ireland. The law simply didn't exist. The best he could expect was a very messy separation agreement which would cause even more confusion in the long run. He put the notion quickly out of his head as the taxi had arrived outside the front door of his house.

The children were delighted to see their Daddy, and were especially thrilled with the presents that he had brought them. They climbed onto his knees and hugged and kissed him and he told them stories about New York, the tall buildings and the Zoo in Central Park. He noticed Geraldine standing at the doorway listening to him, but she did not participate and her body language clearly indicated that she was using the door as a barrier.

He knew that he might not be the easiest person to get along with due to his present working lifestyle which certainly did not suit her and because of this she was not showing any signs of willingness to cross the Atlantic and join him. He needed her with him if they were ever to make a go of things in New York so he made up his mind that plans for the future had to be put in place.

He decided that a game of golf might help him think better, so the following day he phoned Doctor Murphy.

"Hello, Patrick. Gavin here. I'm home for a few days and I was wondering if you would like to try a few holes at Lahinch."

"Try and stop me," came the happy reply, "and if you have time, maybe we will have a go at Ballybunion as well."

The arrangements were made and they met at Lahinch the following morning. After the usual pleasantries were exchanged the doctor asked Gavin if he had looked at any house properties in the New York area. "I suggest you do this fairly quickly, Gavin," commented the doctor, "as house prices are rising and I think it would encourage Geraldine to get herself out there a lot quicker."

"She is showing very little sign of being in any hurry to join me," replied Gavin, "and I can't drag her out by the hair."

"Em," answered the doctor, "I think we will all meet for dinner tomorrow night in the St Gregory where we can discuss this matter in more detail. In the meantime, I will make a couple of phone calls."

"Great," replied Gavin and with that the subject changed back again to golf. The discussion ebbed and flowed as to whether Bobby Jones was the greatest amateur golfer that ever lived, and how well Christy O'Connor and Harry (The Brad) Bradshaw were performing on the Irish Circuit. Arnold Palmer was also mentioned in the conversation.

They arrived at the St Gregory Hotel the following evening. After drinks in the bar they all moved to the reserved table in the dining room, where they enjoyed a traditional dinner of roast spring lamb. When tea and coffee were being served, Doctor Murphy moved Gavin to another room where he very subtly brought up the subject of property in the States.

"Gavin," he said. "An old friend of mine called Jack Greenfield is living in White Plains in Westchester County and you should give him a ring when you get back and tell him I sent you. I was on the phone to him today so he is expecting you to give him a ring. I'll give you his number when we get back to the house."

"Thanks, Patrick, I'll give him a call as soon as I get back," replied Gavin and asked, "Is he of Irish extraction?"

"Oh, second or third generation," came the reply, "but I know he has a keen nose for property and my father and his father were great pals a long time ago."

"Thanks very much, Patrick, I appreciate what you're doing," responded Gavin again.

"He will definitely put you on the right track," continued the doctor as they walked back into the dining room again. When they rejoined the others there was a distinct pause in the conversation.

"Heavens, look at the time," interjected Mrs Murphy, looking at Gavin, "and you have an early flight to catch tomorrow morning."

It had been a very enjoyable evening and at least Gavin was now getting the direction that he so badly needed. He thought to himself that Margaret Murphy looked every inch the doctor's wife and they really were a very nice couple. Geraldine also looked pretty in her little black dress and he asked himself why it wasn't possible for things to be like this all the time.

The following morning he boarded the Aer Lingus flight at Shannon for another transatlantic crossing and approximately seven hours later a taxi was transporting him once again into New York City. As the cab made its way into Manhattan he sat looking out at the various sights but this time he wasn't taking them in. His mind was totally focused on all the events leading up to the forthcoming St Patrick's Day Parade as this was going to be a very important and busy time for him.

All New Yorkers want to be Irish on St Patrick's Day. They look for distant relations with whom they can identify and even use divorced in-laws as a reason for being Irish. New Yorkers not only wear green on St Patrick's Day but also drink green beer as well as copious amounts of Guinness and Irish whiskey, and thoroughly enjoy themselves.

This major event is regarded as the most popular parade in New York City. It starts at 44th Street at approximately 11.00am and marches up 5th Avenue as far as 86th Street, where it disperses around 2.30pm. One of the best places for viewing the Parade is from the steps of the Metropolitan Museum on the east side of Central Park on 5th Avenue. Despite the fact that cars, lorries, exhibits and floats are not allowed in the parade, it still attracts more than 150,000 spectators to see the marching bands and the various representatives from all over the world, including two columns of Aer Lingus air hostesses in their beautiful green uniforms.

Gavin was seated at the Rockefeller Center with other business associates and he felt very honoured to be in such prestigious company. Further up on the right hand side of 5th Avenue, as was traditional, His Eminence Terence Cardinal Cooke, the Catholic Archbishop of New York, and other visiting dignitaries, were taking their seats on the steps of St Patrick's Cathedral.

This was the 213th St Patrick's Day Parade, but it was Gavin's first as a Senior Executive Vice President. He decided to keep a low profile as a political influence was spilling over into this year's event. A procession of marchers carried fourteen coffins, all draped with black flags, commemorating the events of Bloody Sunday in Northern Ireland, when unarmed civil rights protesters had been shot dead during a demonstration.

CHAPTER 21

The clock on Listowel's town hall indicated exactly 2.15pm and Duffy calculated that if he left now he would miss most of the heavy traffic in Tralee. He hoped to arrive in Killarney about 3.30pm. He realised that distances by American standards meant absolutely nothing in Ireland due to its large network of narrow twisting roads. Even if he did get a stretch of open roadway, this could be blocked for twenty minutes or more by a farmer taking his cows home for milking, or his sheep to market. Both of these events were everyday occurrences.

When he arrived in Killarney he drove around the town's one way traffic system, keeping his eye open for a vacant parking space and on his second time around he found one. He parked in Kenmare Place just off the Muckross Road and walked the short distance to the Great Southern Hotel. He was greeted by a cheerful uniformed porter who took his bags inside.

"How long are you staying with us, sir?" enquired the porter.

"Just for one night," replied Duffy.

"Oh, that's not long enough for Killarney, sir. You'll have to come back and see it properly another time."

Smiling at the porter he slipped him a tip, made his way to the reception desk and checked in.

His room was exquisite and overlooked the main street where he could see town folk and tourists mingling freely together. This was a lovely part of Ireland and one that had been made famous in song and verse. From his window he could see four or five of the two-wheeled one-horse vehicles known as jaunting cars waiting to take people on the grand tour of the famous lakes.

"Next time I'll do that," he thought to himself, looking at the jaunting cars, "but this time is strictly reserved for golf."

He had read in American golfing editorials that golf had been played in Killarney since the 1890s. In the late 1940s the course was extended from a nine hole to an eighteen hole course and this encapsulated all the beauty of the lakes and the mountains. The eighteenth par three hole was described as one of the most beautiful and most stunning golf shots in Europe, and it was the club's signature hole. This he had to see and he felt quite exhilarated.

Duffy asked the porter to order him a taxi and as he waited in the drawing room of the hotel he watched as other people were sitting quietly, either reading their daily newspapers or sipping tea or coffee. A couple were chatting happily to each other and he thought that this was indeed a very civilised way to live.

"Your hackney is here, sir," called the porter and Duffy, knowing that this was what the Irish called taxis, made his way outside. He asked the driver to take him to the Golf Club and on the way he received a pleasant commentary on places such as the Gap of Dunloe and Kate Kearney's cottage.

"That will be seventy five pence, sir," stated the driver when they arrived. Duffy gave him a punt and told him to keep the change and walking into the club he introduced himself to the chief steward. After shaking hands, he was directed to the sports shop where he was fitted out with a pair of golf shoes, a sweater, a set of golf clubs and a hand drawn caddy-car, all at a reasonable cost. He was also given a score card which he relegated to his golf bag. He was only here for pleasure.

He walked down to the first hole and admired the view. He could have been in an Alpine country with the proximity of the tall stark slate-coloured mountains reflecting in the lakes below. He had never seen grass so green. As there were a few people watching him, he teed his ball up quite high so as to be sure of hitting it and took a couple of practice swings just to limber up. He always maintained that if he could swing at the ball as well as he could swing at fresh air he would be as good as Sam Snead.

Then he stood quite still, lined himself up and hit a fine shot right down the middle of the fairway, which gave the few people watching something to talk about. As he walked down the fairway of the first hole a smile broke out across his face, his step quickened and he felt he was walking to the top of the world. He was in heaven.

The second hole was a total disaster and Duffy lost three balls one after another. He was beginning to swear at everything and anything that moved, so he decided to skip that hole, and pulled his caddy-car to the third tee.

Standing there with a seven iron, he took his usual two practice swings and with a short back swing, he hit a beautiful shot right onto the middle of the green. He was again beaming from ear to ear but unfortunately there wasn't anyone watching him this time. Taking out his putter he placed the ball twelve inches from the hole and sank the putt for a par three. He felt great.

The next hole was a par five and the fairway was quite narrow. To the left was a copse of small trees and bushes. That is where he hit his first ball. He uttered many choice four letter words, but was determined to find this ball so that he could continue his game. He decided that there was no more room for excuses so he walked in a direct line from the tee to where the ball had entered the small thicket of trees. As he was tramping around in the undergrowth, kicking at this and that, a ball practically landed at his feet. He looked up, shocked. Another foot and it would have hit him on the head. He hadn't a notion where it came from as there wasn't anyone playing behind him. Then it dawned on him that it must have come from another fairway behind the bushes.

Standing in the shrubbery, he was about to let out another string of unsuitable language, when he spotted the owner of the ball walking in his direction. She was a very well-dressed woman in her mid forties. She was wearing brown culottes with short white socks and a short sleeved Fair Isle jumper over a white blouse. A flat chequered cap made up her ensemble. Duffy immediately bit his lip and, walking out onto the fairway, waved at her. She spotted him immediately.

"I'm so sorry," she yelled. "Did I nearly hit you?"

"Oh no, not at all," lied Duffy. "You missed me by a mile. I've marked the spot where your ball is. It's over here."

He saw that she was an attractive woman so under no circumstances was he going to tell her that she had nearly killed him. She thanked him for marking her ball, and they exchanged a few words. Then he asked her if she was playing alone.

"Yes," she replied. "I'm not that good, and it's hard to find a partner sometimes."

"Me too, ma'am, so don't worry," he replied. "I've been in places on golf courses where no other human being has ever stood."

They both laughed and the ice was broken.

"You're from America?" she quipped.

"Well, yes, ah – New York." He decided not to use the old cliché that he had used back in the hotel at Lahinch as it was a bit corny.

The woman spoke again and asked him, "Is this your first time in Ireland?"

"Eh, yes, it is, but it will not be my last." Then he pointed to her golf ball. "Ma'am, could I be so bold as to suggest that I might have the pleasure of playing in with you," he asked her in his very polite American Brooklyn English. "By the way, which hole are we on anyway?"

"I would be very pleased if you would," she replied immediately. "This is the fifteenth hole."

He considered that he had lost enough balls and this was a great way of ending the round. Even if a person had no interest whatsoever in golf, the last few holes at Killarney are magnificent: the scenery is just exceptional. As Duffy played the final hole with this attractive woman he considered himself very lucky to have lost a ball at the fourth hole.

When they arrived back at the Clubhouse he asked her if she would like a lift back into town. She informed him that she had her own car and then Duffy asked her if she knew any good restaurants in Killarney.

"There is a new one just opened called the Forecourt," she replied. "I had a meal there about two weeks ago and it was excellent,"

"Do they serve steaks there?" he enquired.

"Yes, with prawns, mushrooms and onions on the side," she joyfully replied.

He could feel his mouth salivating and, nodding at her, he said, "Wow, I'm hungry already. Would you do me the great honour of joining me for dinner this evening ma'am?"

"I would be delighted," she replied.

"Would 8.30pm suit you, ma'am?"

"Yes, that would be perfect," she responded. "Will you know how to get there?"

"Oh, don't worry about that, ma'am, I'll find it OK," and touching his hat he watched as she reversed her car out of the parking area. He returned all his borrowed goods to the club and requested the steward to call him a taxi.

When he had walked down the first hole at Killarney he had thought that he was on his way to the top of the world. Now as he sat in the Clubhouse waiting for his taxi, he felt that he had just arrived at the top.

That evening Duffy spent much longer than usual getting ready. He bathed, shaved, manicured his nails, shampooed what little hair he had and took out a clean shirt and tie. He asked for an iron so that he could give his suit a press, and then he dithered as to whether to take his hat or not. He decided that the hat went with him as he felt slightly uncomfortable without it. He looked in the mirror again and everything that reflected back looked much better than usual. He asked directions to the Forecourt Restaurant as he was determined to be there on time. It was so long since he had been out on a date that he felt clumsy and self-conscious, but for the first time in many years he felt contented. He was now sitting at the table he had reserved and the time was exactly 8.25pm. At 8.30pm, she walked in.

She was wearing a beautiful pair of beige linen trousers with a cream blouse and a lovely dark velvet jacket. She wore medium high heel leather boots and carried a clutch bag in her right hand. Her outfit was complemented with a topaz necklace and matching earrings. Her make-up was lovely and she looked very eye-catching. Duffy could not take his eyes off her.

As soon as she sat down, she said, "Mr Duffy, I love your American accent but we will have to dispense with all this ma'am business. My name is Siobhan Comiskey and I have lived in Killarney most of my life."

"Eh, my friends just call me Duffy," he replied. "But I would be delighted if you would call me Brendan. And I have lived in New York for most of my life."

"It's a pleasure to meet you, Brendan."

"And you too, Siobhan," came the happy response.

Over dinner he told her that he was working in Ireland on a commission for a young Irishman who was now living in New York. He then informed her that he would be returning to the States shortly and she told him that she was going to Dublin the following day to visit some relations. They promised to keep in touch.

The evening ended all too quickly and as they exchanged telephone numbers and addresses he assured her that he would call her as soon as he got back to New York. They parted company graciously with handshakes and as he replaced his hat and walked to the car, he felt a wonderful glow of contentment within him and wondered if this might be the woman who could give him a real reason for living again.

PART TWO

AMERICA

CHAPTER 22

Gavin took the Harlem and Hudson Line from Grand Central to Ardsley station, where he was met by Jack Greenfield, his father-in-law's old friend. Jack was a sprightly sixty-eight year old who looked younger than his years and, as they drove in the direction of Scarsdale, he talked about life in America and how long it had been since he had visited the Old Country. Jack had been delighted to get the phone call from Paddy Murphy, as he called him, and was only too pleased to be of assistance to Gavin. It was the last week of March 1973.

"I have viewed three properties in this area, Gavin," he said. "One was not really value for money, the second was a bit on the small side, but the third one is really top drawer." He went on to emphasise that it was *out on its own,* so he advised that they drive to it straight away.

"The next left at the crossroads will take us onto the Sawmill Parkway and it's only a short drive from there," he informed Gavin.

As Gavin looked out through the windscreen of Jack's Pontiac, he realised that this was a very classy area and, having travelled for about ten minutes on this beautiful tree-lined road, Jack exited at junction 41 into the borough of Tarrytown. They drove through the town, taking the second right and there it was: one of the loveliest houses he had ever seen.

What he was looking at was a large New England-style two-storey house, enclosed within a beautiful white picket-type veranda fence. The house was only twenty minutes' driving time from Ardsley station.

"Well, what do you think of that?" asked Jack.

"It's fantastic," replied Gavin, as they drove up the short driveway to the steps leading up to the veranda and the front door. "Gosh, I wonder what it's like inside."

"It looks as good inside as it does on the outside," smiled Jack, as he brought the car to a gentle halt on the driveway.

Inside it had a wooden-floored entrance hallway, three large reception rooms, a large modern kitchen, a small but adequate study and a decent sized downstairs bathroom. There was also a door leading to the basement. As Gavin stood in the hall on the wooden parquet floor, he toyed with the idea that this could be an ideal dancing area for the girls in years to come. He smiled to himself at such a thought.

Upstairs there were five bedrooms, all en-suite, and at the end of the long corridor there was a full bathroom suite and an up-to-the-minute shower unit. The house was perfect.

Gavin wasn't worried if he would have to budget on other items. This was the investment of a lifetime and a perfect place to set up home. He knew that he would have large bank borrowings, but these would be well secured by the deeds of the property and with his position and salary he knew that he could adequately finance the monthly instalments. He also knew that he would be well recommended by his bank back in Ireland.

Jack noticed the happiness in the young man's face and was pleased to have been instrumental in helping him find such a property. He knew that Paddy Murphy would be delighted that he had taken such good care of his son-in-law and he felt an inner warmth of satisfaction.

"As soon as you sign the legal papers," he said to Gavin, "you must come up for dinner with Mary and me. She's looking forward to meeting you."

With that they drove back to Ardsley station.

Jack Greenfield recommended an excellent real estate agent and Gavin set about arranging the mortgage. Letters of credit were set up with his Irish bank. To assist with the purchase and because of his status he also received a large refundable grant from the Irish International Tourism Association.

He contacted Ronan, who was now a bank manager in a large Dublin City office. He went over everything with Ronan who, considering the large capital injection being placed up front by the parent company, hadn't any problems recommending the loan. Ronan also spoke to his American counterparts and completed a mutual trust agreement which under American law necessitated Geraldine's name being placed on the deeds. Such a law did not exist in Ireland but as Gavin wanted this property he had no option but to comply, thus granting her joint ownership. Geraldine signed the necessary documents in Limerick and Gavin endorsed them in front of a notary public in the presence of an American attorney. The loan was sanctioned.

The next morning he phoned Jack Greenfield and told him that everything was in order and sincerely thanked him for assisting him in acquiring such a magnificent property. Jack invited him for dinner the following Sunday.

When he arrived he was met at the door by Mary Greenfield, who gave him a big hug. She was bursting to share his excitement and instantly asked how Geraldine liked her new home.

"Oh, she hasn't said very much," hinted Gavin.

"She hasn't?" came the surprised reply. "Jack says it's a beautiful house."

"It is," responded Gavin, looking for a plausible explanation. "Eh, it's just that she hasn't seen it yet, but when she does she will simply love it."

"I'm surprised she's not on the first flight out of Ireland. What's keeping her?" came the lively response. "Can she not get a flight? I thought that with your connections she could get a seat with Aer Lingus any time."

"She can," stuttered Gavin, knowing well that he was running out of excuses.

"Heavens, if I was in her shoes I would be out here faster than you could say Jack Robinson – or should I say Jack Greenfield?" They all laughed and thankfully this turned the conversation in another direction.

Gavin ate his meal and later confided in Jack that even though Geraldine had signed all the papers she was still being quite obstinate about relocating to the States. Jack just shrugged his shoulders and smiled sympathetically, which clearly indicated that he didn't want to get involved in Gavin's personal affairs. However, he did remark that if he needed any help or advice on house purchase in the future, he would always be there for him. Jack suggested that he contact Geraldine again immediately.

This was a clear prompt to Gavin that it was time for him to act positively and he asked if he could use their phone.

"No problem at all, Gavin," came the response and with that he placed a call to Ireland.

When Geraldine answered, he told her once again how lovely the house was and that she should come out and see it immediately. He went on to say that both sets of grandparents would be only too delighted to look after the children for a few weeks, so there shouldn't be any difficulties at her end. He added that after they got things set up in the States, both of them could return to Ireland again to finalise matters before moving over permanently with the children. He told her that he would contact Aer Lingus on the Monday morning and an open ticket would be in the post to her shortly.

When he finished the call, he returned to their sitting room again.

"Thank you very much," he said. "I am just after talking with Geraldine and first thing tomorrow I am going to arrange that an open ticket is sent to her immediately. She should be here within a week or so."

Two weeks later Gavin picked Geraldine up at JFK International and drove directly to Tarrytown. On the way over he told her that Mary Greenfield thought the house was beautiful but with a shrug of her shoulders Geraldine dismissed Mary's opinion as if it didn't matter. She was still showing a definite lack of enthusiasm but as they rounded the final bend and she saw the house for the first time her manner changed dramatically. She actually remarked that the house looked quite out of the ordinary, and this pleased Gavin very much.

The following week they were both invited over to the Greenfields' for drinks and it became quite obvious from the beginning that Mary Greenfield had taken a dislike to Geraldine because of her self-centred attitude. Jack, however, was more conciliatory and quietly suggested to Gavin that since Geraldine was interested in golf, they should both join Tarrytown Golf Club. Mary commented that this was a good idea as it might be the appropriate place for him to meet important contacts. All this appeared quite sensible and was accomplished quickly with the Greenfields' help. After all the documentation relating to their arrival in America was completed, Gavin and Geraldine returned to Ireland to collect the children.

CHAPTER 23

Gavin was overjoyed that the girls were now in America and he felt that they were all a family again. He promised himself that he was going to do his utmost to make the marriage work. Geraldine was making new friends at the golf club and everything seemed to be flowing along quite peacefully. She met other parents whose children were going to attend summer camp later that year and she proposed to Gavin that the girls should join the camp as well as this would make it easier for them to fully integrate into the community. He had no objection to this but he soon realised when summer arrived that this was only a ploy on Geraldine's part to allow herself more free time during the day.

At the weekends they went for picnics to Bear Mountain and on many occasions they crossed the Hudson on the Tappan Zee Bridge and visited the world famous West Point military academy. In the middle of June as they were returning from one of these trips he was shocked when Geraldine suggested that the following September the children should be enrolled in the Sacred Heart preparatory boarding school for young ladies in Galveston.

He was amazed at her suggestion, which he considered outrageous, as it brought back memories of his own school days when he was a boarder at Oakwood. He told her he totally disagreed with her proposal, and that if she pursued the matter further he would contact both their families in Ireland straight away. They drove home in complete silence.

When they got back to the house all hell broke loose and again he threatened to call Ireland.

"Call them if you want," she yelled back at him at the top of her voice. "I don't care. They are my kids and they are going to Galveston in September."

"They are not going to a boarding school," he shouted back at her. "They are my children too and I tell you here and now – they are not going to a goddamn boarding school."

"They are going to this school and that's all I have to say on the matter," she screamed back at him.

"What in God's name has got into you? No, they are not going and that's the end of it," he countered.

"We'll see about that," she snarled, and raced out of the drawing room and into the kitchen.

"Geraldine," he called after her, "I am saying this for the last time. They are not going to Galveston, and that's final." Then he heard her smashing plates on the floor.

"Christ, she's flipped," he muttered to himself. "She's wrecking the bloody house."

Suddenly she stormed past him and ran up the stairs and locked herself in their bedroom. Gavin rushed up after her.

"If you go through with this, we're finished. I will leave you. I promise you that," he shouted at her through the door.

"That would be wonderful," she screeched back and eventually the conversation developed into a slanging match. He felt the neighbours, who lived a quarter of a mile away, could be hearing everything that was going on and as he thumped the door with his hands he suddenly noticed the two little girls standing at the bottom of the stairs. This defused his anger and he calmed down.

"Can we not talk sensibly about this, Geraldine?" he asked her in a quieter tone and after a long pause the key in the door turned and she walked out past him as if nothing had happened.

Sitting in the dining room, she said, "OK. I will concede that they can go to the boarding school during the week and they can return home at weekends. My friends at the golf club have a similar arrangement and it's called day-boarding."

He knew he was getting nowhere with her so for harmony's sake he compromised. This was as good as it was going to get. He realised he had no control over family decisions any more. He just nodded agreement.

"OK," she commented again in a very cool, composed voice.

"That's it settled then."

"Good God, they're only babies" he thought to himself. "They're only six and seven. What on earth am I agreeing to?"

He knew she had manoeuvred him into a corner and won. After much soul-searching he considered an *au pair* as an alternative solution, but he saw no point in pursuing that idea either as he knew the girl would be completely controlled by Geraldine. With his hectic schedules the boarding school arrangement seemed the only option as it guaranteed that he would see the children at home every weekend. However, he was not going to raise the subject again, as this was only June and circumstances might change before the start of September.

Like his suburban neighbours working in Manhattan, Gavin rose at 6.30am every morning, drove to Ardsley railway station, and caught the 7.45am to Grand Central. He then walked the three blocks to his office on Park Avenue and commenced work. This entire procedure was reversed every evening so he seldom got home before 8.00pm, just as the girls were going to bed. Sometimes they were already in bed when he arrived home but that never stopped him from going up to their bedroom and giving them a silent goodnight kiss.

This routine was Gavin's daily *modus operandi*, but also on many occasions he had to travel upstate to Albany and out of State to Boston, Washington and Chicago. He was totally consumed with his work but he always maintained that as a Senior Executive Vice President he did no more nor no less than what was expected from him. Despite his continuing resistance regarding Galveston, at the beginning of September the two little girls were enrolled in the Sacred Heart preparatory boarding school for young ladies.

With all this extra free time, Geraldine was now playing golf every Tuesday and Thursday and she also joined the local bridge club. This occupied her on Monday and Wednesday nights as well. She was also attending a drama centre. Grocery shopping was delegated to Friday afternoons as that evening the girls returned home for the weekend. Her week was now mostly accounted for and Gavin and herself were seeing less and less of each other and were drifting further and further apart.

However, the year passed without any further serious upheavals within the family circle and, as Gavin was still fostering new clients, he was away regularly on business. In October he made a flight to Dublin in order to make a projection on his 1974 budget. He was delighted when he received a further increase in salary. In normal circumstances in any household, this would be a reason for celebration but it barely affected Geraldine, who accepted the increment as something to be expected.

This was their first Christmas in America and when Deirdre and Fiona got their holidays from school great excitement descended on the house. The tree was decorated and placed in the corner of the front room, and cards started to arrive from various friends. The most important ones were those they received from both sets of grandparents in Ireland and they held a special place on the broad mantel above the log fire.

Christmas Eve was a very special day and all four of them went up to Manhattan for lunch. They visited Macy's windows, which were full of wonderful magical toys and games. There were Santa Clauses on every street corner. Rockefeller Center ice rink was full of people of all ages, skating around to the sounds of popular Christmas tunes, and the tall wooden soldiers looked even taller to the young boys and girls who were staring up at them. The lights on the official Christmas tree at Rockefeller Center were switched on at 6.00pm and then various groups commenced singing carols. Later in the evening, crowds of people crossed 5th Avenue to St Patrick's Cathedral for the special Christmas Eve Mass. This was always a very welcoming place at this time of year. The rich rubbed shoulders with the poor, the weak rubbed shoulders with the strong and the cops rubbed shoulders with a mixed assortment of crooks and gangsters, but everyone was happy and contented as they joyfully waited to celebrate the arrival of the newborn King.

Christmas slipped into the New Year and on Wednesday 2nd January Geraldine suggested that instead of sleeping in separate beds, as they had been doing for years, it might be a good idea if they now slept in separate rooms.

"Eh, what do you mean by that?" enquired Gavin.

"Well," she replied, still not looking up from her morning newspaper, "your late comings and early goings are disturbing my sleep. It's as simple as that."

"But these unfortunate early mornings and late evenings are all work-related," responded Gavin. "At least they are not golf-related."

He knew he was being sarcastic but he wanted to provoke some sort of response.

"Maybe it would be better if they were golf-related," she calmly replied.

"What do you mean?" responded Gavin quickly, noticing that she was getting the better of him.

She slowly put her paper down and, looking at him directly, said, "If it was golf-related at least I might see you more often. Sure I never see you from the beginning of one week to the end of another. If it wasn't for the girls coming home at weekends, I wouldn't see you at all. Thank God I have the golf, as meeting people there is the one thing that is keeping me sane."

Gavin knew that there was a certain amount of truth in her words, but in order to maintain his standards and achieve his objectives and targets he had to work a fifty-five hour week. This meant that at certain times he had to stay overnight in the Company's apartment on Central Park West. He felt he was fighting a losing battle with her and saw no point in voicing his opinions as they only fell on deaf ears, so that very evening he moved into a guest bedroom.

The marriage was heading for disaster. He didn't know what to do but for the sake of his children, he decided to seek professional advice. One of his clients suggested that he contact a distinguished psychiatrist he knew in order to discuss his marital problems, but noticing a distinct hesitation in Gavin's voice, the client added confidently: "There's nothing to worry about, Gavin, sure everyone in New York has a shrink these days."

Gavin made sure that he was going to pay strict attention to all the recommendations and directions he was receiving from the psychiatrist, as he got quite a shock when he was informed that his fees were a dollar a minute. Notwithstanding this, he booked three sessions.

Gavin openly told the doctor everything. He even told him that he was considering giving up his position in New York and returning to Ireland but the psychiatrist quickly told him that a decision such as this would not solve his problems.

"Geographical changes never work," commented the doctor and Gavin opened up his heart more and more. He explained that he was very confused by his wife's contradictory behaviour. She wanted the good life, she wanted lots of money, she wanted to play golf and bridge; she wanted to attend drama classes, wanted her big house, wanted her big car and also wanted the children in a boarding school. Her list was endless. She was always bickering and complaining about his work schedules and his unsocial hours and the fact that he was never at home. Yet when he was at home, they were passing each other on the doorstep. Gavin did not condemn her, but he knew that she was forging a life for herself that did not include him or the children. He didn't know what to do.

The doctor listened attentively and suggested that a trial separation might be the best medicine at this moment. This would give them breathing space to think and reflect. Gavin proposed that he could stay in the Company's apartment in Manhattan for the time being and travel up to Tarrytown to see the children on Sunday afternoons. The doctor considered this a good idea and pointed out that, as Gavin was not used to rail travel, the stress of the morning and evening commute might be a contributing factor which could also be affecting his marriage. The doctor also commented that with the commuting out of the way, he would be in a better position to look after his business affairs and there was every possibility that his marriage might even start to improve. This was the final diagnosis.

Gavin felt that he could have given himself the same advice. At times in the past he had thought of taking such action but now that it was validated by a well-known medical man he felt more secure in what he was going to do. Geraldine was delighted with this suggestion and Gavin moved into the Company's apartment on the last day of January 1974. She had successfully moved him out of her bedroom and out of the family home in a single month.

CHAPTER 24

The tiny sovereign state of Vatican City contains not only the residence of the Pope but also the largest church in Christendom. It has countless other treasures as well. Many scholars believe that St Peter was martyred upside down there when Nero was Emperor, and later Constantine built the original Church above the Apostle's tomb. It had survived many centuries of invasion by Saracens until Pope Leo IV ordered large walls to be built around the entire church, and this area became known as the Vatican.

Napoleon's intervention in Rome was also quite significant and it was there that he crowned his son *King of Rome*. The Italian national flag was also designed by Napoleon. He simply substituted the colour green for the colour blue as it exists in the French national flag. Under the Lateran Agreement, the State of Vatican City was officially created after World War One.

This small independent State is symbolically guarded by the Swiss Guards who carry long pikes as tokens of protection and it has only a population of about 700 people. Five of these citizens were Noreen de Silva, her husband and three children.

As she drove her Fiat across the Tiber from Piazza del Popolo, up Via Cola di Rienzo to the main gate of the Vatican, her mind was concentrating on the reception that she was organising that evening for some visiting prelates and local politicians. Inside the walls of the Vatican she followed the cobbled driveway for half a kilometre until it widened into a small square and she parked her car outside the catering building.

Noreen de Silva was employed by the Vatican to oversee the visits of major dignitaries. The Vatican maintained six large houses, or legations, and she was in charge of one of these buildings. These buildings have embassy status and the standards of a five star hotel. She knew everything that was taking place within her house and would not accept tardiness of any description. She was an Orthodox Catholic, a member of Opus Dei and would do anything to protect her faith and her Church. She could never tell a lie.

She was a woman in her late forties and definitely of very high integrity. She was always well dressed and her make-up was so flawlessly applied that sometimes she looked as if she was not wearing any at all. She was originally from Ireland and a native of County Cork. She had been educated in University College Cork where she graduated with an honours degree in Social Science and Italian.

In 1947, just as Italy was recovering after World War Two, she applied for a position with a major catering college in Rome and was accepted. She was only twenty-three years of age. While in Rome she met her future husband Mario, who at that time was an official with Banco Concillio. Within five years they were married and settled on the outskirts of that city. In early 1960 she was head-hunted by a representative from the Vatican Personnel Department and, knowing that this would be a wonderful career move, she entered her new position within a matter of months.

She had been responsible for many changes within the catering systems of the Vatican and had warmed the hearts of many with her Irish charm and personality. She was very popular with her staff and a devoted wife and mother. Signora de Silva and her family held Vatican passports, which generated tremendous respect whenever and wherever they were produced. She spoke Italian fluently without any trace of an accent.

The family lived in a beautifully furnished seven room apartment within the Vatican, and the children had private tutors. Mario when still a young man had been promoted to the rank of area manager of his bank so, coupled with this, one would have to say that by the standards of the day Noreen de Silva was considered one of Italy's most progressive and important women.

CHAPTER 25

Gavin had moved to the Manhattan apartment on the advice of his psychiatrist and it did make a certain amount of sense. However, not for a minute did he consider this to be a permanent move from his home in Tarrytown and he returned to see his family every Sunday afternoon. He even thought that things were starting to improve between Geraldine and himself. He was in closer contact with his work and felt less stressed. Everything seemed to be working out reasonably well.

Being on better terms with Geraldine was a big step forward as this meant easier contact with the children. When he talked to them on the phone he would always ask to speak with their mother. On one such occasion he had an exceptionally long conversation with her and ended up inviting her out for dinner. He could hardly believe his ears when she accepted. He dressed himself meticulously for the event and actually felt that he was going out on a first date with her again.

Just like the night in the St Gregory, her conversation soon drifted to golf but then it went on to clothes and eventually money and how difficult Geraldine found it to manage everything on the allowance she was getting. He asked her why she needed more money, as his accountant assured him he was allocating her more than enough, but she could not be specific. He felt that if he offered her his total income as a net figure, it would still not be enough. She complained in general about the cost of food which was surprising as this was her only major outlay as he paid all the other household bills. He also paid the mortgage, the school fees, the medical expenses and the annual subscriptions to the golf club and her bridge club. He soon realised that her side of their conversation was turning into one very long boring complaint.

He pointed out to her that he wanted to move back into the house as soon as possible, as he was unhappy where he was, and emphasised again that he only considered his present accommodation as a temporary arrangement. In fact he had told no one except the psychiatrist about his switch to Manhattan, which had taken place just a month before. Deep down he was becoming more and more conscious that Geraldine was doing absolutely nothing to heal the rift between them. In spite of her complaining about money, she seemed quite happy to wander aimlessly from day to day.

As he returned to the apartment he knew that the marriage was practically over. She was completely indifferent to anything he suggested. He didn't know what to do next but he did know that they could not continue like this, so in a last drastic attempt to try and rescue the situation he decided to seek help from the family back in Ireland. He rang her father in Kilkee.

"Hello, Patrick, Gavin here."

"Hello, Gavin. Heavens, this is such a great line I would swear you were in the room next door."

"Patrick," Gavin went on, "I have something to tell you and there is no easy way to say it. Things are not the best between Geraldine and myself at the moment."

"Oh, such as? We've always known that both of you have had differences of opinion in the past, but we decided not to take them too seriously. We just turned a blind eye. Sure, true love never runs smooth."

"No, it's not as easy as that, Paddy. This is more than a difference of opinion, this is quite serious. Over the last couple of years our marriage has been slowly rolling downhill, but I think it is now off the tracks completely."

"I knew she was reluctant about going to the States," came the uncertain reply, "but this is astonishing news. I had no idea matters were so serious."

"I know you're shocked," replied Gavin, "and I am very sorry to have to break this news to you so abruptly, but I have been trying very hard to keep things on the straight and narrow. I really wanted the marriage to work and I have tried everything – even been to a psychiatrist – at the moment I'm at my wit's end."

Gavin went on to explain everything to his father-in-law, who was dumbfounded. He informed Gavin that he was going to have a chat with his wife and would phone him back straight away.

The phone rang in Gavin's office approximately thirty minutes later and a gentle female voice simply said: "Hello, Gavin, Margaret Murphy here. Bring her home as soon as possible and we will sort something out."

Those words were like music to his ears. He felt relieved, as if a weight had been lifted from his shoulders.

Gavin phoned Geraldine and told her that he had arranged a short holiday home to Ireland within the next few days, but he neglected to tell her the reason why. He booked a mid-week flight, so that the girls would not be inconvenienced at the boarding school and planned to be back in New York so that he could see them at the weekend. Geraldine was very excited at the thought of going home and proceeded to make plans, but when they arrived at Shannon airport, she was somewhat surprised to receive such a cool reception by her father who was there to meet them.

Hardly a word was spoken during the fifty minute drive to Kilkee and when they arrived and settled inside her parents' home, silence continued to reign.

Margaret Murphy, usually a very quiet woman, entered the dining room. She looked at her daughter sitting in the chair opposite her and shouted at her at the top of her voice: "Who do you think you are, young lady? What do you think you are playing at? How dare you carry on in such a way? You're a disgrace! I'm totally ashamed of you and your behaviour."

Geraldine was taken aback at this outburst. She had expected a warm, loving welcome but this was something else and she was stunned into silence. Her mother continued: "I am shocked beyond belief. Imagine placing your little children in a boarding school. Is golf that important to you? What in the name of God has got into you, girl?"

Geraldine's mouth was now wide open and she was in shock. She attempted to say something in her defence but words would not come out, and then her mother continued. "You have one of the best men in Ireland. Hard working and dedicated. At the top of his career long before his time. Is this the correct way to treat him and your family? I will never be able to face Mary Greenfield again."

By this stage Gavin and her father had moved into the kitchen and were sitting at the table in a hushed silence.

"I have never heard her mother so cross," whispered the doctor.

"I have never seen Geraldine so stunned," responded Gavin. "I'm worried what's going to happen next."

"Don't worry yourself," replied Patrick Murphy. "No one can blame you for the way she has been behaving lately. You did the right thing in bringing her home."

The doctor's words were very comforting, but Gavin knew that he would eventually be blamed for arranging such a homecoming. This was not the time for laying blame, but he felt that he had no choice but to involve her family, and this was the last and only opportunity left to him to try and salvage what was left of the marriage.

In due course, Geraldine managed to speak, what possibly were the first true words she had uttered about this matter.

"But, mum," she spluttered, "maybe I'm not in love with him anymore."

"Aaggh! Not in love with him? What in God's name has love got to do with it?" bellowed her mother. "It's Father Slattery for you in the morning, my girl," and with that her mother left the room and Geraldine was now on her own, sobbing bitterly.

Any words relating to love, affection or emotion were never mentioned by her mother. Frightening her daughter into clear-headedness was the traditional Irish way of dealing with these matters and, as if the Catholic Church had all the secret formulae, it was involved immediately. The following morning, after she had recovered from her jet lag, Geraldine was driven up to Lahinch and reintroduced to the parish priest who had married them.

After an hour's conversation, it was decided that she should enter into a *Course of instruction in Faith and Morals* under the guidance and discipline of Father Slattery, so her stay in Ireland was extended for an indefinite period.

This was not the time for playing golf so, making his excuses to the doctor, Gavin made arrangements to return to New York on the EI 105 departing Shannon at 2.30pm on Friday afternoon. This time he had been in Ireland for only two nights.

CHAPTER 26

Seated in the front row in window seat 1A on this Friday afternoon's departure from Shannon to New York was a woman of about thirty years of age. She was dressed in a deep blue two piece business suit. When she handed her jacket to the hostess, her beautiful lemon blouse with a lace collar only added to her elegance. Her leather high-heeled shoes emphasised her sophistication and contrasted delightfully with her shapely tanned legs. Her make-up was perfect and her lovely auburn hair was cut in the latest fashion. Her nails were immaculately manicured and the colour matched that of her lipstick.

During the aircraft's taxi to the main runway, she sipped champagne from fine Waterford crystal and looked through *Paris Match*. She exuded confidence. Just after take-off she opened her briefcase and withdrew some papers.

Gavin was watching her every movement from his seat across the aisle at 2F and the way her briefcase was positioned he noticed the gold CD insignia embossed on the black leather. He could not help admiring her because of her self-assurance. There was no doubt whatsoever, Gabriella de Leon had turned into a beautiful woman. Having graduated with an honours degree from Trinity, she had recently completed a post graduate degree course in Politics and Economics at the Sorbonne in Paris, and was following her father's footsteps into the Spanish Diplomatic Service.

After dinner was served and tables cleared, the first class passengers settled down to watch a movie. Gavin sat and watched the film, but instinctively his eyes kept returning to the person sitting in seat 1A. He tried to read his book, but the distraction was too strong and he continuously felt his head turning in her direction. About halfway through the flight she left her seat and moved toward the spiral staircase and, as she passed his row, their eyes met briefly, resulting in both of them smiling politely at each other. Neither of them spoke.

Gavin's mind was in overdrive as he tried to overcome his instantaneous attraction for this woman. He knew very well that he had no right to feel this way, nor was he in a position to even speak to her as he was still faithful to his wife and his marriage vows. Deep down he was quite a conservative person and he knew that it was only these solemn promises that were stopping him from introducing himself. As the flight progressed on its transatlantic crossing, he dozed off.

He was awakened about an hour from touchdown by a smiling hostess who offered him afternoon tea consisting of scones and clotted cream. She also handed him a hot towel. When he wiped the sleep from his eyes, the first thing he did was to check if the passenger was still sitting in 1A. She was.

On arrival at Kennedy, Gavin joined the long queues of people lining up for immigration clearance and as he stood and waited he watched as this elegant young woman was ushered quickly and quietly through the VIP doorway into the special section that dealt with all diplomatic clearances. As the door closed behind her it was as if a brief chapter in his life was over and he wondered why he felt such a strong attraction to someone he didn't know.

He regretted that he had not spoken to her when the opportunity presented itself on board the plane. He tried to rationalise his thoughts and reckoned that there would have been no harm in saying "hello", but it was too late now. As he slowly moved forward in line, he consoled himself by thinking that he was left with a brief but very pleasant memory.

CHAPTER 27

Just as the first daffodils started to appear in the shadows of watery sunshine, Gavin found himself alone again in New York. Thankfully he was fully occupied with the events that were leading up to the St Patrick's Day parade.

He drove up to the boarding school every weekend to see his daughters and it saddened him to see them in such an establishment. He knew he was not in a position to look after them personally and they were too young to fully understand what was happening within the marriage. On every visit they asked about their mother.

"When is mammy coming back?" enquired Deirdre. "We miss her very much."

"It will not be long now," he replied.

"Is mammy sick?" asked Fiona, still holding her teddy and looking at her older sister with her large blue eyes.

"No," he immediately responded. "Mammy is staying with granny and grandad for a short holiday and will be home very soon.

"How do you like school?" he asked them and they replied by telling him that they had great fun in the dormitories and on Wednesday and Saturday afternoons the tuck shop was always open. They added that they went for lovely walks during the week and had great fun playing ball and skipping in the recreation area. They went on to say in a childish manner that Matron was very nice. He knew that the Matron was a very kindly person and well used to dealing with young children and when she appeared, he kissed his daughters goodbye. He got into his car, all the time waving at the girls.

During his drive back to Manhattan, he reflected that the children appeared to be reasonably happy in the school, but all he could think about was history repeating itself. He had crossed from the Sawmill Parkway to the Henry Hudson Freeway before his tears stopped flowing. He tried to bury himself in his work, but most of his nights were lonely and he felt that his life was over. He missed the girls more than he missed his wife, but he knew that he could not have one without the other. At the beginning of April, he decided that it was time to contact her parents once again to find out what was happening. He dialled the number and the phone rang about five times before it was answered in a very professional manner.

"Good afternoon, Doctor Murphy speaking. How may I help you?"

"Hello, Patrick, Gavin here."

"Oh, hello, Gavin. It's good to hear from you. As a matter of fact, I was going to ring you tonight. I have some good news for you. I think some sort of a compromise has been reached and Geraldine would like a quick word with you."

A slight pause followed and then he heard her voice. "Hello, Gavin, how are you?"

"Very well," he responded, "but the children really miss you. I think you should make some plans about coming home soon."

"I was thinking the same thing myself," came the reply, which surprised Gavin but brought a happy smile to his face. "I have a proposition to make to you," she continued, "and considering all the circumstances, it's all for the best."

"Go on, Geraldine," he encouraged, "what is it?" and she continued, "Well it's like this. I have been taking marital guidance counselling twice a week with Father Slattery, and he has suggested that I continue this counselling with a Monsignor Fagan when I return to America. Monsignor Fagan is attached to the Archdiocese of New York."

"That's OK with me. I'm delighted. I have no problem whatsoever on that score," he replied, but before he could say another word she interrupted him again.

"But there's more. I want you to continue with the psychiatrist in Manhattan, so that both of us can benefit equally."

"OK, OK, if that's what it takes," he replied hesitantly.

"That's the deal, Gavin," she stated, "and if you agree, I will come back to the States at the end of April and we can start sorting things out."

"Does that mean that I can move back into the house again?"

"No, not quite yet," she countered immediately, "but we can talk about that later. I have to say, this is a positive start."

With that the phone call came to an end and he was left wondering what was going to happen next.

He drove out to JFK International on 28th April and as he parked his car he wondered what sort of a reception he was going to get. It was nearly two months since he had seen his wife.

He was waiting for her at the other side of the customs area and, when they met, he made an attempt to kiss her but she turned her head away immediately and all he got was the side of her cheek. He consoled himself by thinking that it was better than nothing and as they commenced their drive back to Tarrytown he asked her to go over everything once again, so that he had it clear in his mind. He was determined to try his best to communicate.

"As you already know, I have been taking religious instruction with Father Slattery," Geraldine replied, "but he is getting very old now, and as I told you on the phone he has recommended that I should return to America and continue this instruction under a Monsignor Fagan. Monsignor Fagan is a much younger priest, and he is stationed here in the Archdiocese of New York. It is as straightforward as that."

"When can I move back into the house again?" enquired Gavin who was preoccupied and only half listening to what she was saying. She replied in a condescending tone that they would both know what to do when an appropriate time presented itself.

He said all his goodbyes, and as he was driving back to Manhattan it struck him that he did not understand what she meant by saying *when an appropriate time presented itself*, and came to the conclusion that her statement was just a very carefully composed jumble of words. When he left the Henry Hudson Freeway to take West 57th Street to Columbus Circle, he was more confused than ever.

He arrived at his apartment puzzled and generally upset at the way Geraldine had behaved and the off-hand way that she had treated him once again. However, he was determined to go along with what they had agreed, as this was his very final effort. If this didn't work, nothing else would. With this in mind, he made an appointment to see his psychiatrist the following Friday.

Gavin was away on company business in Chicago and San Francisco during the months of May and June, but he made it a point to be home in time for the girls' summer holidays, which continued from July until September. He arranged to have most of his schedules in the New York area during this period, and this ensured that he would see them every weekend and sometimes during the week.

During his trips to Tarrytown, he noticed that Geraldine had taken on a life that totally excluded him from all her interests. It was getting to the point that as he arrived at the house, she was leaving. On one occasion, when he had a seminar to chair on a Saturday morning, she made him feel guilty about not coming up to see his daughters that weekend so immediately he cancelled the seminar. As it transpired her only arrangement was with the local golf club, and she was using him as a babysitter for this social appointment. That cancellation cost his company a major contract.

Gavin knew that this type of behaviour could not continue indefinitely and divorce was now presenting itself as an acceptable option, but he kept putting it to the back of his mind. He knew if he took the first steps without proper grounds, it would mean financial suicide. He did not want to lose his house, nor was he in a position to pay Geraldine a massive private income for life, so he had no alternative but to continue the present arrangement. As she never mentioned divorce or legal separation, he often thought that he was locked into this loveless marriage for the rest of his life.

These present arrangements suited Geraldine completely, so why should she change anything? He managed to bring the children down to New York for a couple of special occasions, but unfortunately family vacations were out of the question as their mother did not want to go anywhere that necessitated an overnight in their father's company. Very quickly the summer was over and the girls were back at boarding school again.

Gavin sat in his apartment and reflected on what had gone wrong with the marriage. Then he realised that from the very beginning, nothing had gone right.

He poured himself a large whiskey and recalled his wedding night. He recalled that when they finally got to bed Geraldine had insisted on switching off all the lights. Not even a romantic candle was allowed. He recalled that he had never actually seen her totally naked. He recalled that sometimes during love making she could adopt the sexiest positions and the following day when he went to give her a kiss or caress her, she would shrug him off as if he were a total stranger. He also recalled that he always felt rejected, sexually confused and emotionally unfulfilled. It was a life of frustrations.

He felt that his marriage had been a waste of time. The only redeeming features were his two children whom he loved dearly, even though they were not a product of true love.

The Christmas holidays were approaching and in mid-December Gavin visited the house unannounced, a few days after the girls arrived home from Galveston.

"Where's your mum?" he asked as he entered.

"Don't know, daddy," came Deirdre's reply. "She has been out a lot since we've been home."

"Who has been looking after you?" he enquired.

"Mrs Lawson from next door comes in and checks us every hour and then we go to bed," came the innocent response.

"So mammy has been out most nights since you came home?" he asked. This was answered by a simple "yes," by both of them. With that he helped them get undressed and ready for bed and waited until Geraldine arrived home.

"Where have you been to this time of night?" he asked when she eventually arrived home.

"None of your business," came the curt reply.

"Indeed it is my business when it concerns the children being left on their own."

"They were not on their own," she answered sarcastically. "You were with them."

"You're well out of order, Geraldine. You know that. You're out at the golf club two nights a week, the bridge club two nights a week, your drama circle whatever that is and with your attendance at religious instruction, are you ever at home?"

"I can do whatever I want," she countered. "You are not my father. Don't you ever lecture me, Gavin O'Neill."

"That's it," he shouted at her. "I've had enough," and with that he walked out of the sitting room and into the hallway. As he opened the front door to leave she yelled after him, "And don't come back for Christmas Day, you're not welcome here."

Those words echoed in his ears as he drove back to Manhattan. He rehearsed in his mind what he was going to do, but nothing seemed to make much sense. He felt hurt that she was once again treating him in such an outlandish fashion. However, he resolved to find out why she was out of the house so much, especially when the children were at home.

That Christmas was a very lonely time for Gavin, but he rang the girls every day until it was time for them to return to school again in early January. He knew that his visit in December had activated a spark of guilt within Geraldine, and while the children were at home for the three-week period she curtailed her evenings out. At the end of every phone call he asked if mammy was there, and he was always told that she was, although she never wanted to speak to him. At least he knew she was around. He was now starting to feel very depressed and wondered how he was going to cope.

In early New Year he sensed he was losing his grip on the job as his mind was jumping all over the place. He told his psychiatrist everything, but he felt he was only getting lip service. As he sat in his apartment in early February, feeling very sorry for himself, he decided to accept the offer that had been made to him by Bill O'Malley, the second generation Irish Police Chief with whom he had had lunch over the Christmas season. He rang him and explained all his frustrations once again. At least he had a sympathetic ear at the other end of the phone.

"Leave that with me," advised the Chief. "I think I have the very man you need."

CHAPTER 28

In his better times he drank bourbon in 42nd Street and beer in the Bronx. He was acquainted with most bartenders in saloons of all shapes and sizes. He knew the pecking order of every gang leader in New York City, kept in contact with conmen and ex-convicts and knew the right people in the NYPD.

As a private detective, his name was often mentioned in station houses throughout the city, and before the booze got the better of him he had been highly respected by many. He had been divorced for more than fifteen years and never considered remarrying. He was just out of rehab for the third time and it was frequently said that he was on his way out. Few thought that he would ever make it back, or even work again, and all he had left were a few hangers-on who were not true friends. However, it was this aimless character that the Police Chief recommended to Gavin as one of the greatest noses in the business.

The phone rang in Gavin's office. It was Friday 7th February.

"Hello, is that you, Mr O'Neill? My name is Duffy, Brendan Duffy."

"Hello, Mr Duffy. I would like to meet you if that is possible. Chief O'Malley speaks very highly of you. Can you come over to see me?"

"The Chief and I go back a long way," came the courteous reply. "I could be with you in forty-five minutes, if the INT Subway Line is running to schedule."

"My office is on the thirty-fourth floor of the McKenzie Building," advised Gavin, but before he could continue his statement, he was gently interrupted by a polite "I know that, sir; I'll see you in forty-five minutes."

With that the call ended.

Duffy was exactly as the Chief had described. Gavin proceeded to explain his concerns and in the meantime they had the club sandwiches and the pot of coffee that he had ordered earlier.

"I think I have the gist of it, Mr O'Neill. It would appear that you are anxious to know what your wife is up to in your absence. You do understand, however, that she is entitled to go out and about without your permission, but I'll soon find out if she is up to something or if it is all harmless stuff. You'll never get a divorce from naming a bridge club or a golf club as a co-respondent, so it's better that you leave that to me. Can I confirm that your daughters are at a boarding school and they come home at weekends?"

Duffy, despite his appearance, cringed his lips as he finished the last sentence and Gavin could see that he did not approve of young children being sent to boarding school either.

"Yes, unfortunately they are," replied Gavin, "and I try my utmost to get up to see them as often as I can. During terms I see them nearly every Sunday."

For the first time Gavin felt a hollow feeling within himself. He was employing a private detective to spy on his wife who more than likely was completely innocent of anything. At this stage, however, he simply had to know what was going on.

Looking at Duffy, Gavin asked him about his fees and how long it would take to get some results.

"I charge one hundred dollars per day plus expenses and it should take me the best part of a week to come up with some positive information," came the honest reply. This was not considered expensive for investigative work in New York.

"OK, Mr Duffy, the job is yours. See you in a week's time."

"Sure, Mr O'Neill, a week should see me all done," and as he walked out of the office, Duffy raised his hat as a mark of respect and thanked Gavin for the commission. Gavin was relieved that he had made a decision, no matter where it was going to lead, and he knew that he would soon know the outcome.

He decided that it would not be proper for him to go to Tarrytown while a private eye was investigating his wife's whereabouts, but when Duffy presented himself in his office the following Thursday afternoon, he was surprised at the speed of his investigation. He had expected that it would take much longer.

"Hello, Mr O'Neill, I think you could have a slight problem on your hands." announced Duffy and with that both of them sat down.

"It's like this, Mr O'Neill," he continued. "Mrs O'Neill attends the golf club every Tuesday and Thursday from mid-day to evening, and the bridge club on a Wednesday evenings from 7.00pm to 10.30pm approximately, and that's very much her social arrangements. She doesn't go to drama classes."

"OK," replied Gavin, "I know mostly that and I don't see a problem. I was just wondering if she was out wining and dining or having an affair with someone at one of these clubs, due to the irregular hours she keeps. That was my concern."

"She is not having an affair with anyone at the clubs, Mr O' Neill, but it's not as simple as that."

"Thank God for that," responded Gavin.

"Hold your horses, Mr O'Neill, I'm not finished yet," retorted Duffy. "I repeat, she is not having an affair with anyone from the clubs but I regret to have to tell you that she is definitely having an affair with the young Monsignor. It would appear that they have been seeing each other two or three times a week for the past seven months."

"What?" exclaimed Gavin. "I don't believe you!"

"It's true," responded Duffy. "He's having his wicked way with her."

"Sexually?" gasped Gavin.

"I'm afraid so," replied Duffy.

"He's actually…?"

But before Gavin could finish his sentence, Duffy shrewdly interrupted him: "Exactly, Mr. O'Neill," he said.

"Merciful God," exclaimed Gavin. "I don't believe it."

"I'm so sorry, Mr O'Neill. It's all true."

Gavin collapsed into his armchair like an empty paper bag and when he regained his composure he asked: "Where the hell were they meeting to do this, may I ask?"

"In the Archbishop's house in New York," came Duffy's reply.

Gavin was shaken in his tracks. His mouth dropped. This was not the news he had been expecting. How could she be doing this to him? It took him a few minutes to gather his composure. Then anger set in and various thoughts flooded his mind. His old nightmare returned, and his mind flashed back once again to Sheila Maguire's words in Trinity College. It was exactly the same thing all over again and he felt totally outraged at hearing such news. He thanked Duffy for his work and, even though his fee was less than a thousand dollars, Gavin slipped ten single hundred dollar bills into his hand.

"Thank you for your generosity, Mr O'Neill. I am very sorry to be the bearer of such bad news, but that's the way the cards fall sometimes."

"Oh, it's not your fault, Mr Duffy. You were only doing your job."

"Maybe this is a good time for us to drop the *Mister titles*," suggested Duffy in a sympathetic voice. "My name is Brendan."

"OK, Brendan, thanks."

Raising his hat once again, Duffy replied: "I'll stay in touch, Gavin," and with that he left the office.

Gavin was in a state of shock. He was shaking uncontrollably and the palms of his hands were soaking wet. Eventually, after two hours of pacing up and down, his mind started to calm down and he realised that this might be his passport to freedom. He had stopped shaking. He phoned the lawyer he had used when he was purchasing the house in Tarrytown and, revealing all that had just transpired, he was immediately informed that he had an open and shut case.

"Gavin, you now have the grounds for divorce," assured the

attorney. "It hasn't been done before as far as I know, but let's name this priest as the material co-respondent. We're on a winner."

CHAPTER 29

During the last week of February 1975 news bulletins were blaring out from every radio station in Manhattan. It had just been announced that His Holiness the Pope was very seriously ill and a thought flashed into Duffy's mind as he sat in a diner off Canal Street.

"Shit," he thought to himself. "If what I'm thinking comes to pass, the Catholic Church can pack its bags and run. This sure is serious."

The Holy Father had been in his eminent position for nearly twelve years and even though he had been ill on many occasions it was thought that this time he would not survive. The entire world was praying for his recovery. In the early years of his Pontificate people thought that he might make a few changes. Most Catholics favoured a moderate Pope, with the exception of Opus Dei who sought a more traditional Pontiff. The present Pope hadn't made any major changes but he hadn't imposed any new restrictions either. He was *a very middle of the road man* in his thinking.

If the Pope did pass away, this would mean that the College of Cardinals would meet again in Conclave and it was felt that a free thinking leader would definitely be ruled out.

As Duffy listened to the radio, it was becoming obvious that the Vatican Civil Service had taken over the everyday running of the Church. The Cardinal Secretary of State, or in layman's terms the Pope's Prime Minister, had very obviously taken control within his Ministry, and was actively appointing new Ministers.

Even at this early stage, speculation was rife regarding a possible papal successor and a consensus was emerging as to who that cardinal might be. Candidates from North and South America, Africa and Australasia were ruled out. There was little chance that a cardinal from behind the Iron Curtain would be elected as that would possibly indicate a Pope in exile.

This brought to the fore five very eminent churchmen, all quite intellectual on the surface, but very cautious. They were the Archbishops of Vienna, Bordeaux, Venice, Milan and Naples. At the moment the bookies were giving odds on the outcome being an Italian Pope as usual, so Austria and France were regarded as complete outsiders.

Duffy thought that if the past was anything to go by, either Milan or Venice would probably win and, in accordance with tradition, two or three young Monsignors would be elevated to the position of bishop. One of these probably would become a new Minister of State to assist an elderly Cardinal with his Treasury duties. It was then that Duffy's horrible thought fully materialised.

Monsignor Fagan could be elevated and called to the Treasury as all outward appearances indicated that he was an ideal candidate for such an elite position. In years to come, he could be appointed Archbishop, a Cardinal or even elected Pope.

"Fucking hell," Duffy thought to himself. "Imagine that scumbag Fagan having his fingers in the pie. Something has to be done about this real fast."

CHAPTER 30

It was now Wednesday 23rd April and Gavin had just left his attorney's office at the junction of 3rd Avenue and East 52nd Street. He was again assured that he had an open and shut case and was told not to worry about anything. As he sat in the traffic on the way back to his apartment, he was wondering what it would be like to face Geraldine in a divorce court. He was dreading the confrontation. Accusing her of infidelity in open court would be difficult and might possibly affect the children. But he was still hurting at what she had done to him and knew that this was the only way out of his dilemma. Although determined to end the marriage, he silently prayed that the divorce might not be as painful as he feared. The case was fixed for Wednesday 7th May, which didn't afford him much time to arrange everything. Deep down he thought that things were moving too fast.

On 7th May he arrived in the court. It was a large room with a small seating area and he sat beside his attorney, Larry Grimshaw. Geraldine was also present, seated beside her attorney. He was advised not to look at her but to fix his gaze straight ahead at all times. Once again he was informed that he had nothing to worry about *as it was all in the bag*.

He was very fidgety and uneasy and wondered if he really had a cut and dried case at all. He had only had two appointments with this lawyer, who seemed to be very busy with other cases every time he called to see him. He was told over and over again that there was nothing for him to worry about, but he couldn't help wondering why Geraldine was defending the divorce in the first place. Through her solicitors, she had already admitted her relationship with Monsignor Fagan. She had admitted fault and this seemed a very odd course of action.

He had hoped that when the word divorce was mentioned she would have sought a compromise and some sort of honourable settlement could have been reached. This would curtail their court appearance to the compulsory four minutes that is mandatory in all divorce hearings in the United States. He just couldn't understand why she was putting herself through so much pain, considering that she had admitted open adultery. Gavin hoped that the proceedings wouldn't take too long.

"All rise for the Honourable Judge Rosemount," called the bailiff and, as soon as the judge was seated, there was a shuffle of chairs and within seconds Gavin heard his name being called to take the stand.

He was duly sworn in and waited until his attorney rose to his feet, asking Gavin if he would explain to the judge why he was in court today.

Gavin had not been well briefed and stumbled through his opening remarks. However, he managed to get most of the information out, signifying that he wanted a divorce from his wife because she had been unfaithful to him.

"Thank you, Mr O'Neill," said Gavin's attorney. "I have no further questions for this witness."

"But I have, your Honour," immediately interjected Geraldine's lawyer. It was only then that Gavin noticed that she seemed to be flanked on either side by a full legal team. He was very surprised. He had not expected to be questioned since she had already admitted culpability. What was going on here? He looked at Grimshaw for guidance, but just received a vacant expression and a shrug of the shoulders.

Geraldine's attorney had dated records of everything Gavin had done, and every place he had been, over the past two years. He was amazed at the detail they went into, and the way they selected appropriate points and meticulously picked them clean. The way the questions were being phrased and asked made Gavin feel that he had done wrong instead of Geraldine. Why wasn't his lawyer jumping out of his seat and shouting "objection", he thought. Then it suddenly dawned on him that his lawyer was as unprepared as he was. The more Geraldine's attorneys painstakingly stripped him bare, the worse it looked for him. At times he wasn't sure which one of Geraldine's attorneys was questioning him, as they seemed to pop up and down continuously, but as long as Grimshaw was not objecting, there was nothing he could do.

They got Gavin to freely admit that he had to travel away on business trips at least three or four times per month. They went to great pains to point out to the judge that on certain occasions when Mrs O'Neill had phoned the hotel where her husband was supposed to be staying, there had never been a response from the phone in his room. They were inferring that he was *out on the town*, and all that Gavin could answer was to say that he had possibly gone out for a walk or was having dinner somewhere in that particular city. He was asked if he paid by credit card as this would confirm the dates, but he pointed out that as the bills for his meals were so small he paid for them all with cash.

"What you are actually saying, Mr O'Neill," commented the attorney, "is in fact that you have no credible alibi for where you were when your wife was desperately trying to contact you. Not even a credit card receipt to show that you were in a restaurant."

"No," replied Gavin. "I wasn't aware that I would need to keep a log of where I ate."

"On the contrary Mr O'Neill, it's most unusual for a senior executive not to keep a record of his meals for tax purposes."

He knew they were correct but he still expected Grimshaw to come to his defence.

Geraldine's lawyers could produce telephone dockets indicating that at least six to eight telephone calls had been made by her on different days and at different times, and still he was never in his room. This, they suggested, seemed too many to be a coincidence. To add to his trauma, he even noticed the judge making notes, which clearly indicated that doubts were settling into his mind also.

The questioning continued: "You openly and freely admit that you left the marital home, Mr O'Neill? Am I correct in saying that?"

"I didn't freely leave the marital home. I left under doctor's orders."

"Would you mind repeating that again for the record?"

"OK," replied Gavin. "I was advised to leave on doctor's orders."

"Doctor's orders?" came the response. "Could you be a little more explicit?"

"The psychiatrist I was attending suggested that I leave the family home on a trial separation basis which might help improve the marriage in due course."

"He advised you or suggested to you or ordered you to leave the family home?" enquired the lawyer. "Let me inform you, Mr O'Neill, these expressions are not similar and advised and suggested is not the same as being ordered. These have two very distinct and different meanings. Let me repeat the question for the judge's attention. I put it to you that you were advised to leave the family home, not ordered to do so. Would that be correct, Mr. O'Neill?"

"Yes," replied Gavin.

"No further questions for this gentleman at the moment, your Honour."

After what seemed an eternity, Gavin was excused from the stand and when he returned to his seat he was in an agitated state.

"Why the hell didn't you object or do something?" he asked Grimshaw.

"There was nothing I could do," came the reply. "They were basically asking legitimate questions."

"Why isn't my psychiatrist here to give evidence?"

"He would only agree with what was said by the defence lawyers," responded Grimshaw. "He confirmed that he only advised that you go to the apartment in Manhattan so having him here wouldn't do you any favours."

Following that, an Anthony Fagan was called as the next defence witness instead of Geraldine.

"What the hell's going on here?" commented Gavin, looking around to see that there was only one other person sitting in the public area of the courtroom.

"Is that Fagan?" he asked his attorney. "What the fuck is he doing here?"

"Relax, Gavin, they are entitled to call him," came the response, "but once he has admitted everything, we will be home safe and dry."

A very tall handsome man in his early thirties walked up from the middle of the empty courtroom and took his seat on the witness stand. He was wearing a dark brown double breasted suit with a white shirt and maroon coloured tie. His slightly tanned skin highlighted his well-oiled jet black hair, which was parted at the side. He was very well groomed. He looked relaxed and it was quite obvious that he was well prepared for this occasion. He was duly sworn in.

One of Geraldine's lawyers stood up and asked him to describe his relationship with Mrs O'Neill.

Fagan immediately admitted that he had had sex with the lady and, treating his answer as *no big deal*, the attorney skilfully led him from one question to the next.

"Why isn't this all over now?" Gavin whispered to Grimshaw. "He's after admitting that he had sex with her." But there was no answer forthcoming from his attorney.

Fagan went on to tell the court that until very recently he had been a Monsignor in the Roman Catholic Church, but the moment of truth arrived for him when he fell passionately in love with Mrs O'Neill. He went on to say that this was one of the most difficult decisions he had ever had to make in his entire life as Mrs O'Neill unequivocally returned his love and this made his choice even more difficult. He stated that he still loved the Catholic Church, but that love was totally different from the love he had for Mrs O'Neill. He found Mrs O'Neill not only attractive but also intelligent and he looked forward to seeing her at every consultation when she visited him in the Archbishop's house in New York.

"Good God," remarked Gavin to Grimshaw. "Object for Christ's sake."

Grimshaw just sat there shaking his head.

Fagan admitted that the Church would not tolerate a married cleric, so he had to make this life changing decision. He told the court that he still considered himself to be a priest, even though he did not practise openly any more, and Mrs O'Neill accepted and understood this. He concluded by saying that the Church had respectfully reviewed his situation before releasing him from his vows.

"I would say that you're a very honourable man," concluded this attorney and with that another one of Geraldine's lawyers continued the questioning. With great skill he suggested that Mr O'Neill was not really a fit father and this was one of the reasons why Mrs O'Neill had to send her young children to the Sacred Heart boarding school.

"Would I be correct in suggesting that?" he asked Fagan.

"Absolutely correct," came the assertive response.

Gavin was horrified and astonished at such a suggestion. He could not believe that Grimshaw was still sitting in his chair, doing nothing.

"Do something," he anxiously urged Grimshaw, but once again nothing happened.

Geraldine's solicitor encouraged Fagan to mention that had it not been for his intervention the young girls could have been badly affected by the behaviour of their father, as he had started to neglect them.

The lawyer went on to say that Mr Fagan was a tower of strength to this lady in her hours of desperation. What else could he do but look after her and care for her and as the weeks slipped into months he had fallen deeply in love with her. She was a full-blooded woman who needed sex and affection, which was quite normal since her husband had deserted her.

"Could you be more specific, Counsellor?" asked Judge Rosemount and it was fully explained once again in great detail that Gavin O'Neill was not ordered but only advised by the psychiatrist to leave the family home at the end of January 1974. This was well over a year ago and, in the State of New York, this constituted desertion.

"Object for Christ's sake," Gavin whispered to Grimshaw. "I never once neglected the children."

"Objection, your Honour," yelled Grimshaw. "The attorney is leading the witness."

Carefully sidestepping his derogatory remark implying that Gavin was a bad father, Geraldine's lawyer continued, "Let me enquire if the court requires a verbatim explanation of the three words, advise, suggest or order," he enquired.

"No. Not at all," responded the judge, clearly indicating that he knew the distinction between them. "Objection overruled."

Gavin realised that he was being hung out to dry in open court. These attorneys knew every trick in the book. Everything they said was true but their skilful use of words deflected the burden of guilt from Geraldine's shoulders to his.

"Your witness, Mr Grimshaw."

"I have only one question for this witness, your Honour," stated Grimshaw, rising to his feet. "I would just like to ask Mr Fagan to confirm again that he had sexual intercourse with Mrs O'Neill."

"Yes, I did have intercourse with her," came the confident response. "I have already admitted that."

Larry Grimshaw sat down and Gavin's mouth started to go dry. He wondered if his ears had deceived him. The very issues which he was told would win his case outright seemed useless and were being used to discredit him. This arrogant scoundrel freely admitted that he had had sex with his wife, yet his lawyers were making him out to be a paragon of virtue.

Then the judge intervened and commenced his summing up. He accepted that Mrs O'Neill had been intimate with Mr Fagan and he did not condemn her for this, as she was entitled to seek her conjugal rights from whoever she found fit, since her husband had deserted her for more than a twelve month period. He also accepted that Mr Fagan was a perfectly honourable gentleman, and the fact that he had been promoted so young to the rank of Monsignor in the conservative Catholic Church meant that his superiors were very impressed with him at that time.

He concluded his short address by saying that he had heard enough and had reached a decision. Looking directly at Gavin he said, "Mr O'Neill, you can have your divorce, but I am unreservedly awarding it to Mrs O'Neill, on the grounds that you deserted her without due cause. Since she still has two young children, I also award her the family home. It is in joint names so I hereby direct that your name is stricken from the deed forthwith. I also declare that you are an unfit husband and father, and from what I have heard today, these selfish tendencies could manifest themselves again at any time. Since you abandoned your wife and your children, I am placing the children into the safe custody of Mrs O'Neill, who is their birth mother, and Mr Fagan, who will act as their legal guardian. I am also placing a restraining order on you, Mr O'Neill, and you are only to see the children at Mrs O'Neill's pleasure.

"In due course this court will issue you with an official letter setting out these details and fix the monthly maintenance schedules. In the meantime you are to continue to pay the mortgage on the house in Tarrytown and all medical expenses for your family, together with the children's school fees."

With that he banged down his gavel and adjourned the court. The entire matter was over in less than thirty minutes.

Larry Grimshaw quickly shuffled his papers together and, as he stuffed them into his briefcase, muttered to Gavin that he was lodging an appeal immediately and would be in touch with him in due course. He then left the courtroom.

Gavin just sat there completely stunned and speechless. He couldn't believe the verdict. He had done nothing wrong and the judge had awarded the case to his wife and her clerical lover. It was incredible. He had lost everything, his house, his home, his children and his reputation. The irony of the situation was that his wife didn't even have to take the stand and Fagan, who was only the material witness, stole the show. Gavin was dumbfounded.

As he was getting out of his seat, Duffy entered the empty courtroom and appeared in front of him.

"What in God's name were you thinking of, Gavin? Don't you know that there is no such thing as a *sure thing* in this man's town?"

"What are you doing here?" asked Gavin, still shocked after the morning's events.

"Never mind what I'm doing here. What are all those clergy doing sitting outside?" he asked, pointing to the door. "I never saw so many together before, not even in a bloody church. Why the hell didn't you get a decent lawyer instead of that two-bit amateur?"

"I don't know," groaned Gavin. "I am completely devastated with this result. It's even worse than her adultery."

"Aaggh," moaned Duffy and, noticing that Gavin was in a state of shock, told him that he had tried to gain access to the court to give him some moral support, but he hadn't been allowed in as the case was being heard *in camera*.

Gavin was still stunned and couldn't answer.

"Furthermore," Duffy continued, "About two months ago I had this bloody awful thought about Fagan which didn't do me much good. Christ, I really got spooked again today when I saw those priests sitting outside the courtroom. There must have been about five or six of them together. Clergy don't attend divorce courts in

New York unless there is something big happening."

Gavin wasn't really interested in Duffy's mumblings, as he had too many worries of his own to contend with, so he just sat there with his head in his hands, and said nothing. Duffy continued talking.

"Gavin, are you listening to me? I am going to introduce you to a real lawyer. His name is Mark Sutherland and he is good. I will explain everything to him and he will get in contact with you shortly. Put all this behind you and have nothing more to do with Grimshaw."

Gavin stood up and nodded. They walked out of the courthouse together and crossed Lafayette.

CHAPTER 31

On 14th May, exactly one week after the divorce hearing, the phone rang in Gavin's office. He was still in a state of shock and every time the phone rang it startled him. He knew he would have to overcome this reaction so, taking a deep breath, he picked up the receiver. Just when he thought matters could not get any worse, he was informed by a relative that his father had just passed away. He didn't know what to do, or who to contact, but instinct directed him to go out and buy a dark suit, a couple of white shirts and a black tie. He called Aer Lingus and reserved a seat on that evening's flight to Shannon.

On arrival in Ireland the following morning he got a taxi to Lahinch and booked himself into the local hotel. He thought this would be a better choice than staying with his mother in the family home. He then made his way out to the farm. As is traditional in Ireland, his father was laid out in an open coffin in the best room of the house. All pictures and mirrors were draped with black veils and continuously throughout the day people were walking in and out of the room. Some just stood at the side of the coffin while others knelt for a few moments in silent prayer.

That evening when all the mourners had paid their final respects, he privately went into the room, closed the door and stood at the end of the coffin. He looked at his father lying there and realised that he had never really known the man, but he did know that he was a very good and quiet person who had seldom raised his voice in anger.

He thought of Ronan's jokes at his wedding reception and hoped that it hadn't offended him too much, but then again he thought that there was a distinct possibility that his father hadn't understood the meaning of them anyway. Gavin knelt down beside the coffin.

"Well, Da," he whispered, "I've made a right bloody mess of my life. I have no wife here today to see you off, and no grandchildren here either, and I've no home to go back to in America. It's desperate, bloody desperate. Da, I'm so sorry for not being a better son to you," and then he burst out crying.

Later the parish priest arrived and all the family went into the parlour again to say a decade of the Rosary before the undertakers prepared the coffin for the hearse. That night his father was resting in the parish church in Lahinch.

When they returned to the family home later that evening, his mother was behaving as if nothing was wrong at all. She was making sandwiches and boiling kettles of water to make tea for all those that were calling at the house. She indicated that she was very busy and hadn't time to talk to anyone in particular, and when she saw Gavin, she asked him if he would be able to get home for his dinner during the week. She was in a state of denial and really didn't know what she was doing or saying.

Patrick and Margaret Murphy attended the removal that evening, and were staying overnight in the hotel for the funeral Mass and burial the next day. Gavin didn't have much to say to them. They were embarrassed at what their daughter had done but he knew that they had to remain loyal to her. However, they fondly asked after their grandchildren. Paddy Murphy shook him firmly by the hand and remarked that *there would be happier days ahead.* Gavin wasn't quite sure if he was referring to his father's death or to the situation between himself and Geraldine. Notwithstanding this, he acknowledged the comment with a nod but said nothing.

As he sat there accepting kindness and sympathy from those that visited, he noticed that not one person asked about Geraldine. It was as if the entire county of Clare knew what had happened in America, and nobody knew what to say to him.

The following morning the parish church was packed with mourners. The priest's homily outlined his father's life and what he had achieved and assured everybody that he was now in the Kingdom of the Lord.

Ronan drove from Dublin for the funeral Mass and after leaving the cemetery they all drove down to the St Gregory for lunch. Gavin was delighted to see Ronan and after they had exchanged compassionate handshakes they sat down together. When Gavin related all the details arising from the divorce proceedings, Ronan was not entirely surprised.

"I always had my reservations about that bitch," he remarked. "She was no fucking good."

"I should have known better," replied Gavin, knowing full well that it was only the truth he was hearing. Then the conversation quickly changed.

"Hopefully I will be over in Boston early next year," continued Ronan, "and you can introduce me to some of those great fish restaurants they have over there."

"I certainly will – that's if I still have a job with the IITA."

"You will," responded Ronan confidently, "and you will be feeling much better by that time. By the way, when are you returning to the States?"

"Tomorrow afternoon from Shannon," came the reply. "I think it's better that I get back to work as quickly as possible. Do you know something, it wouldn't surprise me if my replacement was on the same fucking plane as me."

"Don't talk that shite to me, Gavin," remarked Ronan. "You'll be in that job for a hell of a long time to come."

"I hope so as I need the money," came the reply. "And how's your own job going?"

"Oh, I'm still hanging in there. It's a long story but it will keep until Boston."

With that they moved into the dining room for lunch. At about 4.00pm Ronan stated that he had better get on the road as it was a long drive back to Dublin. The two friends embraced each other, shook hands again and Ronan's extended arm was still waving from the driver's side of his car as it disappeared down the road.

Totally dejected, Gavin boarded the EI 105 the following day at

2.15pm Irish time. He knew that he would be in New York at approximately 5.00pm EST but this was not a flight that he was looking forward to. This was not like the other transatlantic crossings which had always seemed so full of hope and opportunity. This flight was a flight of doom and gloom as he had no idea what the future held in store for him.

CHAPTER 32

The last thing on his mind at night, and the first thing on his mind every morning, was the divorce case. He found it difficult to sleep and during the day he always felt tired. His eyes were continuously sore. He was not sure if this stress related to the anguish of the case that he had just been through, or the fear of the one that was coming up in the near future. Life was becoming unbearable as on top of everything else he was still mourning his father.

He found it difficult to concentrate on his job, but he knew that this was his only legitimate escape. He tried to live as normal a life as possible on the small disposable income that he had left, and he even considered selling his car. All luxuries were now a thing of the past. He had no idea how he was going to make ends meet, and he felt extremely concerned about his future. He was overwhelmed with grief at losing his children and he was not at all sure where he was going to find the money to pay the mortgage on the house that technically was not his any more. He repeated to himself what he had told his dead father the night before the funeral in Ireland: "My life is now a bloody mess."

The tourist business was approaching one of its busiest times, and he knew that the best remedy was work so he decided to get fully involved and try to put everything else out of his mind. He got into a routine and started to go to the same familiar places for meals; he became quite well known in the neighbourhood diners.

In America the last Monday of May is Memorial Day and everything closes down for the duration. In view of this he decided to attend the tourism industry annual dinner in Boston, so he booked himself into the Back Bay Hilton for four nights. The few days away would help recharge his batteries. He took the Amtrak from Penn Station and when he arrived at Union Station in Boston he took a cab to the Hilton Hotel at 47 Dalton Street. He had dinner in Boodles restaurant and retired early.

The following morning he met some other delegates and

exchanged the usual small talk and gossip. Later that day he went for a walk along the Charles River, visited Quincy Market and returned to the hotel at about 6.30pm. After he had showered and shaved he made his way down to the ballroom where the annual dinner was taking place and checked where he was sitting on the large billboard that was located outside the door. He was pleased to see that he was sitting with some people he knew from Chicago, as he found some of these black tie functions rather boring.

As he looked at the menu his eyes wandered around the room and he saw to his utter amazement, sitting at a large circular table in front of the stage, the woman he had seen on the flight when he was recently returning from Ireland. His heart started to palpitate and he could hardly think straight: "Imagine seeing her here," he thought to himself and throughout the dinner he kept looking in her direction. Eventually, when their eyes met, she smiled as if she recognised him. He didn't know what to do.

After a few minutes, when coffee was being served, he gathered his thoughts and decided that he would go over and introduce himself. Standing up and buttoning his dinner jacket, he walked over to her table.

"Hello, how are you?" he smiled. "It's nice to see you again. My name is Gavin O'Neill and I think we have met before."

She smiled back at him. "Yes, I know, on the plane."

He was suddenly stuck for words and there was a lump forming in his throat. He asked if she would like a drink on the veranda and she agreed. He thought her Spanish accent was lovely. He told her that he was with the Irish International Tourist Association, stationed in New York and that he usually attended this function.

In turn she introduced herself very politely. "My name is Gabriella de Leon and I am with the Spanish Embassy in Washington but I also rent a small apartment in New York," she said.

"Wow," replied Gavin. "That's great."

She went on to explain that she was attending this function on behalf of her father who was now the Spanish Ambassador to the United Nations. Conversation between them was easy and she told him that over the next couple of days she was organising some events for the local Hispanic community. They continued chatting and when it was time for him to return to his table, he asked her if she would like to join him for breakfast in the morning.

She nodded politely and he asked: "Would 8.30 be OK?"

"Perfect," she smiled.

For the first time in many months, Gavin felt almost happy again.

The following morning after breakfast, they exchanged more information about themselves, and agreed that they would meet for a meal later that evening in the Legal Fish Company in the Prudential Centre of Boylston Street. Gavin couldn't explain the warm glow he was feeling. Could there be such a thing as love at first sight? Gabriella was definitely a ray of sunshine in his life. It was just what he needed at that moment.

After dinner, as they walked back to the hotel, he stopped at a small bar and asked her if she would like to have a "nightcap" as there were some things he wanted to explain to her. He needed to tell her about his present situation so that it would not present a major problem if they decided to see each other again.

He outlined the events of the past few weeks and told her that he had two children. He kept it very brief as he didn't want to frighten her away altogether, but he knew that the sooner she knew about it the better it would be.

"You do have a divorce, don't you?" she asked in a quiet tone.

"Yes, I do," he replied positively.

"OK," she responded but said no more. She was obviously surprised at what she had heard, and she informed him that it might be better if they didn't meet for a day or so. This he readily agreed.

He walked her back to her room and said goodnight.

He didn't see her for the next two days and thought that she had probably checked out without telling him. He wouldn't have been surprised at all as his saga would have scared anybody away. Then, totally unexpectedly, as he was standing in the hotel shop, his heart jumped when he noticed her walking out of Boodles into the lobby. When she saw him she waved.

"Hello, Gavin," she said. "How are you? I have been very busy and tomorrow I am driving back to New York. It's a long journey and I was wondering if you would you like to join me?"

"Would I what?" he replied excitedly. "I would be delighted."

This suggestion came as a complete surprise and he didn't need to be asked twice. He made his final arrangements in Boston that evening and the following morning they took the "T" to Copley Square, where her car was garaged. She suggested that it would be better not to discuss his divorce case, and this he gladly accepted. He was simply enthralled to be in her company.

They left Boston on Highway Three, and at the Sagamore Bridge took a left turn onto Cape Cod.

"How would you like a trip in a light aircraft?" she asked.

"You fly planes as well?" he enquired, astonished.

"Yes, it's a lovely day and we could fly up as far as Provincetown."

"Wonderful," replied Gavin, who couldn't believe the fun and excitement that he was having with this young woman.

They lunched at the Henry Webster Roadhouse and after passing through the village of Sandwich they arrived at Hyannis Airport. She walked into the operations area and spoke to one of the instructors.

"Good afternoon," she said. "My name is Gabriella de Leon and I was checked out three weeks ago on the Piper Series. I have over 300 hours on that particular type," she said, pointing to the aircraft on the ramp. "I was wondering if I could hire it for about an hour."

"May I see your licence and logbook, please, ma'am?" asked the instructor and she opened her briefcase and handed him both documents. He meticulously examined the books, noting that the logbook was stamped by the Washington Flying Club and signed by their Chief Flying Instructor.

"All appears to be in order, Miss de Leon. Are you familiar with the area?"

"Not really. Could you please explain the circuit pattern as I just want to fly up to Provincetown and back."

"That's not a problem at all. It's very straightforward. Outbound traffic exits at Brewster and inbound traffic calls the field at Yarmouth," he said, "and you will find charts and headsets in the plane. There's no other traffic in the area at the moment, so you will have nothing to affect you."

The instructor confirmed that he would have an engineer refuel the Piper on the apron and then, placing her credit card in the machine, he swiped it forward and backwards to get an imprint.

"We will settle everything when you return," he concluded.

She thanked the instructor, and Gavin and Gabriella walked out to the aeroplane. Gavin felt like a kid with a new toy. He watched her as she made her external checks. She touched everything with such authority that he marvelled at her skill. Before getting into the plane she dipped the fuel tanks with a graduated rod and was satisfied that she had sufficient fuel. Then they boarded the aircraft.

Picking up the checklist she examined all the instruments, the seats, the harnesses, the radios, the controls, and all the gauges. She took out a chart and drew a red line along the track that she was about to fly and also circled the exit and entry points. She fired up the single engine and, turning the plane into the wind, completed her power checks. She told Gavin exactly what she was doing each time she moved from one thing to another and he was very impressed.

After confirming with the control tower that she was ready, she was cleared for take-off on runway 29. She asked Gavin if he was all right as she made her last visual checks before easing the throttle full forward. As they speeded down the runway over seventy-five miles an hour, the ground slipped away and after climbing to five hundred feet she commenced a gentle right hand turn and continued the climb. At two thousand feet, even though the aircraft was travelling at over a hundred and fifty miles per hour, there was no sensation of movement at all. She called Hyannis at Brewster and was cleared north. She made everything look so easy. Gavin had only known this woman for a few days but he felt as comfortable with her as if he had known her all his life.

They flew up the western side of the Cape which according to locals resembles a man's elbow. They flew over Wellfleet and Truro, before circling at Provincetown. The beaches and sand dunes below looked beautiful. Then following the eastern side of the Cape they flew south over Tonset and Naeset Beach before circling again over the famous Chatham Lighthouse. Then they headed west towards Yarmouth and called the tower for re-entry into the control zone. She throttled back, lowered the wheels, extended the flaps and landed smoothly. She taxied the aircraft to the apron and stopped outside the small terminal building. The entire trip had taken less than forty minutes, but for Gavin it was a wonderful experience.

As evening was approaching they decided to stay the night, so they booked into a guest house in Falmouth which had originally been an old sea captain's home. They had dinner and retired early to their separate rooms as they wanted an early start in the morning.

The following day they left Cape Cod, promising to return some time in the near future. They took Highway 195 which joins Interstate 95 at Providence Rhode Island and this roadway runs all the way to New York City. At the fishing village of Mystic they stopped for lunch, all the while chatting about their few days together.

They re-joined the Interstate which passes through Connecticut and, just before reaching the junction at the George Washington Bridge, they turned left on to the Henry Hudson Parkway and exited at 57ᵗʰ Street into Manhattan. The street lights on Central Park West were just coming on as Gabriella parked outside Gavin's apartment building.

"When is your appellant hearing due?" she asked out of the blue.

"I am not sure," replied Gavin, slightly surprised as she had distinctly said that she did not want to talk about the divorce. "It's either September or early October."

"I think I would like to be around for the result of that," she smiled.

"Really? Do you mean that? Are you serious?" he asked.

"Yes, I am serious" she replied. "I am a woman of the world and I have lived a very full and active life in Paris for many years. Besides, can you not see that I'm slightly interested in you?"

With that he leaned over and gave her an affectionate kiss. They talked for another few minutes and then Gavin stepped out onto the pavement. He watched the red tail lights of her car as it turned left and when they were no longer visible he made his way up to his apartment. He was feeling extremely happy.

Being with Gabriella was entirely his decision without any family influence, and without fear of interference from anyone. Being with her was so different from any other women that he had ever been with in the past. The feeling was so special that he knew this was real love and every time he thought of her he imagined that the Earth had just moved.

PART THREE

THE CONSPIRACY

CHAPTER 33

Fewer Catholics worldwide were attending Mass on a weekly basis. Vocations had dropped drastically. The churches were virtually empty. To many people the sermons were pointless and uninteresting. There was never any good news in them and many were asking why priests were preaching in the first place, as their words only assisted in driving people away. If the truth were known some of the older priests were missing the halcyon days of the fifties and sixties when the Church was such a powerful organisation. However, this was the seventies and people were no longer afraid to stand up against them. The clergy were losing their grip over their faithful, and it was for this reason that Fagan had been fast-tracked upward, as part of its revival campaign.

After he was appointed a Monsignor in 1971, he had had dinner with an acquaintance called James Reid. They had been at university together and James was now married with four young children and had to work very hard to support his wife and family. Fagan took great delight in telling him that being a priest within the Vatican was one of the best jobs in the world. He referred to his position as *the job* and bragged that no matter who starved he would always have three full meals prepared for him daily by the best chefs available. As dinner progressed he also remarked that he would never have to sleep rough, would always have clean sheets to stretch out on at night and pompously admitted that he had done very well for himself. James was shattered and disgusted at such revelations. So much for being the humble priest, he thought to himself. At the end of the meal they shook hands politely, and James Reid decided that he never wanted to meet this man again.

Immediately after the divorce case Fagan moved all his belongings into Geraldine's house and parked his red mustang sports car in the driveway. He had always liked fine wine, gourmet food and fast cars and now he had ample opportunity to sample all at his leisure. He always regarded his former life in the Catholic

Church as a good training ground and looked on his early promotions as career moves which had nothing to do with a vocation. During his time in the priesthood, many hands had assisted him in various ways onto the long ladder of Church hierarchy.

It was quite evident that he was used to the good life and it did not take him long to settle down in his new environment. Needless to remark, he no longer wore his clerical gear. Now that the divorce was confirmed he began setting his own agenda.

He immediately started controlling Geraldine by every means possible and, whether he was applauding her or chastising her, she had fallen completely under his spell. Now that the house was scheduled to become hers solely, his next task was to have it transferred into his name exclusively. This was on the pretext that he would always keep it safe for her and the children, just in case her ex-husband was successful in the future appellant hearing. He was astute enough to know that possession was nine tenths of the law and he needed the house as a legitimate front for what he was organizing. He also wanted the authorities to know that he was a pillar of society.

During the month of June, it had been noticed by some of Geraldine's friends at the golf club that she was not looking well and she confided in them that she was feeling very tired at times. She often complained of headaches and about having a pain in her left side, but Fagan laughed it off by saying that she must have strained herself when she was swinging her golf club.

By early July her tiredness and apathy were such that she was not able to cope with the children, even at weekends. This did not unduly worry Fagan, but since she was becoming so lethargic he decided to call a doctor. Gavin continued his weekly visits to see the children in the boarding school and it was during one of these visits that the Matron subtly informed him that the children's mother had become seriously ill. Because of the forthcoming appellant hearing, Gavin decided that it was not his place to intervene, for fear that it might jeopardise his case. He contacted his new lawyer, Mark Sutherland, who instructed him to visit her only if she specifically requested him, but he was never to go alone. Even though he didn't love her any more, he kept telling himself that she was the mother of his children who dearly loved her, but he was also their father, and they dearly loved him as well. It took him some time to get his head around this confusing fact. Very shortly after that, he heard that Geraldine had an inoperable brain tumour. It was only a matter of time.

While he felt very sorry for Geraldine, he found it difficult to understand why he did not feel any outright grief for her in her present condition. Whatever flickering flame of love had existed between them many years ago was now completely extinguished.

CHAPTER 34

Milan is so full of vitality that many have said it should have been the capital of Italy instead of Rome. It is indeed the business heart of Italy and compares equally with all other financial centres in Europe. It is flanked by motorways and railways that radiate out through tunnels to France and Germany, and is so strategically positioned that it is serviced not only by the Mediterranean but also by the Adriatic.

The Cathedral, or Duomo as it is known, is one of the largest gothic churches in Europe. Its marble turrets, flying buttresses and lacy pinnacles are awesome sights. Across the arcade, in the Piazza della Scala, is the world-famous La Scala Opera House, which seats more than 3,000 people and is celebrated for its performances of Verdi, Rossini and Donizetti.

This is also the city where Catholic clergy, in non-clerical garb, mingle discreetly with Mafia members. In its various fashion houses they sit and watch as provocatively draped sexy supermodels in revealing designs from the Houses of Versace, Armani and Dior *strut their stuff* on the famous Milanese catwalks.

Tonight, however, two very senior gentlemen from totally diverse professions were being driven, not to the famous fashion halls of Milan, but to the renowned church of the Santa Maria della Grazie, which houses the famous Leonardo da Vinci fresco of the Last Supper.

A large black Alfa Romeo slowly glided to a stop outside the church and the driver quickly got out and opened the rear door. Out stepped a man in his early seventies, well tanned, with silver grey hair and immaculately dressed in a dark blue handmade suit. His black shoes were also handmade. His spotless white shirt was complemented by a powder blue tie, sculptured in the famous large Italian knot. His appearance radiated authority and the butt of a .38 protruded from his shoulder holster. His name was Don Luigi Alberto Fagione and he was from Sicily.

A few minutes later a large black Lancia 2000 edged its way quietly and smoothly to the footpath. Out stepped another very tall well built senior gentleman also dressed in a hand crafted black suit. In Milan the colour scarlet is often seen in public, but the two vertical red stripes and the small red buttons on the front of his black shirt indicated something different. The gold cross on a thin gold chain discreetly tucked into his waist belt and the large signet ring on the third finger of his left hand clearly designated that he was a cardinal of the Roman Catholic Church. The small band of white that was fitted unobtrusively under the lapelled collar of his black shirt revealed about two inches of brilliance which contrasted completely with his black ensemble. Two gold cuff links held his starched white cuffs in perfect position.

As they entered the grounds of the church the first man's driver was on hand to open the large mahogany doors and the two mature gentlemen sat down in the second to last row. Silently they eyed each other in the shadowy darkness. This was not the night for admiring the famous fresco; this was the night when some straight talking had to be accomplished.

The cardinal, almost princely in appearance, quietly stated that there was still sufficient time before the appellant case came up for hearing in New York. He reassured the Sicilian Don that everything was very much under control and the best lawyers in the United States were looking after everything. He went on to say that as soon as the case was won, it would be filed away in the annals of history.

"It had better be," came the deep menacing reply. "He was a very stupid man to get mixed up with that married woman. He was one of the best sleepers we ever had."

"And he will be again," replied the cardinal instantly, "but there is nothing we can do about the past. He won the first case outright and there is no reason why he will not win the second. As you know we need this money now so that we can be assured everything is still going according to plan."

"I cannot understand why so much money from previous transactions has disappeared into thin air," came the mumbled response. "I certainly hope that there is no funny business going on."

"There's been no funny business going on," countered the cardinal, trying desperately to sidetrack the last suggestion. "We have invested too much time and energy into this project, so it would be very foolhardy for either of us to take chances at this late stage."

"This is the last payment you are getting until I can see some positive responses," came the throaty reply.

"Don't worry, everything is under control," the cardinal assured him again, and with that the Don clicked his fingers. His driver appeared again, this time carrying a small rectangular suitcase.

The Sicilian nodded, and the suitcase was placed on the pew beside the prelate.

"Open it up," groaned the Don, and the cardinal moved the two small catches simultaneously. The lid sprung open.

"It's all there," came the husky voice once again. "Eight hundred thousand dollars in used bills. Exactly as you requested."

The cardinal closed the lid of the attaché case and bowed his head as if in thoughtful prayer. "Thank you," he said in a low whispered tone.

"It's a lot of money to request in one session."

"Yes, it is," replied the cardinal, "but we need it urgently and it will pay great dividends."

Moving down the pew the Sicilian leaned forward and spoke softly into the Churchman's ear. "I want to tell you something once again," he whispered, threateningly. "I don't want any more glitches in this matter and if any *members of my family* have any mishaps visited upon them by any individual, I will have no hesitation in authorising an extermination immediately. It doesn't matter to me who they are. Is that understood?"

The cardinal knew exactly what he meant and drew a deep breath as if a chilled invisible hand had reached out and touched him on the shoulder.

That evening in total secrecy another illegal deal had taken place, and this transaction was just as ominous and mysterious as any that had occurred in the past.

"In view of the circumstances surrounding everything at the moment," stated the cardinal, "I think it might be better if we are not seen together for the time being. I will be in touch with you shortly."

"Suit yourself, Cardinal Babatisto," came the raspy response. "Just make sure the money gets to the places that it's meant to be going." Standing up and slowly walking towards the door, the Don stopped while his driver draped a camel coloured overcoat across his shoulders. He stood there motionless for a second and muttered, "This place is too far north for my liking. If we are going to have another meeting, let's do it in Palermo. Ciao."

For a few seconds they both stood in stony silence and then parted quietly without even a handshake.

CHAPTER 35

Gavin realised that even though Geraldine was terminally ill, it was of the utmost importance that he win the forthcoming appellant case. If Fagan were considered to be her common law husband, he could inherit her entire estate. Worst of all, the judge had appointed him legal guardian of the children. This was the most shattering fact of all – if it suited him in future dealings Fagan could use the children as pawns.

The phone in Gavin's office suddenly seemed to ring louder than usual and he answered it instinctively in his usual brisk manner. It was now the last week in July.

"Hello, Gavin, Mark Sutherland here. The date for the appellant hearing case has been fixed for Tuesday 2nd September so I would like to see you in my office next Monday at 11.00am. Cancel all your appointments. It's going to be a long day."

"OK, Mark, I'll be there. Thanks."

As he replaced the receiver he noticed that his hands were starting to sweat, and that the clammy feeling was returning to his body. He had just been through one divorce case, and the prospect of another was daunting. However, he knew that he could not continue under the punitive payment conditions that were set out in the court letter which he had received from Judge Rosemount's office.

The letter confirmed his worst fears. It stated categorically that if he was unsuccessful in the appellant court he would have to continue the mortgage repayments on the house in Tarrytown, which was now solely in his wife's name, as she had no visible means of support. Since the divorce, a temporary maintenance order had been in force but it would now be made permanent and index-linked. Not only this, he had to pay all medical fees for the children, together with their school fees, until they were eighteen years of age.

At the moment he was allowed only limited access to see his

children. He was hoping that this would be increased, so that he could take them down to Manhattan again. He often wondered what he had done to deserve such a harsh punishment. He always looked forward to seeing the girls, but when he was leaving them he felt very upset. He shook every time he read the contents of the court letter and now he was convinced more than ever that his new attorney had to do something to overturn Judge Rosemount's decision.

He arrived in Mark Sutherland's office.

"We have a difficult battle ahead, Gavin," announced Mark, who sat opposite him in his large leather chair. "We cannot let the Church get away with this. Brendan Duffy has filled me in with all of the details and, as far as I can see, there is something very sinister going on. With that army of clergy outside the door of the court fully supporting the first divorce case, and the size of the legal team assisting your ex-wife in court, the Church definitely wanted to win that case outright. It has to be some sort of cover-up. They knew that there would be an appellant hearing so I am hoping that they think the next case is just a formality. We will do our best to surprise them. I have read the transcripts of the original trial and Grimshaw only made two serious objections. He just hadn't the ability to think on his feet. He was not a courtroom lawyer.

"Now, I have to tell you, I was stunned when I heard that the Archdiocese of New York paid Mr Fagan's legal expenses and they will probably pay them again this time, so as far as I am concerned there is much more at stake than just a simple divorce case. They are doing all in their power to put this trial behind them, so that they can get the elegant Mr Fagan out of the limelight. The Catholic Church opposes divorce in their teachings and I have the feeling that something big is going on, otherwise they wouldn't blatantly be displaying such a show of strength. We have to really disgrace them. There definitely appears to be some sort of a conspiracy developing and, by the looks of it, you are the fall guy."

He poured himself a glass of water before continuing.

"It's at times like this I ask myself, where does the money come from to finance these court cases? New York attorneys don't come cheap. They say that nobody breaks the rules more often than the Catholic Church and the Mafia and I know that *The Mob* operates brothels in Latin America as there is definitely big money in sex. The top is creamed off, laundered and ploughed back into legal companies that look completely clean and are tax compliant. However, one of their big problems is the *set-up money* which has to be released from Mafia accounts in Italy and this is commonly referred to as *Mattress Money*.

"From what I have ascertained, these monies find their way out of Italy by every means possible to cities such as Boston, Chicago, Los Angeles and New York. Their *modus operandi* includes the diplomatic pouches that travel under the seal of immunity from places such as Milan, Rome, Florence and even from Shannon. These monies are often referred to as *Money for favours*. There is no doubt about it, the Church is certainly involved.

"For instance, is it by strange coincidence that the Catholic Church always features prominently in the homes of high profile well-known Mafia members, especially at births, marriages and deaths? Can this be accidental or, as I said, is there something more sinister going on? I am really convinced there is.

"So, Gavin, are you ready for what lies ahead? This is what we have to substantiate. Just bear in mind that when your back is firmly on the ground, the only way you can go is up."

This part of the meeting lasted nearly an hour.

"I think we should break for lunch now," suggested Mark. "There is a small restaurant across the street that does a superb New England chowder."

CHAPTER 36

When they finished lunch Mark excused himself for a few minutes to speak to a colleague he hadn't seem for some time and once again Gavin was left alone with his thoughts. The glimmer of hope that had flickered in his heart while he had been talking to his lawyer did not last very long, and morose feelings consumed him once more.

"What the hell's happening?" he thought to himself. "If Mark Sutherland is correct and if there is a major conspiracy or cover-up going on within the Catholic Church, where the hell do I fit in?"

He started to wonder more about this *elegant Mr Fagan*, as Mark referred to him, but he couldn't find any answers. Mark returned to the table and insisted on paying for lunch, and it was about 2.30pm when they returned to his office.

"Now, Gavin," persisted Sutherland when they resumed their meeting. "We have to adopt a positive attitude. I maintain that every monster has its weak spot, and very shortly we will find this monster's Achilles' heel. Over the next couple of weeks I am going to look very closely at the Church and I strongly recommend that you get a private investigator to do a bit of spade work."

"I would like to ask Brendan Duffy," commented Gavin. "He seems to be on our side."

"Brendan is OK," came the reply. "That is, when he's sober, but he has had a very bad track record recently and he has only been out of rehab a few months. The doctors have said that they don't think there's another recovery in him if he ever hits the bottle again."

"He seems OK at the moment," answered Gavin.

"Oh, don't get me wrong," replied Sutherland. "He's the best in the business, but I was thinking more of an investigator that you could rely on to send abroad and I am not sure if Brendan would be the best choice at the moment. He just hasn't been dry long enough."

"I still think he's good. He found Fagan for me within a couple of days and gave me a very concise report. I would like to trust him to do this – if it's OK with you, of course?"

"As I said, Gavin, he's the best in the business and when he is switched on there's nobody that can touch him. Just remember that you're only getting one crack at this appellant hearing and it's up to you to decide if you want to place your entire future in the hands of a recovering alcoholic. But if you really want him, then he is yours."

"He's grand, I want him," insisted Gavin. "I think he will be OK."

Gavin thanked Mark. They shook hands and arranged another meeting for early the following week. Mark told Gavin not to go anywhere unusual or to do anything out of the ordinary without contacting him. Gavin was delighted that somebody competent had taken control of the situation and he felt that his back had already risen a couple of inches off the ground.

The next day Mark phoned him. "I have good news for you, Gavin. I was speaking to Brendan and he is delighted to accept the assignment. I have filled him in with everything, and he would like to meet you again. I gave him your apartment address on Central Park West, so you can expect a visitor on Thursday night about 8.00pm."

"That's fine," responded Gavin. "He's very welcome any time. Anyway, I have someone special that I want him to meet."

"Great," responded Mark. "Give him as much background information as you can. He feels the same way about this case as I do. Oh, Gavin, I forgot to mention, I am taking this case on a *no-win-no-fee basis*. Is that OK?"

"It certainly is. Thank you very much, Mark," responded Gavin.

The following evening the doorbell rang at exactly 8.00pm. It was Duffy and as soon as he entered the sitting room, Gavin introduced him to Gabriella. When they sat down Duffy looked at Gavin and remarked, "You're looking much better than you did the last time I saw you."

"So are you," replied Gavin.

Gabriella had prepared a lovely supper and Duffy ate real home-cooked food for a change, instead of his usual daily diet of fast foods. Gavin told him all about Gabriella, how he had seen her for the first time on a flight from Ireland and how they had met for the second time in Boston.

They talked until well after midnight and it was agreed that the Atlantic had to be crossed again in order to do some spade work. As Gavin walked with him to the elevator, Duffy shook him firmly by the hand and thanked him for the commission.

"How long did you say you guys have been together?" enquired Duffy.

"Almost three months."

"She's beautiful, Gavin, and for Christ's sake hold on to her, she's a real gem."

Gavin knew exactly what he meant and, patting him on the shoulder, he wished him well with all his investigations.

Duffy's life was surrounded by hunches that led him from one clue to another. He was seldom wrong and the next day as he sat in the taxi on his way to Kennedy, various thoughts flashed through his mind. Something wasn't right. Gavin was just a young man who worked extremely hard at his job and who now suddenly found himself in this dreadful situation. His ex-wife and children were being cared for by a former priest, and it all seemed too ridiculous.

A divorce court in the State of New York does not attract such heavyweights as an auxiliary bishop, four priests, and the Cardinal Archbishop's secretary, together with three or four attorneys. As Mark Sutherland stated, there was definitely more to this case than met the eye and it definitely involved the Catholic Church.

That was why Brendan Duffy was flying to Ireland: in order to see if he could track down any solid evidence against this pompous former Monsignor Fagan.

191

CHAPTER 37

Duffy had only been in Ireland for four days but he felt that he had been there for ages. He left Killarney at 10.00 am and it took him over two hours to drive forty-five miles. He stopped at Skibbereen for lunch, and arrived in Clonakilty at about 3.00pm. After making enquiries, he proceeded to the retirement home and parked his car. Inside he asked if he could see Father Joseph Slattery. He was shown to a room at the end of a long narrow corridor and when he knocked on the door a feeble voice answered: "Come in."

He entered the room and, looking around, saw the lonely figure of Father Slattery slumped in an armchair. Looking out of the window he noticed that it had started to rain again.

"Good afternoon, Father," he said. "My name is Duffy, Brendan Duffy."

Father Slattery nodded and Duffy continued, "How're ya doing, Father? Are ya doing OK? It's a damp day outside."

"It's what we call a soft day in this part of the country," acknowledged the priest quietly. "How can I help you, Mr Duffy?"

"I was just wondering if you ever hear from a Monsignor Fagan these days, Father?" asked Duffy, getting straight to the point.

This was followed by a long pause. "No," eventually came the quiet reply, "but I've received a few letters from him over the years. He's a Monsignor in New York and he was very good to me and every so often he sent me some American money. It must be two years since I last heard from him. Would you like to see some of his letters?"

"Yes, Father, I would," replied Duffy, not wanting to appear rude.

The old priest slowly stood up and made his way to his bureau.

"Did you know I used to be the parish priest in Lahinch?" he proudly asked.

"Yes, Father, I did," replied Duffy, and with that the elderly cleric took six or seven letters from a drawer in the writing desk.

He showed these to Duffy. All the writing was in longhand on official letter headed notepaper typical of a Catholic Archdiocese. Some of the letters were dated more than two years before and the majority had only a few lines of writing on them enquiring after the priest's health. Duffy respectfully handed the letters back to Father Slattery.

"How well did you know Monsignor Fagan?" enquired Duffy, and once again silence followed, which made Duffy suspect that something was not quite right with the elderly gentleman. Then looking closely at Father Slattery, Duffy realised that he was suffering from dementia. After a few moments, Father Slattery once again repeated that Father Fagan was a kindly person, and he had been appointed to the Vatican Congressional Office at a very young age. He just assumed that he must have been a very intelligent person.

"I met him when I was in Rome about seven years ago," he commented, "but I don't think he was a Monsignor then. He was with other young priests and a lot of them had Italian names, I think. I'm not really sure. They all looked the same. There was an awful lot of them."

Then, looking at Duffy, he poignantly asked, "Who did you say you are?"

"Brendan Duffy."

"Brendan who?" enquired the priest again.

"Duffy, Brendan Duffy."

"Oh, OK, thanks, Mr Duffy," he continued and as he was coherent again for a few minutes he kept referring to the previous question which he had already answered. "I only knew him as Father Fagan. He was a kindly man and he went to New York about four or five years ago, I think."

"Is there anything else you can tell me about him?" prompted Duffy who felt that the old priest had more information to tell but unfortunately was unable to bring it to the forefront of his mind.

Duffy realised that he was getting nowhere fast.

"No, nothing. That's all I know," replied the priest and apologised that he was now getting tired.

Duffy appreciated this, said goodnight to him and made his way back to the hotel. He knew it was pointless asking Father Slattery about Geraldine O'Neill, as sadly he could see the first signs of the dreaded Alzheimer's disease taking its hold. For this reason he could not rely on him to remember anything correctly. He was aware that Father Slattery would probably agree with most things anyone suggested, so he felt he had drawn a complete blank on this occasion.

When he returned to the hotel there was a large country wedding taking place, which would have totally captivated any onlooker's attention, especially when the bride got stuck in the small downstairs toilet without toilet paper. The entire hotel knew what had happened as the screaming coming from that small room was unbelievable. The problem was they couldn't push in a toilet roll, either above or below the door, as there wasn't sufficient space, so the bridesmaid had to slip single sheets of paper underneath the door, one piece at a time.

Eventually when the bride appeared, she was wearing the large traditional white meringue wedding dress in spite of the fact that she was heavily pregnant. Duffy couldn't imagine how she had managed in that small cubicle but she looked totally unconcerned at her situation. She noticed her groom leaning against a nearby wall with a cigarette in one hand and a pint of beer in the other and she shouted a few words of abuse at him. In response he could only manage a stupid smile as he was completely drunk. The incredible thing about this situation was that the bride's mother was also heavily pregnant and Duffy overheard someone saying that neither mother nor daughter really knew for sure who the fathers were. Apart from this welcome diversion, which he really enjoyed, he couldn't get Fagan out of his mind for one solitary moment.

He rehearsed over and over again the quandary of how a young good-looking priest could rise to a top position within the Vatican in such an exceptionally short space of time. This was most unusual in an organisation such as the Catholic Church, where everyone of importance was generally middle-aged and everything concerning them was comprehensively examined at least a hundred times. Fagan was only thirty when he was appointed a Monsignor, and the next step after that was to the status of Bishop. He perished that thought immediately as Fagan becoming a Monsignor was bad enough, but Duffy suspected that most of the secrets surrounding these matters rested in Ireland.

The following morning, after a fitful night's sleep, Duffy walked up to the retirement home, which was situated beside the large Cathedral. He once again met Father Slattery, who was a little more alert. In the course of conversation he informed Duffy that he had a niece who had a very important job in the Vatican. He went on to say that she was a very clever girl, that she was very well educated and he was very proud of her. He added that she was happily married to an Italian gentleman called de Silva, but she still maintained her family connections with County Cork. He rummaged through his bureau once again and found her name and address in an old notebook.

"My sister is married to a Collins," he said and tearing the page out of the notebook he handed it to Duffy. "They live in the small town of Carrigaline, just outside Cork City," he concluded.

He once again asked Duffy who he was, and when Duffy heard this, he realised that it was time to go. He stood up, nodded very courteously to the elderly gentleman and shook hands with him. He told him that he would call again to see him before he returned to New York and thanked him for his time and patience. On the way out he called aside the Head Staff Nurse and, slipping an Irish twenty punt note into her hand, he suggested that this might go a little way towards the old priest's favourite "tipple". He thanked the nurse and, with his usual nod, replaced his hat and made his way down the steps, along the cobbled path and out into the street.

The following morning he contemplated the information acquired from Father Slattery and decided that it was definitely worth investigating. He set off for Cork City, passing through the villages of Bandon and Ballinhassig before taking the turn off for the town of Carrigaline. He booked himself into the large modern hotel that was situated at the top of the town and checked out the comfortable bedroom before walking down the two flights of stairs to the dining area. Duffy never minded stairs as long as he was not walking up them, as he firmly believed that there was no value to be gained from such an exercise. He recalled that an old South American doctor had once told him that workouts of any description only added a few hours to one's life and when it was time to go you simply had to comply. This probably explained why he was so overweight, especially from his many days of heavy boozing and carousing. Apart from this, Duffy was nobody's fool.

He entered the bar where food was being served and this was something that he still could not get used to since coming to Ireland. This was so unlike America, where food is only served in restaurants or in diners. He found it difficult to understand and wondered why the majority of people in this green and pleasant land were not all roaring alcoholics. After his near miss in Lahinch he had decided that he would vacate all licensed premises by 8.30pm every evening, as it was not correct for him to be in such a place once the lights were dimmed. He was determined to keep this rule for Gavin's sake, as he owed him so much for affording him the opportunity of regaining his dignity by working again. Only a few months earlier he had thought that he had completed his very last job and would never be considered trustworthy enough to be given another assignment. A young waitress approached him and, with a pleasant smile, he ordered an open smoked salmon sandwich on brown bread and a pot of coffee.

CHAPTER 38

Duffy decided that there were two establishments where there might be someone who knew where the Collins family lived: one was the local pub and the other the local police station. He decided to ask the barman of the Crowing Cock Inn rather than arouse the suspicions of the local Gardai.

He was informed that the Collins home was the red brick house at the bottom of the Main Street and it would be impossible to miss it. He raised his hat as usual, placed a few coins in the charity box on the counter, and made his way in that direction. The door was answered by a very elegant woman.

"Good morning, ma'am," Duffy greeted her, raising his hat once again. "I'm looking for a Mrs Collins and I am wondering if she might be at home."

"Mrs Collins is very seriously ill at the moment," came the polite response.

"Oh," responded Duffy. "I am very sorry to hear that."

"My name is Noreen de Silva, I am her daughter," came the cultured reply.

Duffy had not expected to find the person that he was actually looking for answering the door! "My heavens, I can hardly believe this. You are the lady I am here to enquire about," he exclaimed.

Noreen de Silva was a very attractive woman. She was dressed in a beautiful cream suit and when she spoke the slightest hint of an Italian accent percolated through her Cork brogue. As it happened, two days before she had received an urgent message that her aged mother had suddenly taken ill and she had travelled home immediately to be with her.

"My name is Duffy, ma'am, Brendan Duffy. If it's not too much of an imposition, I would welcome a few words with you."

"That's OK, Mr Duffy. My mother's sleeping at the moment so I have a few minutes to spare but I really don't know how I can help you. I have never heard of you before."

"I am doing some investigations for a young Irishman who lives in New York," continued Duffy. "I was speaking to your uncle, Father Joseph Slattery, yesterday and he mentioned your name. He's a fine gentleman and he is really enjoying his retirement in Clonakilty."

"I haven't seen him for years," came the reply. "It must be a serious matter if he gave you this address in Cork. Is he all right?"

"Yes, yes," replied Duffy. "I was informed by the parish priest from Lahinch that he had retired to Clonakilty, and when I was talking to your uncle he told me that your mother might be able to assist me in some enquiries. I am delighted that I have met you. May I come in?"

"Yes, of course," came the welcoming response, "and please forgive me for keeping you standing so long on the doorstep."

"Not at all," remarked Duffy. "You're a real lady."

Blushing slightly, she ushered him into the parlour, and asked him if he would like tea or coffee.

"Coffee would be fine," responded Duffy, knowing that it would probably taste dreadful, but anything was better than tea.

"I will not take up much of your time, ma'am," continued Duffy. "I am really only interested in one fact."

"And what would that be, may I ask?"

"Have you ever heard of a young priest called Anthony Fagan?" he enquired.

"I come in contact with a lot of clergy." she replied. "It would not be appropriate for me to know any one of them on a personal basis."

"I understand that, ma'am, and I am not suggesting you do, but this priest is quite unique," responded Duffy. "He is reputed to be very distinguished and also very intelligent. He's in his early thirties, and he is already a step up the ladder within the Catholic Church, as a few years ago he was appointed a Monsignor."

She paused for a moment which indicated to Duffy that he might have struck a chord somewhere, but she quickly side-stepped his remark, as she poured his coffee.

"Sugar and cream, Mr Duffy?"

"No, thanks, ma'am, I take neither."

She eventually settled herself and sitting opposite him she started to explain her occupation within the Vatican. Most of the information he already knew, but it was good to hear it again and only helped to establish her credibility.

"Well," she continued, "in my position I am in charge of a Papal Legation in Rome. It's run on the same lines as an Embassy. I see a lot of priests coming and going at all times but before I say any more, could you please explain who you are actually looking for?"

Duffy took his time, explaining only what she needed to know and did not mention that Fagan was now a defrocked priest and involved in a divorce case. He knew that as a devout Catholic such information would instantly put her on her guard and his interview with her would be a complete waste of time. He continued very cautiously.

"All I know is that your uncle met Father Fagan in Rome about seven years ago."

"Really," she replied, "I wouldn't know anything about that."

"I understand, ma'am, I am only trying to establish Monsignor Fagan's connections."

"As I have already told you, Mr Duffy, I'm in charge of the Santoni Legation and, yes, I could have seen a young priest there periodically. I cannot say that it is the same man that you are referring to as he only stays a couple of nights and he's normally with other clergy."

"Let's assume it is the same man? How would you describe this young priest?" asked Duffy inquisitively.

"Well, if this is the man you're asking about, he is pleasant, he is polite and he is very well mannered. Just as you describe, but I have to point out that I am not actually sure that we are talking about the same person."

He knew that she was being evasive and he realised that he would not get anywhere if he did not tread carefully. He also knew that she was being thoroughly protective of all those she came in contact with.

"Again assuming that we are speaking about the same man, would you know when he was last in the Santoni Legation?" asked Duffy cautiously.

"Not off hand," came the protective response.

"Have you no idea at all, ma'am? This is very important. A young Irishman's reputation depends on it."

When she heard the word *Irishman* being used for the second time coupled with the word *reputation*, she became slightly more reflective.

"Now that you mention it, I think I saw a young Monsignor in the legation with a Cardinal on one or two occasions but that's not unusual."

"You're doing fine ma'am, that's a big help."

"Thank you, Mr Duffy," she replied, "and on one instance if my memory serves me correctly, I think there was a mature Italian gentleman talking to them as well."

"Excellent ma'am, that's great."

Duffy felt that at last he was getting somewhere and made a few notes. He asked her again about her duties in the Legation essentially to get her to talk more freely. She said that she had a staff of ten, which included four chambermaids, but she supervised everything herself. The maids were not allowed to touch anything without her express permission, and it was the *done thing* for clerics to leave any clothes that they needed for dry cleaning on the table in the sitting room the previous night. She went on to say that she always checked the pockets of all the suits before they were collected by the cleaner's van-man.

"Did you ever find anything interesting?" enquired Duffy.

She said that she found many things in various pockets and smiled discreetly. This was a dead giveaway to Duffy.

"Can you remember what you found?" he enquired again.

"Oh, mostly handkerchiefs, coins, rosary beads, medals, combs and keys, nothing of much importance but just in case I always place what I consider important in the *lost and found box* that I keep on the sideboard in the sitting room."

Duffy thought for a few seconds and realised that something must be triggering her memory to that day in question. Her responses now were becoming more positive and less cautious.

"Can you recall anything you might have found in the pockets of the suits that were left for collection that morning?"

"Suits are left out all the time so it's impossible to answer that question," she replied assertively.

"I appreciate that, Ma'am," countered Duffy, "but is there anything at all that rings a bell anywhere?"

"There are a few things on occasion."

"Such as, ma'am?"

"Well, one morning I recall finding a thousand lira note, a small key on a ring, a ferry transit ticket and another thing in the pockets," she admitted with embarrassment.

"May I ask what the other thing was?"

"It was an unused condom," she bashfully replied, and turning her head sideways, she raised her eyes and stared at the top right hand corner of the room. She was totally mortified that it was the condom that prompted her memory to the morning in question.

"Do you know who owned these items?"

"Absolutely not," she replied indignantly. "I have to emphatically point out that I have no idea which suit any of these items came from, and considering what was found, it would have been very unethical and imprudent of me to have pursued the matter further. All I can tell you is that most of the suits have the owner's name printed on their inside pockets and if they don't we always tag them with their room number. I am sure there was a very good reason for that thing being there."

Mrs de Silva was now starting to hear herself talk and, realising that she was using the wrong words to try to express herself, she tried desperately to rephrase her last statement.

"Eh, eh I'm sure that the unused condom was probably found in a most unusual place, and was removed by a priest so that it could be destroyed later," she suggested.

"I'm sure you are correct, Mrs de Silva," commented Duffy, not believing a word of her explanation. "But can you recall if the Monsignor left clothes out to be cleaned that morning?"

"Again I am not sure. There could have been a suit belonging to a young cleric on the sitting room table with the others."

"Did any of these reverend gentlemen return to collect any of the things that you found?" enquired Duffy, deliberately not asking if the condom was also placed in the *lost and found* box in the sitting room.

"No," she replied. "They seldom do. On this occasion, I put the thousand lire in the poor box, the condom went straight into the bin together with the ferry transit ticket, and that's all. Generally small items of no importance remain unclaimed and are eventually thrown away."

"Pardon me for asking again, ma'am, but do you think that one of those suits could have belonged to Monsignor Fagan?" interjected Duffy, trying to establish facts. "You need not answer that question directly. A nod would be sufficient."

She raised her eyebrows and continued. "Perhaps one could have, but as I said, these things could have belonged to any of the priests who stayed in the Legation that night. I have no idea which pockets any of these items came from and that's a fact."

He knew he was up against a stone wall and getting nowhere. He decided to change his line of questioning.

"Thank you, ma'am, for being so helpful, and if I understand you correctly, was the small key also placed in the *lost and found box* as well?" asked Duffy in his broad Brooklyn accent.

"Yes, it was, and it was there for some time. Only the other day I decided to lodge it in the Vatican Archives as no one had claimed it. They have hundreds of boxes there, full of all types of sundry items that have been lost over the years and haven't been claimed. I never attached any importance to the key as it looked so insignificant. The same morning that I intended returning the key, I received the phone call from Ireland telling me that my mother, who is eighty-five years of age, was very seriously ill. I just dropped everything. Mario drove me straight to Rome Airport where I managed to get a business class ticket with Aer Lingus, and here I am. I will hand the silly key into the Archives when I return to the Vatican in a couple of weeks."

"Did I hear you correctly, ma'am? Did you say you will return it when you get back to the Vatican?" interrupted Duffy immediately.

"Yes," came the quick response. "I will lodge it in the Archives when I return."

"You mean to say that you have the key with you?" stuttered Duffy.

"Yes," she replied, somewhat surprised. "It's here somewhere in my handbag. There is nothing unusual about it, and it looks like something a child would play with. I don't think that it is of any importance otherwise someone would have been back for it by now."

"It's in your purse, ma'am?" gasped Duffy, and, as she searched in her handbag, she produced the small key and handed it to him.

Duffy examined the small single key on the tiny ring and had to admit that it meant absolutely nothing to him, but his instinct told him that it could be the link to something else.

"I am going to ask you an enormous favour, ma'am. I would like to borrow this key for a short period of time and I assure you I will return it to you as soon as I am finished with it."

"You can have it," came her instant reply. "I don't want it back. I'm sure it's absolutely worthless, otherwise, as I said, someone would have been enquiring about it by now."

Duffy stood up, bowed gently and, sincerely thanked her for her kind assistance. She was not a woman who could be taken for granted. She had answered all his questions politely and positively and he accepted that the items found in the suits could have belonged to any of the priests. She had no way of knowing, and though he had established that Fagan could have been in the Legation that day he needed more proof. He asked her if he could visit her again if it was necessary and she agreed.

He enquired after her mother and she told him that she had suffered a severe stroke and it was touch and go as to whether she would survive. He sympathised with her misfortune and as they stood to shake hands she smiled in the knowledge that a real professional had skilfully questioned her. Before he left town he arranged with the local florist that a bouquet of roses be sent to Mrs de Silva as soon as possible. On the card he wrote the words,

Thank you for all your kindness. Brendan Duffy

As he walked back to the hotel he thought to himself that she was a real lady and there were very few like her around any more. He decided that he had to return to Clonakilty, as there were a few important questions that needed clarification from Father Slattery. He prayed that the reverend gentleman would be lucid enough when he arrived, but it was a chance he had to take.

He continued along the river path which eventually led him back to the hotel. While walking he asked himself – who was this cardinal in the Legation with young Fagan and who was the other Italian gentleman? Could it be that the old priest was correct when he said that when he was in Rome all the young priests had Italian names? He had no answers to these questions and cursed the whiskey for dimming his brain but now he was more determined than ever to avoid the "demon drink". He knew that he had more leg work to do in order to establish reliable facts.

He was delighted to be staying the night in this fine hotel in Carrigaline as the food was good and the bed very comfortable. This ensured that he would be well refreshed for his drive to Clonakilty the following morning.

CHAPTER 39

It was after 4.00pm on Thursday 14th August when Duffy arrived in Clonakilty and, before going up to the Retirement Home, he checked himself into the local hotel and reviewed exactly where Clonakilty was situated on the map of Ireland. He thought to himself that if he managed to get things cleared up this evening he could drive to Shannon Airport the following morning via Mallow and Limerick. As this necessitated a 7.30am start, he decided that he would have a good meal and retire early. Thankfully he was now starting to sleep much better.

He arrived at the retirement home about 4.45pm, asked once again if he could see Father Slattery, and was very courteously shown to the same room as before.

"Hello, Father, it's me again, Brendan Duffy."

"Hello, Mr Duffy, do I know you from somewhere?" asked the elderly priest, moving slightly in his chair. "Who are you? I don't get many visitors these days. Did I ever meet you before?"

"Well, Father," smiled Duffy, politely disregarding the priest's last remarks so as not to cause him any embarrassment, "It's a pleasure seeing you again and I was wondering if I could examine some of those letters that you showed me the other day when I was here. That's if it's not too much trouble."

"I don't remember showing you anything, Mr Duffy. Did I show you my letters before? Let me get them again. It's no bother at all. I get them from America all the time. Have I ever told you that I am the parish priest in Lahinch?"

"Yes, I know that, Father," replied Duffy as he very gently helped him out of his large armchair.

"Thanks," responded Father Slattery. "I have all the letters in the bureau over there against that wall. That's where I keep everything."

The feeble gentleman opened a drawer in the desk where the letters were kept and handed about nine of them to Duffy.

"You can have them all if you want. There will be more in the post soon," he said.

"No, Father, it's OK. If I may, I will take these four."

"Certainly, take as many as you like. What did you say your name was?" asked the old priest once again.

"Brendan Duffy, Father" and with that Duffy neatly folded the four pages and placed them safely in his inside pocket.

"Eh, OK, Mr Duffy. As you can see I am very busy at the moment so you will have to excuse me. I'm preparing my sermon for parish Mass next Sunday"

"I'm sure it will be excellent," responded Duffy, who fully understood this dreaded illness, and he chatted to the frail gentleman for some time before leaving.

Duffy sincerely thanked him for all his kindness but he knew that within a few minutes he would probably not remember who had been in the room with him. He promised Father Slattery that he would visit him again very soon, as it was his intention to return to Ireland in the near future.

On his way out he once again saw the Head Staff Nurse and, after more pleasantries were exchanged, he gave her another twenty punts which might assist towards Father Slattery's modest luxuries. He felt unhappy seeing the elderly gentleman in this condition, but he knew he was not suffering pain, and that he was well cared for.

He walked back to the hotel and made his way to his room. He phoned Mrs de Silva and once again asked about her mother. He was advised that there was no change in her condition. He then told her that he had seen her uncle again, and he had been very helpful. Duffy politely asked her if she could clear up a problem that was playing on his mind.

"I will, if I can and I was waiting for you to contact me," came the pleasant response.

"Ma'am, assuming that Monsignor Fagan was the young priest you saw in the Santoni Legation that particular morning, I was just wondering if there is any way you could remember or verify the names of the people that were talking to him."

"Yes, I could" she answered, much to his surprise. "I have been giving this matter a lot of thought so I decided to phone the Legation this morning and ask my assistant to check the register on the day in question. When I was speaking to you I wasn't sure of names or exact dates but I made a phone call this morning and now I am quite certain. Last year Easter Sunday fell on 14th April and I can positively tell you that the young priest was definitely Monsignor Fagan and he was talking to Cardinal Babatisto. Both of them were in residence for Easter. Their signatures are in the register and during the course of the day I noticed them talking to a very well dressed older Italian gentleman."

"You can definitely confirm what you have just told me, ma'am?" he enquired.

"Yes, I can positively confirm what I have just said. It's recorded in the register and I will repeat it again if you wish."

"No, ma'am, that's fine – thank you very much indeed. The fact that you have confirmed it is quite sufficient," he quickly responded, remembering her strong Catholic beliefs and, even though she was over a hundred miles away, he instinctively touched his hat. That was all the information he needed to know.

"Oh, Mr Duffy, before I forget, thank you very much for the flowers."

"Not at all, Mrs de Silva. It was totally my pleasure."

With that he replaced the receiver, but picking it up again almost immediately he asked for the local telephone exchange operator.

"Good evening, ma'am," he said when she answered him. "I was wondering if you could place a transatlantic telegraphic wireless message for me please. It's to a Mr Gavin O'Neill, Apartment 627, Central Park West, New York.

"The message is simply to read – *I will be home tomorrow on the EI 105 – Duffy.*"

CHAPTER 40

Gavin and Gabriella drove out to Kennedy International Airport to meet Duffy. On Friday afternoons the traffic is normally of gridlock proportions, and that day it was hardly moving at all. They ruled out trying to leave Manhattan by way of the Queens Midtown tunnel or the Queensboro Bridge and decided on the slightly longer route over the Triborough Bridge, which connects with the Grand Central Parkway just short of La Guardia Airport.

This would leave them with a choice of intersections which join the Van Wyck Expressway that goes all the way to Kennedy. Unfortunately, one route was just as bad as the other and when they reached the Expressway they were just inching along.

It was after 6.00pm before Duffy emerged through the customs hall exit doors as he had had to wait in a long line at the Immigration Desk. He was delighted to see them both and told Gavin that he'd had a very enjoyable time in Ireland. He went on to say that he had done so many wonderful things he felt like the mayfly that packs a lifetime into one solitary twenty-four hour period.

"Well," he announced when he had finished relating his adventures. "I think we've something to go on, but first we have to contact Mark Sutherland." Holding up the key he continued. "Secondly, we will have to get our heads together to unravel the mystery surrounding this key. If we solve this puzzle I am positive we will crack this case wide open. I also have some letters to show you."

Duffy asked if he could telephone Mark, who was delighted to hear that he was back, and after a few minutes Mark asked to speak to Gavin.

"Hi, Gavin. I just want you to ensure that Brendan gets some valuable sleep over the weekend so that he can get rid of his jet lag. We want him back on tip top form by early next week."

"No worries, Mark," replied Gavin. "I have the very person here who is going to take real good care of him."

He was of course referring to Gabriella, who was nodding that she understood every word he was saying. When they were all seated around the table for supper Duffy had the feeling that he had never been needed on a personal level in quite the same way before. There were superficial acquaintances and people he knew through his business; there had been women, of course, including his ex-wife, but he felt no one had cared for his true self. He was feeling hopeful that his relationship with Siobhan would prove different, and he felt grateful to Gavin and Gabriella as they had been indirectly responsible for bringing about that meeting. He also knew they wouldn't think he was being over-sentimental when he honestly told them: "I just want to say one thing: this is the first time in my entire life that I've ever had such good friends."

CHAPTER 41

Mark phoned Gavin again on Monday morning to see how things were going and, as the trial date was approaching fast, he suggested that all three of them should literally lock themselves up in the apartment for the next few days and try to unravel everything that Brendan had to offer. He was pleased that he was over his jet lag.

"When you come up with something," he said, "give me a buzz, but one way or another I will see you for our appointment on Thursday 28th. We can then go over everything again in great detail, so that it will be fresh in your mind for the following Tuesday. You'll be OK, Gavin – just try not to worry too much."

Gavin acknowledged what he said and they hung up.

At 11.00am Gabriella produced a large pot of coffee and all three of them sat around the dining room table. Duffy related everything he had discovered while in Ireland, and it was after 3.30pm before they decided that it was time for lunch.

"Let's go over it once again and see if you can highlight the most important parts of your trip," suggested Gavin.

"It was all great but I think my time in Killarney was definitely the best."

"I suppose it was," agreed Gavin, with a smile on his face.

"I'm going to make some more sandwiches," suggested Gabriella, "and then we can start off all over again."

After they had eaten they felt better and it was decided that they would keep going until 7.00pm. Nothing new emerged that evening and at about 6.30pm they were all mentally and physically drained. They decided to call it a day, go for a walk and meet again the following morning at 11.00am.

The next day, Gavin was up at 8.30am and at about 9.30am Gabriella arrived. He had deliberately waited for her so they could have breakfast together. Giving him a gentle kiss, she informed him that she had placed all her appointments and commitments on hold until after the court hearing. He was wooing her in the old-fashioned way as he had great respect for her and no one would ever be able to point a finger of indiscretion at either of them. She simply loved his attentions. Duffy arrived at 10.45am.

"OK, let's start again," said Gavin, getting everyone organised. "Brendan, can you go over everything once again that you consider the most important parts of your investigations in Ireland?"

"The most important part of my enquiries was my conversation with Mrs de Silva and the meetings I had with Father Slattery. I have the letters here to prove that."

"OK, Brendan – so let's start with Mrs de Silva. Tell us again what she found in the pockets of the clothes."

"An unused condom, a thousand lira note, a key and a ferry ticket," responded Duffy.

"Yes," commented Gavin, "and you say that the lire went straight into the poor box and the condom and the ferry ticket went straight into the bin."

"Correct," said Duffy, "and out of that little bunch, all we have is this key and the letters from Father Slattery."

"I cannot see any connection between them," commented Gavin, "so let's take a closer look at the key."

The key was about an inch and a half long with the lettering 216L engraved on its shaft.

"My experience definitely indicates that it's a key to some sort of bank deposit box," stated Duffy.

"Gosh," remarked Gabriella, "we cannot check every bank in New York."

"It might not even be in New York," commented Gavin. "There are over a million boxes that this key could open."

"It might not belong to Fagan at all," Gabriella pointed out. "You said there were other priests staying in the Legation that night."

"You could be right, Gabriella," agreed Duffy, "but it's all we've got to go on, so we must assume that it did belong to him."

"I'm only trying to be the devil's advocate," she replied, and Duffy agreed with her and told her to keep thinking that way, as it kept him on his toes.

"OK, folks, I think tomorrow we should start by checking the local banks where Fagan lived," recommended Gavin. "At least it's a starting point."

On Wednesday afternoon they drove up to Tarrytown and walked down its main street. There were two banks in the town; one was the New England Banking Corporation and the other was the Bronx and Queens Banking Federation.

"Which one did Geraldine bank with?" asked Duffy, looking at Gavin.

"I'm not really sure," he responded. "I think she had accounts with both of them."

They decided to enter the two banks and enquire about their branch networks. They were most disheartened when they discovered that one bank had over ninety-eight branches mostly in the metropolitan area and the other had a hundred and seventy-eight scattered all over New York State and into New England up as far as Boston. The small key bore no marking whatsoever except for the engraving, and in post war America, even though many smaller banks had been taken over by larger conglomerates and reborn again out of mergers, their deposit box systems were never updated. The problem looked unsolvable. The deposit box could be anywhere. They drove back to the apartment in complete silence.

"Let's go over it all once again," suggested Gavin for a third time. "There was a condom which was thrown away, a port ferry ticket that was also thrown away, a thousand lira note which went into the poor box and this key. There must be some connection."

"Which ports have ferry services?" asked Gabriella.

"Nearly all of them," responded Duffy. "And there must be thousands of them."

Just then the phone rang and Gavin answered it.

"It's for you, Gabriella. It's Suzy Baxter."

Gabriella made a face as if to say she wasn't there, but there was nothing she could do as Gavin had already called her by name. She had to take the call.

"Hello, Suzy, what can I do for you?

– I'm very busy at the moment;

– No, I am not going out of town;

– Yes, I'm staying in New York;

– OK, Friday at 2.00pm in Saks restaurant;

– Yes, lunch on the balcony would be lovely;

– Me, too, Suzy;

– Bye for now."

Looking up she said quite seriously, "Gavin, she is the one person I could do without at the moment, but if I don't meet her for lunch she will continue to pester me."

Gavin just smiled pleasantly at her, knowing how she must be feeling.

Suzy Baxter was an all-American girl. She was a cheerleader from the beginning to the end of her High School days and had never really grown up. She went through men the same way as she changed her socks, and she lived on a private income from her mother, who had just re-married for the fourth time. Her mother had told her that the allowance was part of an alimony settlement awarded to her from one of her former husbands. Suzy didn't really care which one it came from as long as she received the allowance every month. She had never known her father.

She was the sort of person you could throw out of the back door and within seconds she would be knocking at the front door again, trying to get in. She was very untidy and her apartment was always in a mess. She loved talking about holidays, clothes and make-up. She was giddy and scatterbrained but for some reason Gabriella liked her very much. Perhaps at this moment, Suzy was the tonic she needed.

On Thursday evening with only twelve days to go, everything was still at a stalemate. They were not any wiser. Gabriella told them that she would see them for dinner on Friday night and perhaps if they gave it a rest over the weekend something might pop into their minds on Monday morning. They rang Mark but he only suggested that they kept on trying. His meeting for the following week still stood as scheduled.

On Friday just after one o'clock Gabriella took the cross town subway to 5th Avenue and walked the short distance to Saks. When she arrived at the SFA restaurant on the eighth floor, Suzy was already seated at a window table overlooking St Patrick's Cathedral. When Gabriella saw her she walked over to the table and was greeted with a kiss on each cheek. Suzy's blonde hair was clipped up on each side, she was wearing too much make-up and as usual she was a bundle of energy. Before Gabriella could open her mouth, Suzy was bursting with chat.

"You look radiant. Are you in love? Go on, admit it," she eagerly enquired in her high pitched New York accent, but Gabriella successfully steered her away from anything that even remotely related to Gavin. They ordered identical lunches which consisted of sweetcorn and mushroom soup with an open prawn sandwich. It was served by a very pleasant young man who informed them that he was only a part-time waiter and was really an actor waiting for his big moment. This brought smiles to their faces. Suzy told Gabriella that she had been feeling stressed out of her mind recently and had decided to join a bongo drum class.

"Gee, honey, it was great fun," she continued, "but I couldn't hear too well afterwards. All those drums pounding. I think I killed my left thumb as well on the third trip. After the fourth session my fingers ached like hell, so I quit. What a way to kill stress. Still, it was fun while it lasted."

Gabriella couldn't help laughing at her description and knew that this would be the major element of the conversation. They soon talked about the latest fashions and how stupid the models looked. Over coffee they chatted about the latest hits, and the musicals that were playing on Broadway. When the bill arrived, both of them tried to grab it at once. Suzy won.

Opening her large bag she looked for her wallet and in doing so numerous items fell onto the table including a lipstick, a powder compact, a pen, a book token from Barnes and Noble, some eye shadow, a comb, some hair pins, three subway tokens, and a slightly crumpled ferry ticket.

"What books are you reading at the moment?" asked Gabriella, looking at the book token, and Suzy informed her that she was really interested in reading a book on moral psychology and was going to get it on her way home.

"Gosh, wow, I'm very impressed," commented Gabriella, somewhat taken aback, "and I see you have been on a ferry as well recently."

"Pardon?" asked Suzy looking slightly puzzled. "What ferry?"

"That ticket you're putting in the ashtray."

"Oh, that. That's not a ferry ticket, honey; that's a bus ticket."

Gabriella was curious as she had distinctly noticed the word port written across the top of it. "Do you mind if I look at it?" she asked. "It looks like a ferry ticket."

"Be my guest, honey," came the chirpy response, "but it's useless without the other half. It's only a bus ticket."

Gabriella picked up the partially crumpled piece of paper and straightened it out. It was cream in colour and there was a dark blue margin around its edges, except for the perforated side on the left where it had been torn in two. She looked at the three words starting at the top and read it downwards –

- PORT
- TRANSIT
- SYSTEM

and on the bottom line was a number. The print was large and the ticket was about an inch and a half square.

"It looks like a ferry ticket. Can I have it?" asked Gabriella. "It reminds me of something."

"Sure, honey, you can have it, it's no use to me. I got it the day I travelled down to see an old aunt of mine who is in hospital. I'm not really sure if she is my real aunt or not but I was always told to call her that. Anyway, who cares? When I arrived down to see her I got the bus from the train station to the hospital and that's it."

When Suzy said where the hospital was, Gabriella inhaled a deep breath in silent surprise, and then she said, "I hope your aunt gets better soon."

"She'll be OK, honey, she's a tough old bird."

"Thanks, Suzy. It's been great seeing you and I will give you a call in a few weeks' time. We will do this all over again and the next time I will pay."

"Sure, honey, any time would be great," came the instant reply.

With that they put on their coats, gave each other big hugs, and took the lift back to the ground floor. They walked through the perfumery and accepted various free sprays before reaching the exit doors. Then they hugged each other once again before disappearing into the crowds on 5th Avenue. Gabriella could hardly wait to get back to the apartment and hailed a cab, but cursed the traffic as it took over thirty minutes to get to Central Park West. When she reached the apartment, she turned her key in the door and entered. She very excitedly announced that she had had a great lunch with Suzy, and what's more, she had something very important to show them.

They all stared at the ticket in amazement and when Gabriella explained everything to them, Duffy remarked, "Well, let's get down there straight away. Thank heavens for Suzy Baxter."

CHAPTER 42

On reaching the town they went directly to the bus station and purchased a ticket. Clutching it like a prized possession, they walked to a nearby diner and ordered coffee and doughnuts. They wiped the table clean with a paper napkin, placed the ticket face up and examined it completely. Then they tore it in two to make it even more authentic and convincing to the eye, and bringing the two pieces together it read across with two words on each line:

BRIDGE -- PORT
INTER -- TRANSIT
METRO -- SYSTEM
136576 -- 136576

The perforation mark running down the middle of the cream ticket split the word BRIDGEPORT and the other words in two. The words on the left side of the ticket meant absolutely nothing on their own but the words on the right side read, - PORT - TRANSIT - SYSTEM - 136576 and indicated a totally different meaning. There was no doubt whatsoever, it was a bus ticket but when torn in two the right hand side could easily have been mistaken for a ferry ticket.

Could this have been the type of ticket that Mrs de Silva had found in one of the pockets of the priests' jackets when she was getting the clothes ready for the dry cleaning that morning in Rome? Could she have mistaken this and thought that it was a ferry ticket? Could Fagan have been in Bridgeport?

The coffee and doughnuts arrived but these and other questions they would have to ponder over throughout the weekend.

CHAPTER 43

It was now Monday morning and time was beginning to move very quickly. After an exhaustive weekend of reflection and contemplation, they were back in the apartment again at 11.00am.

"As I see it," Duffy commenced, "we can't afford to get too over-confident as we don't have that much to go on, but one thing is for sure, we are definitely running out of time. If we don't do something fast we are going to miss out. I believe in hunches and I think we have to act on what we've got.

"We do have a lot more today than we had last Monday and, even though what we think is a ferry ticket might be a shot in the dark, we have no other choices but to go with it. I think it's worth taking.

"We have a key that fits a bank deposit box somewhere in America and, whether by accident or by design, we have been led to Bridgeport, Connecticut. I know that there is a Newport Rhode Island and I am only ruling that out for the time being on account of distance. My mind will not go there at the moment but that doesn't mean anything. Bridgeport is a town that is within easy driving distance of New York, and it has good train connections, so Fagan possibly considered it quite accessible. That is of course if it is Bridgeport and not Newport but I think it's too good a hunch to throw away. Anyway, no more negative thoughts! I say we go for Bridgeport and go for it now."

They all agreed, and it was time to set up a strategy.

"As I said," continued Duffy, "we only have one bite at this cherry and if the bank is in Bridgeport, then we have hit the jackpot. If it isn't, we are back to where we started so we've lost nothing."

"What do you suggest we do?" asked Gavin. "Are you going to call Mark?"

"Not at the moment," replied Duffy. "What we are going to do might not be one hundred per cent ethical, so it's better that Mark is not in the frame just at the moment."

"What do you propose?" asked Gavin.

"Well, it has to be handled in stages. First, the bank has to be cased, and that's my job. Secondly, you have to take on the role of Fagan and thirdly, Gabriella, you have to act as a distraction and *play the room*."

"Go on," responded Gavin and at the same time Gabriella was nodding.

"I will go down to Bridgeport today and nose around the three banks. If I come across the one that I think is *the mark,* then I will try and open a bank account. By doing this I will be able to see what is required. It will make things easier when you two arrive."

With that he fully outlined his plan.

That afternoon Duffy arrived in Bridgeport at 3.30pm. It took approximately one and a half hours to drive from Central Park and he realised that this town was very conveniently situated to New York. He was feeling more and more convinced that Fagan could have opened an account at one of these banks. He parked, put a quarter in the meter and entered the first bank. He was out on the street again within fifteen minutes as that bank did not have deposit box facilities. He moved into the second one and after ten minutes he was back in his car scratching his head as that one didn't have them either. He couldn't understand why modern banks did not have this service any more, and even started to wonder if they had selected the right town. Maybe it was Newport, Rhode Island after all. He was starting to perspire.

His search was now narrowed down to the one remaining bank and if this office did not have deposit safes then they were back to square one. He was beginning to doubt everything and acknowledged the fact that even if this bank had such a facility, it guaranteed nothing. An exasperated Duffy entered the third bank.

CHAPTER 44

Inside the bank there was a staff of five. Some people were standing in line for the cashier and a security officer stood at the doorway. The building looked pre-World War Two and as he approached the enquiry section of the counter, a young man got up from his desk immediately.

"What can I do for you today, sir?" he asked politely.

"I would like to open an account with deposit box facilities," replied Duffy.

"No problem, sir. Opening both entails exactly the same procedures."

Duffy breathed a sigh of relief. "You have deposit box facilities?"

"Yes, sir, we do. How much are you lodging?"

"Four hundred dollars," replied Duffy, looking at the money which Gabriella had given him to set up the scam.

The young man returned with a form which contained a lot of small print and resembled a legal agreement, which he asked Duffy to read. Duffy glanced at the form. Then the clerk commenced filling in a small pink rectangular signature card. Duffy watched some female clerks filing these cards in special cabinets and noticed that some were checking signatures.

"May I have your name, sir?" enquired the clerk,

"– and your address,

"– and your date of birth,

"– and your occupation?"

Duffy answered with the appropriate information and rearranged the truth slightly when it came to his age and occupation. When all the information was complete, the clerk pushed the pink card towards Duffy.

"Would you mind signing the card where I have indicated and I will witness your signature."

"Not at all," retorted Duffy and he scribbled his signature, which was duly witnessed.

"All that remains now, sir, is for me to issue you with a deposit account book and a receipt. I will make out a lodgement docket, and we're all set."

"Is that it?" enquired Duffy.

"Yes, sir," came the reply. "Quite painless."

Duffy was issued with an account number, which he wrote on the lodgement docket, and handed over the $400.

"It's all there, sir," the official confirmed and he handed Duffy a brand new deposit book.

"Thank you, but are you not forgetting something else?" enquired Duffy. "What about the deposit box facilities?"

"Oh, that takes a week to issue, sir. I will see you again next Monday, all being well."

"Shit," Duffy muttered under his breath. "They will have to play it blind."

He thanked the young man and put the deposit pass book into his inside pocket. Before leaving the bank he cast his eyes over all that he could see and remember, particularly the staircases, which he assumed must lead down to the vault. He wasn't at all happy when he returned to Gavin's apartment at about 6.30pm. He sat down and explained all that had happened.

"I never got to the fucking safety deposit room," he muttered. "It takes a bloody week to open an account like the one we think Fagan had. We will have to play this very clever, as Fagan must have made two visits to the bank and someone might have noticed him. I don't know. I'm only speculating. We can only hope that it wasn't the clerk who attended to me. It might not even be the right bloody bank."

Gabriella could see that he was frustrated and annoyed with himself for not getting all the information he required. She disappeared into the kitchen and reappeared a few minutes later with some soup that she had prepared earlier. She assumed that

Duffy's annoyance resulted from a drop in his blood sugar level as he had not eaten anything since breakfast time. She assumed correctly. Without hesitation, he devoured the soup and the bread, wiped his mouth with a napkin, and was ready for action again.

Once again, he felt blessed with such friends and looking up at her said, "Gabriella, you certainly know me better than I know myself. That soup was delicious and just what I needed."

Duffy commenced telling them about the inside of the bank and proceeded to draw a sketch on a large sheet of paper.

"The enquiry section," he said, "is to the left of the teller's box and to the left of that again is a staircase leading down to a basement and I believe that is where the strong room is located. I'm not a hundred per cent sure of course but I am as positive as I can be. It's just a guess but Fagan might have been in clerical gear when he opened the account so, Gavin, I want you to wear a dark suit and a hat. It's not that anyone would easily remember him. It's just a precaution. Nothing more, so don't worry."

With that he went on to explain the plan.

"The strategy is quite simple really and you can see from the sketch, when you get inside the bank you walk directly to the enquiry counter which is on the left side of the teller's box. A young man will bounce out of his seat immediately. He will ask you your name and you will say Anthony Fagan. Your signature will then be checked against a pink signature card that is kept in a cabinet beside the back wall. In the meantime, Gabriella will be acting as a major distraction and hopefully the clerk will be paying more attention to her than to you. Your signature will be checked but that should be OK if we do everything according to plan. He is quite a young man so that is in our favour – he will be easily sidetracked. You just have to be totally confident, so start practicing Fagan's signature from the letters that I obtained from Father Slattery. If it happens that there is an account in Fagan's name, don't get too excited. This does not guarantee anything. It only means that he has already been there, so don't relax your guard. Speed is of the essence. Don't dilly dally. Be positive. Remember, you are in control. If this is the correct bank we could be *in the money*, if you excuse the expression."

As he became more forceful, his Brooklyn accent got stronger and stronger and without having to be told everything in detail, Gabriella knew exactly the role that she had to play. She didn't comment, only to say, "Maybe I should have borrowed a few pieces from Suzy Baxter."

That said it all!

Duffy then went over every detail with both of them again and again until they knew it backwards. This was a chance in a million but it was all they had to go on. Furthermore, they only had one crack at it. They considered that there was nothing more they could do that evening and decided to retire for the night and meet again the following day as usual at 11.00am.

CHAPTER 45

On Tuesday they arrived outside the bank shortly after midday. Gavin was dressed in a dark grey suit with a light blue shirt and a dark blue tie. He was dressed seriously enough to look respectable, but stylishly enough to be appropriately attired. He also wore a hat. Gabriella's clothes were also slightly different from the ones she usually wore. Her suit was a light two-piece, comprising a box jacket which had a small fur collar, and a very short skirt. The previous night she had spent an hour shortening the hem so that it fell about four inches above her knee. Under the jacket she wore a pink blouse which had an open collar. Her shapely legs, clad in a pair of tan coloured tights, narrowed into a pair of patent leather four inch stiletto heels.

Her nails were polished the same colour as her lipstick, and she looked very alluring. She carried a leather shoulder bag that matched her gloves. Her make-up was perfect and she wore a gold necklace and matching earrings. Her perfume was exquisite and she was attracting looks and admiring glances from the very moment she stepped out of the car.

Duffy remained in the car while Gavin and Gabriella made their way into the bank. There was nothing more he could do as he had played his part, and now he found that waiting was the hardest thing of all.

Remembering all their instructions, they walked straight up to the open enquiry section of the counter where the young man was sitting at his desk. As soon as he saw them, he was up and out of his chair.

"Good afternoon, sir, good afternoon, ma'am. How can I help you?" he asked.

"We would like to look at our safety deposit box, please," said Gavin.

"Certainly, sir, have you the number of your account?"

"I think the number could be on this key," replied Gavin.

"OK, sir," came the quick response. "What is your name, please?"

"Fagan, Anthony Fagan," replied Gavin.

"Very good, Mr Fagan, I will have to check your signature, if you don't mind."

"Not at all," responded Gavin, full of confidence. As he was talking, he noticed that the clerk was casting admiring glances towards Gabriella. She noticed this as well so deliberately she moved a few steps back from the counter so that he could get a better view of her. She was letting him see her full height which was accentuated by her high heels and she was definitely *working the room*. It looked as if her legs went up forever. The clerk returned with a form and a small pink rectangular card.

"Would you mind signing this form where I have marked in pencil, sir, so that I can check your signature against the card?"

At the very moment the form was placed in front of Gavin, Gabriella commented that it was very warm in the bank and proceeded to slowly remove her jacket. Gavin looked twice when he noticed that she had undone the top three buttons of her pink blouse to reveal a very ample cleavage. The young man could not take his eyes from her even for a second. His eyes were almost bulging and during this distraction Gavin signed the form.

Gabriella surreptitiously dropped a coin on the floor and keeping her knees straight, bent over from the waist to pick it up. This certainly drew a lot of attention from other customers in the bank and even Gavin was amazed. Once again the clerk's eyes were firmly fixed on her short skirt as it moved slowly further up the backs of her elegant legs. He didn't want to miss anything. When Gabriella straightened up the clerk refocused immediately, glanced at the corresponding signatures and through his embarrassment, said, "Er, eh, thank you very much, Mr Fagan. Would you both like to follow me down to the vault?"

They were in.

All three of them walked down the staircase to the basement and into the strong room that contained, ground to ceiling, wall to wall, safety deposit boxes. In the middle of the room was a solitary table with four chairs. The clerk walked over to box number 216 on the left hand wall from the entrance, and placing his *master key* in the keyhole, he twisted it and invited Gavin to insert his key. This was the moment of truth and, taking a deep breath, Gavin inserted his key and turned it.

Giving the brass handle of the box a slight tug, the clerk withdrew the long drawer and placed it on the table.

"Thank you, sir. When you want me again just press the buzzer on the side of the desk."

He then looked at Gabriella and commented, "I trust Mrs Fagan is feeling all right again. Is there anything I can get her?"

"No, it's OK, I'm fine," Gabriella replied, and he nodded respectfully in response.

The young clerk looked quite uncomfortable, and was relieved to be exiting the strong room. With that, they opened the box and gasped at what they saw.

A few minutes later Gavin pressed the buzzer on the side of the desk and the same young man reappeared.

"Are you all through, sir?" he asked

"Yes, thank you, we are finished here for the moment," replied Gavin, and the box was securely placed back into its original slot in the wall. They all walked up the stairs together and out into the banking hall. They shook hands in a businesslike manner, said their goodbyes and Gavin and Gabriella walked very determinedly out into the street.

"Before you ask me anything," she said with a broad smile on her face, "I never want to be called Mrs Fagan again, a push up bra is a wonderful invention but very uncomfortable and these shoes are killing my feet."

They smiled at each other, knowing that what they'd done had been very successful.

They returned to the car, where Duffy was sweating profusely. They told him what had happened and he was very relieved. He commented that he would phone Mark Sutherland as soon as he got back to the apartment.

"That's wonderful news, just wonderful," exclaimed Mark when he got the phone call, "and I want to see all three of you in my office on Thursday morning at 10.30am as arranged."

This had been a very successful day and without doubt all four of them were extremely happy and satisfied.

CHAPTER 46

On Tuesday 2nd September, Gavin and his lawyer made their way to court number 18 and took their seats. Duffy and Gabriella remained outside and sat on the highly polished veneered benches. The last time Duffy had visited a court was in Ireland, and this was definitely a far cry from that remarkable day.

Both of them sat very subdued, lost in their thoughts, wondering what was going on inside, as the only persons legally entitled to be in the court were Gavin, his ex-wife, and Fagan as the material witness.

Inside the court the bailiff was already on his feet.

"All rise," he called. "Be upstanding for the Honourable Judge Buchannan."

"This is Family Law Appeal Case number 36, in the litigation of O'Neill versus O'Neill," he continued. "This court is now in session."

"I would like to call on Mr Sutherland immediately, for his opening remarks," requested the judge.

The entire Appellant Court went into a stunned silence when Sutherland stood up and without making any opening remarks immediately called the Cardinal Archbishop of New York to take the stand as his first witness. The Judge's eyes opened wide in shock as he leaned forward in his chair and, placing his elbows on the top of his desk, he removed his glasses and beckoned the lawyers forward. He covered the microphone with his left hand and, looking directly at Mark Sutherland, said:

"What in tarnation do you think you are playing at, counsellor? I certainly hope you know what you are doing, as calling such a witness is a very serious matter. I am adjourning this case until 2.00pm, so that you can come to your senses. I should really be calling the bailiff to have you arrested for gross contempt, so consider yourself a lucky man and this is the only leeway that you will be getting from me today. The single reason I am hearing this case at all is to see what you have got to offer and it had better be good to convince me. Is that understood, counsellor?"

"Yes, your Honour. Thank you, your Honour," acknowledged Mark, and with that the judge banged down his gavel, instructing all parties to remain in the immediate vicinity of the courtroom. The next case on his list was called immediately.

Gavin and Mark walked out into the hallway and rejoined Duffy and Gabriella.

"What the fuck was going on in there?" exclaimed Duffy. "There was a lot of commotion and if it's all over I sure as hell have wasted a lot of time."

"It's not over," replied Sutherland, who considered all this play-acting *good policy,* as now the judge, who was renowned for being an eccentric, was showing a distinct interest in the case.

"It's far from over," Mark repeated, "and you, Brendan, you have played an essential role in getting us this far. We couldn't have done it without you."

Sutherland had planned this very skilful strategy and, by calling a *Prince of the Church* as a witness in a divorce case, he had definitely got the attention he wanted, and as a result, brought a very sombre note to the entire proceedings.

With all the fresh evidence at their disposal, they hoped that it would be only a matter of time before Fagan admitted culpability, and that was going to be difficult to prove. It was only proper for them to hope for a total reversal of the former verdict, but facts were facts; they were guilty as a result of the first trial, and judges did not like overturning the decisions of their peers.

It would be an uphill battle to prove themselves innocent, but Sutherland intended doing all he could, no matter what. Unfortunately, he was only getting one chance in this appeal court, so he had to prove that the evidence previously presented was inconclusive. He also needed to implicate and prove that the principal witness was part of a complicated illegal conspiracy and this he intended to do.

From that moment forward, everything had to be very carefully orchestrated. Mark Sutherland had to make sure that the judge listened to his every remark, otherwise, if there was any doubt whatsoever he would be ruled against immediately. If he was closed down, Fagan would walk away a free man and that would be a disastrous situation.

CHAPTER 47

Natasha the whore made an outstanding entrance into the adjacent courtroom. She was wearing a very short blue denim skirt that revealed the snaps of her black garter belt that clipped onto the lace at the tops of her stockings. Her low cut bright orange blouse was tied in a bow at the front, and it was unbuttoned so as to reveal most of her massive silicone breasts, which bounced freely with every step she took. She was not wearing a bra. Her make-up was a heavy bronze shade, her lips were vivid red and her eyelashes looked even more unrealistic than they actually were. Her hair was dishevelled in an arranged sort of a way, and she was wearing five inch stiletto heels. She was quite a sight.

The policeman who was escorting her could hardly believe his ears when she actually tried to chat him up as he was conveying her across the hallway to court number 12. As far as he was concerned this was the wrong time and definitely the wrong place for such an interaction, and he tried to act as nonchalantly as possible. However it was quite obvious that he could not keep his eyes from the front of her blouse, possibly hoping that one of her extremely oversized boobs might pop out at any minute. Looking up at him, she drawled in a strong southern accent,

"What ya looking at, horse face? Ain't you never seen a lady before?"

He reacted to this remark as if a mule had kicked him in the head, the result of which returned his brain to a reasonable state of sanity. With a wide amazed expression on his face, he wondered how he could have allowed his mind to have wandered so far from centre. He looked down at her in stunned silence as he was now suffering what could only be described as uncontrollable embarrassment. Everyone had heard what she had said. Without answering or acknowledging her remarks, he pushed the hooker through the doorway of number 12 court as if she were a piece of garbage that he couldn't wait to get rid of.

"Christ, it takes all kinds," smiled Duffy, as he looked at the other two.

CHAPTER 48

Gavin's appeal case resumed at 2.00pm.

"All rise," the bailiff called out once again, and everyone stood up, waiting for the Honourable Judge Buchannan to enter.

Mark Sutherland was sitting beside Gavin, and Geraldine's lawyer, Ken Thompson, was sitting alone at the other table on the left hand side of the court. Apart from the court officials, the only other person present was Fagan, who was sitting in the public area. The attorneys eyed one another like gladiators ready to fight in the arena, and indeed this was an arena. This was the arena of Law and Justice.

The judge was not taking any chances this time and breaking with all protocol, he called on Ken Thompson to open the proceedings instead of Mark Sutherland. Sutherland did not object.

This time there was only one attorney representing Geraldine but Thompson was an able and excellent defence lawyer, who had graduated from Harvard with a first class honours degree. He was very good at his job and did not come cheap. Mark Sutherland maintained that the Catholic Church would once again pick up all Mrs O'Neill's costs in due course. This well-groomed lawyer stood up and walked directly to the middle of the floor. Taking a deep breath, he positioned himself in front of the judge and commenced his opening address.

"Your Honour, I want to point out for Mr Sutherland's benefit, just in case he is still in any doubt, that this is not a civil court, nor a criminal court. This is simply a divorce court and for that reason, your Honour, I see no reason to rehash what has already been tried and proved conclusively in Judge Rosemount's court.

"I am positive that my client has done everything possible to comply with all his decisions, and has been an exemplary figure in every way. I am representing Mrs O'Neill, but as she cannot be with us today due to illness I will be directing all my remarks to her principal witness, Mr Fagan.

"During the past eighteen months, Mr Fagan has looked after and cherished Mrs O'Neill in a very special way. By doing so, he has placed himself in the position he rightfully deserves, and now she wishes to legally sign over all property rights to him. The court is aware of this from her sworn affidavits and this will take place immediately after we successfully defend this appeal. Mr Fagan has an exemplary track record that can stand up to any cross examination that Mr Sutherland has to offer or propose.

"It's been proved without doubt that Mr O'Neill stayed away from his wife and the family home for over twelve months, thus failing in his matrimonial duties. This caused Mrs O'Neill mental stress and amounts to emotional cruelty. The fact is, your Honour, he simply deserted her. He literally dumped her and walked away. Under these circumstances she had no one to turn to, and as she was entitled to seek protection from whoever she could, she turned to Mr Fagan in whom she had great trust and respect. This is well-documented.

"The fact that Mr Fagan was previously a Monsignor in the Roman Catholic Church should have no bearing whatsoever on this case, and should not be admissible evidence, as his career at that time has nothing to do with the facts before you today, and what he testified previously is still on the record.

"I state categorically that all actual events as previously sworn remain in place and it's impossible to argue fact against fact, so I rest my case by asking your Honour to uphold the previous verdict and dismiss this lawsuit accordingly."

With that he returned to his seat.

"I will be the one to make that decision, counsellor," interjected the Judge, "but before I make any ruling, I am very interested to see what Mr Sutherland has to offer us."

Mark Sutherland remained in his seat and it was only when the judge looked at him with an enquiring glance and a nod that he stood up. Mark was determined to use every means possible to get and retain the judge's attention.

"Your Honour, I am not here today to argue facts," he commenced, "nor to argue the decision reached by the Honourable Judge Rosemount in the previous case of O'Neill versus O'Neill. That honourable gentleman had no option but to return his just and fair verdict on the evidence that was presented to him on that day.

"I am here to tell you that the evidence given on that day by Mr Fagan, the principal material witness in this case, was flawed. I am here to tell you that what was said before Judge Rosemount was an imaginative creation of the truth, and not the truth itself. I am here to state that Mr Fagan manipulated Mrs O'Neill, who as we all know is now very seriously ill. I am here to tell you that Mr Fagan used her for his own selfish needs, and the evidence I will produce will show him to be a very unreliable witness. What I will show the court will discredit him in every way possible.

"Finally, I fully appreciate that we are guilty before you today, your Honour, but when Mr Fagan takes the stand you will immediately see that he is totally untrustworthy and an unreliable witness, and you will have no problem whatsoever in overturning the former verdict."

Mark Sutherland, knowing that he had countered well in his opening address without any reprimands from the judge, unbuttoned his jacket as he returned to his seat.

"Gentlemen," said the judge, "I think it's time for a ten minute recess in order for me to absorb these opening remarks. Please be back in court at 2.45pm."

With that the court rose as the judge exited to his chambers. When the court resumed after the short recess, the judge leaned forward and spoke into the microphone.

"Before we move further in this matter," he said, "I want both attorneys in my chambers immediately. This is off the record so the stenographer is excused."

The two lawyers walked in single file behind the judge into his chambers.

"Don't bother sitting down, gentlemen, this will only take a couple of minutes and the only answer I want to hear is, *yes sir*. Do I make myself clear?"

"Yes sir," they both responded.

"Now, I want no further surprise witnesses in this case, and if you have any up your sleeves, this is the time to show them. Also if there are any further disclosures, I want them discussed here and now so that we can dispense with all this jiggery-pokery of jumping up and down and shouting objection all the time. Are you both perfectly clear about this?"

Neither of them spoke.

"Well, I'm waiting!" inquired the judge impatiently, looking at both of them.

"Yes, sir. I am quite happy with disclosure as it exists," replied Ken Thompson. "We are resting our case on previous evidence which we feel is quite sufficient in this matter, and one cannot dispute the facts."

"Am I therefore correct in assuming," commented the judge, "that you are waiving your right to any new disclosure which I feel Mr Sutherland might produce, as I think he has definitely got something, otherwise he would not be standing here today. I am giving you every opportunity to speak as it will be too late when we get back inside."

"Yes, your Honour," came Thompson's reply. "Anything that Mr Sutherland might produce at this stage would only be a fabrication of the truth, and he can prove nothing. His client abandoned his wife and that is a fact. That has already been proved."

Switching his attentions to Sutherland, the judge said, "Those are the facts, counsellor, as Mr Thompson has so eloquently stated, but I am wondering if there is anything else that you need to tell me, before we move on?"

Mark thought very carefully before answering the judge's

question. According to the law, the discrediting of a material witness in court in order to show that evidence which was previously sworn under oath might be unsafe does not come under the privilege of open disclosure. He replied very attentively,

"I will be putting Mr Fagan on the stand, your Honour, and as I said in my opening address, I will be endeavouring to break him down, and discredit him in direct and in indirect cross examination, but I have no further surprise witnesses."

"Are you happy with that, Mr Thompson?" asked the judge.

"Yes, your Honour," came the reply. "We realise Mr Sutherland will be doing that but as he has nothing tangible that he can produce we are fully prepared to counter his direct and indirect cross when required."

"OK, gentlemen," commented the judge. "Let us return, and let the court decide the outcome of this case. Mr Thompson, since you have already led with the opening remarks, perhaps you will continue when we resume inside?

"Certainly, your Honour," replied Thompson politely and both attorneys bowed to the judge, who responded graciously. With that, all three of them returned to the courtroom and took up their respective positions.

Order in Court was once again called by the bailiff and Ken Thompson rose to his feet and called Gavin O'Neill to the stand.

CHAPTER 49

"Take the Bible in your right hand and swear after me," instructed the Clerk of the Court. Gavin complied in a very dignified manner, read aloud the oath from the card, nodded to the Clerk and sat down.

"Mr O'Neill," began Ken Thompson. "Where did you live from January 1974 to May 1975?"

"I lived in an apartment in Manhattan, under my doctor's instructions," responded Gavin, "but I always regarded the house in Tarrytown to be my home, so I never considered that I ever deserted Geraldine."

Gavin's answer was very well structured and rehearsed. It was short and polite enough not to give Ken Thompson an opportunity to ask him to rephrase it, but long enough to inform the judge of his sincere feelings. Mark Sutherland always insisted that once a judge or jury heard distinct answers from a witness, it was impossible for them to disregard such comments even if they were ruled out of order. Gavin was also directed to use the word *instructions* rather than the word *orders* when referring to the doctor's directives, so as to quash any objections that might be forthcoming from Thompson.

Gavin had hardly pronounced the last syllable in the name Geraldine, when Ken Thompson spoke again.

"Just answer the question, Mr O'Neill. I will repeat it for you once again, so that you fully understand it perfectly. Where did you live between January 1974 and May 1975?"

"I lived in Central Park West, Manhattan," replied Gavin.

"Thank you, Mr O'Neill," and, looking at the judge, he continued, "I have no further questions for this witness at this time."

Before Mark got to his feet the judge looked at him and commented, "Your witness, Mr Sutherland, and following our little conversation inside a few minutes ago, I take it that you will not be calling the Cardinal Archbishop of New York?"

"Not at the moment, your Honour," remarked Sutherland, with a slight smile on his face. "But I am excusing Mr O'Neill from the stand and I am calling Mr Fagan to take his place."

"I object, your Honour, this is direct and not cross, and Mr Fagan is my witness."

"Mr Thompson, let me inform you that Mr Sutherland can call anyone he wishes to call so long as they are sitting inside in my court. I think Mr Fagan fits into that category. Objection overruled."

With that Ken Thompson sat down knowing full well that Sutherland was entirely within his rights.

Anthony Fagan was duly sworn in and he looked very relaxed as he sat in the witness chair.

"Good afternoon, Mr Fagan, would you kindly state your name and present address for the record."

"Anthony Joseph Fagan, Riverside Road, Tarrytown."

"Oh, I see you're living in the home of Mr O'Neill," interjected Mark.

"Objection, your Honour, Mr Sutherland is badgering the witness."

"Objection sustained," bellowed the judge and, looking directly at Mark, he stated in a sharp tone, "Mr Sutherland, I will only give you a little leeway in this line of questioning, so be very careful."

"Have you ever been to Ireland?" continued Sutherland quickly, almost ignoring the judge's last remark.

"No," came the abrupt response.

"Have you ever been to Italy?"

"Yes, of course," came another abrupt response.

"Objection, your Honour, Mr Sutherland already knows the answers to these questions."

"Objection overruled, Mr Thompson. I want to see where he is going with these questions but, Mr Sutherland, please be very cautious as I already have you on a very short leash."

"Thank you, your Honour," remarked Sutherland and continued, "Mr Fagan, just a simple yes or no will suffice as an answer to the following questions, do you understand?"

"Yes," commented Fagan.

"Do you know a Cardinal Babatisto?"

"Yes, I do."

"Do you know any eminent senior Italians?"

"Yes," came the reply.

"Are you a member of Opus Dei?"

"Yes, I am."

"Is Cardinal Babatisto a member of Opus Dei?"

"Yes, he is, but what's that got to do with anything?"

"Thank you, Mr Fagan," acknowledged Sutherland. "And now will you tell the court the last time that you saw these two gentlemen together?" asked Sutherland.

"Which two gentlemen?" asked Fagan.

"Cardinal Babatisto and a certain senior Italian gentleman."

There was a long pause and the silence was broken by the judge asking courteously, "Do you not understand the question, Mr Fagan? I can always get him to rephrase it for you."

"No, it's OK, your Honour," he replied. "I understand the question."

"Then please answer it," instructed the judge.

"I saw them together last year."

"Where?" followed Mark immediately.

"In Rome, when I was visiting Vatican City."

"What did you discuss?" continued Mark.

"Many things," came the reply.

"Did you discuss Roman Catholic Church annulments, by any chance?" enquired Mark.

"No," came the definite response. "Why should I be discussing annulments?"

Looking directly at the judge, Mark asked that the stenographer re-read the witness's last remark, and note it particularly for the record.

"Your Honour," continued Sutherland. "I have a key in my possession, and I am not entirely sure who owns it, but I think the witness can help and I am wondering if he can identify it."

"Objection, your Honour," called Ken Thompson, and the judge immediately overruled him again and reminded him of the meeting that they had in his chambers concerning continuous objections.

"But this is new evidence, your Honour," protested Thompson, "and I assumed that you would not allow this to be introduced."

"You are very wrong to assume anything in my court, Mr Thompson. I am the only one who can assume anything here. Objection completely overruled. Please show the key to the witness, Mr Sutherland."

"Permission to approach the witness?"

"Permission granted," replied the judge.

"Mr Fagan, can you identify this key?" enquired Mark as he approached Fagan and handed it to him.

"No," answered Fagan quite emphatically.

"I offer this key as *exhibit A* in this case, your Honour," stated Mark, and with that the judge called for a fifteen minute recess.

Outside in the corridor Mark informed Duffy and Gabriella that everything was moving exactly at the correct pace, and he had to be careful how he introduced the fresh evidence as he knew that he was walking a legal tightrope. So far the judge seemed to be on his side, mainly because he was keeping the case interesting, but all that could change if a piece of evidence did not fit the proper place in the jigsaw. The most important thing to do was to keep Fagan on the stand as long as possible and hopefully he would break down and admit culpability. They resumed again at 3.45pm.

"Continue, Mr Sutherland, and, Mr Fagan, you are still under oath," instructed the judge as proceedings restarted.

"Mr Fagan, you tell me, and the court of course, that you have never been to Ireland."

"No, never," came the reply.

"Do you know anyone in Ireland?"

There was a genuinely vacant look on Fagan's face. "I don't understand the question, your Honour," he remarked, looking at the judge.

"Don't snap the thread, Mr Sutherland, you're on dangerous ground. Kindly rephrase your last question for the witness as I don't understand it either."

"Do you know a retired parish priest in Ireland called Father Joseph Slattery?" asked Sutherland.

"Objection, your Honour, where is Mr Sutherland going with this line of questioning?"

"Overruled, Mr Thompson. I am also anxious to see where he is going myself and, as you already know, the two principal protagonists in this case are Irish, so, answer the question, Mr Fagan."

"Yes, I know Father Joseph Slattery," came the reply.

"Can you explain how you know him?" asked Sutherland.

Mark was waiting for Ken Thompson to jump up and object again, and was surprised when he did not get out of his seat.

"I knew him through Mrs O'Neill," he continued.

"Can you be a little more specific?" asked Mark.

"I met him in Rome many years ago when I was a priest in the Roman Catholic Church, and then I received a letter from him saying that he was giving a course of marital instruction to Mrs O'Neill. He asked me to take over this instruction on his behalf when she returned to New York from Ireland. That's my only connection with him. After that, I wrote to him a few times when I heard that he had retired, but I didn't know him personally. I just felt sorry for him, as I heard that he was unwell and I sent him a few dollars from time to time. That's why I was hesitant in my original reply, your Honour, as I just didn't understand the question."

Fagan was now looking at the judge, whose glance back was sympathetic, as the witness had definitely scored major points with that reply.

"That was a perfect answer from Mr Fagan. Counsellor, you better know where you are going with the next question. I am getting impatient with you"

"I also would like to thank Mr Fagan," remarked Sutherland, now looking directly at him. "You have answered very well, but for the record I would like to ask you this question – what was your association with Cardinal Babatisto?"

"Cardinal Babatisto was my superior when I was a Monsignor in the Vatican."

"I see. Thank you, Mr Fagan. And now could you enlighten the court as to your relationship with the other senior Italian gentleman who was talking to Cardinal Babatisto?"

"Objection!" yelled Ken Thompson. "I don't understand why he is asking my client these questions."

"Please let me withdraw my last question, your Honour, and move to another piece of evidence. I only want to establish the connection," countered Sutherland,

"Continue, Mr. Sutherland. Strike the last question from the record. Objection overruled."

"I put it to you, Mr Fagan, that your parents changed their name from Fagione to Fagan by deed poll after their arrival from Italy as they wanted to start a new life without the shadow of the Mafia hanging over them. There is a deed poll document.

"I would also like to put it to you, Mr Fagan, that at the time of your ordination into the Catholic Church, your name was Antonio Fagione. I think I am correct on this point, Mr Fagan – don't you? Will you now tell the court if you knew the other Italian gentleman that you saw with Cardinal Babatisto and if he is related to you?

The court went silent.

"Please answer the question, Mr Fagan," ordered the judge.

"Yes, I know him. His name is Signor Fagione," came the muffled response.

"I can't hear you," interjected Sutherland.

"Be more specific, Mr Fagan," instructed the judge.

"Luigi Fagione is my grandfather," came his reply in a much louder voice.

No one in the court moved except Fagan, who shuffled his feet as he sat in the witness chair, and for the first time he didn't look so relaxed.

Ken Thompson was on his feet again and requested a recess as he saw that his client was badly shaken with this exposé. The judge looked at the clock on the far wall of the courtroom and it was indicating slightly after 4.30pm. With that he announced "OK, Mr Thompson, I will allow you some latitude, and as the case is running on much longer than I expected, and with the time now at 4.35pm, I am concluding proceedings for today. We will resume again in the morning, at 10.00am sharp. Try and get finished by lunchtime tomorrow, gentlemen, as I have a golfing appointment at 2.30pm."

With that he banged down his gavel and walked into his chambers.

CHAPTER 50

Mark Sutherland explained in great detail the events of the day to all three of them as they sat together for dinner in the Riverview Restaurant, which overlooks the Hudson.

"How did you connect Fagan to Fagione?" asked Gavin.

"Just after the War there was a large influx of Italians into New York City and, when I checked the register, much to my surprise there were a lot called Fagione."

"And the deed poll you referred to?" enquired Gavin. "Where did you get that from?

"What deed poll?" smiled Mark. "I only said there was a deed poll document, I didn't say I had one. I'd say it's impossible to get hold of such a document at short notice and we simply hadn't the time. In the "New Name" column of the register I noticed that most of the people called Fagione had changed their names to Fagan but I had no idea why. I played a long shot to get Fagan to reveal his birth name, and the judge did the rest. All this information is only circumstantial and needs to be well substantiated so it's pretty useless at the moment. Ken Thompson will argue that Fagan's parents had every right to change their name, which is correct, but with the Italian connection we have raised suspicions in the judge's mind, which is of the utmost importance.

"Fagan played directly into our hands, and I was acting entirely on the information received from Brendan, after his visit to Ireland. This time putting two and two together certainly made four. We should all be feeling very pleased with the results this afternoon but, remember, the outcome depends on how I can load the questions for tomorrow morning's session. Even though Luigi Fagione is rumoured to be a Mafia Don, we haven't enough evidence yet at hand to overturn the original verdict."

They all said goodnight and went their separate ways. Gavin and Gabriella hailed a cab but Duffy decided to take the subway. He always reckoned that he thought better on the subway and he maintained that the brightness of the stations, coupled with the rumble in the tunnels, encouraged him to sleep better when he eventually arrived home.

He went through his usual routines when he got to his apartment. For convenience, his coffee pot and television were connected to the same adaptor, so as soon as he flicked the switch, both came to life at the same time.

He sat back in his large leather easy chair and within seconds he was asleep. He woke up cold and stiff a few hours later and after going to the bathroom he stumbled into bed. He knew that when he awoke in the morning he might be a little tired but at least he would wake up sober and without the curse of a hangover. His thinking was definitely better and he was making a great recovery.

Tonight he was simply exhausted.

CHAPTER 51

They met the following morning outside the courthouse at 9.30am. Mark again stated that this court case was much more than just a simple divorce hearing, even though that in itself was very important. He knew if they were successful today, it would guarantee Gavin's future. He also pointed out that this hearing was vital and nothing was over until it was finally over. With that, all four of them walked up the steps of the courthouse. As usual Duffy and Gabriella took up their places on the long wooden benches outside.

When Gavin and Mark walked into the courtroom, Fagan was already seated beside Ken Thompson. When the judge entered from his chambers the bailiff ordered everyone to be upstanding.

"May I remind you that you are still under oath, Mr Fagan?" announced the judge as Fagan took the stand. "And, Mr Sutherland, you can continue your examination immediately. Just bear in mind that I have a golf appointment today at 2.30pm."

"Thank you, your Honour, I will bear that in mind," acknowledged Mark and, eyeballing Fagan, he commenced his questioning.

"You say you have never been to Ireland, Mr Fagan?"

"Correct," came the positive response.

"Yet you say that you knew Father Joseph Slattery?" retorted Mark.

"Yes, I met him at a conference in Rome some years ago."

"Objection, your Honour, Mr Sutherland is only rehashing old ground that was fully discussed yesterday," interjected Fagan's attorney.

"Objection sustained. I agree with you, Mr Thompson," boomed the judge, and he advised Sutherland to get to the point.

"I am just trying to establish credibility, your Honour," came Sutherland's reply.

"Well, don't go too far off track, Mr Sutherland, as I'm getting exasperated with you."

"OK, your Honour," responded Mark, and quickly asked Fagan if he had ever had an occasion to correspond with Father Slattery.

"Yes. I had," answered Fagan.

"I have to object again your Honour," stated Thompson, "as yesterday Mr Fagan admitted that he had written to Father Slattery."

"Just let him answer the question, Mr Thompson. Now that you mention yesterday, I gave you some leeway last evening by closing down early, so you will just have to put up with my tolerance a little longer. Overruled. Continue, Mr Sutherland, but please be quick. Remember I'm playing golf at 2.30pm."

"Yes, OK, thank you, your Honour. Mr Fagan, how many times would you have written to Father Slattery?" enquired Mark.

"Oh, I would say seven or eight times. I'm not really sure."

"Why were you corresponding with him so frequently, may I ask?"

"Well," replied Fagan, raising himself up in the chair, "as I said before, he was a retired gentleman and I sent him a few dollars from time to time."

"Very commendable of you, as I remarked yesterday," commented Sutherland and with that he held up a sheet of notepaper which had a very distinctive banner heading.

"In that case, Mr Fagan, would you recognise this letter heading?"

"Yes, that is the notepaper I used when I was writing to Father Slattery," replied Fagan confidently.

Holding up another sheet of paper, Mark asked him a similar question.

"In that case, you would also recognise this letter heading, Mr Fagan?"

"Objection, your Honour," yelled Thompson. "Mr Sutherland is asking my client to identify the same piece of paper for the second time."

"I will allow it, but watch your step, counsellor," commented the judge looking at Mark, and then turning to the witness he said, "You may answer the question, Mr Fagan."

"Yes, it's the same as the last one, your Honour," replied Fagan abruptly. Sutherland quickly countered and asked Fagan if it was his handwriting on the letters.

"Yes, it is," came the curt reply.

"If it pleases the court, your Honour, can I read out what it says on each page of notepaper?" enquired Sutherland, hoping that the judge would show some interest in what he was doing, and overrule any objections that might be forthcoming from Ken Thompson. As it happened this time again, there were no objections.

"If it is relevant to the court, please read it," remarked the judge, "but I must warn you, Mr Sutherland, if I find this to be another one of your delaying tactics, I will close you down immediately, and award this case to Mrs O'Neill. I am not taking any more nonsense from you today. Is that understood?"

"Understood, your Honour, eh, this point is very relevant."

"Carry on, then," ordered the judge with a deep sigh.

"Thank you, your Honour. The wording on the first sheet of headed notepaper reads as follows:

Dear Father Slattery, please find enclosed $20 which might come in useful some time. Hope you are keeping well – Sincerely, Monsignor Anthony Fagan

and, your Honour, the other sheet of notepaper has exactly the same transcript."

"Is that it, Mr Sutherland?" commented the judge, looking quite aghast. "Is that all you have to offer?"

"No, your Honour. I would like Mr Fagan to verify his signature on both sheets of letter heading, and I am now passing them over to Mr Thompson, for his full scrutiny and examination."

"Yes, that is my signature," stated Fagan, without looking at his attorney.

"Correct," agreed Ken Thompson examining the sheets of paper.

"We have no objection with this, your Honour. Perhaps it might speed matters up if I were to confirm that this is Mr Fagan's signature on both sheets of notepaper and add that Mr Fagan was very generous in sending Father Slattery these funds in the first instance. In doing so he has clearly indicated his calibre."

"Your points are well noted, Mr Thompson, and for the last time, Mr Sutherland, I am now informing you that if this is all you have to offer the court it is not enough, nor is it conclusive. I am now going to close you down and rightfully uphold Judge Rosemount's verdict and dismiss this Appellant hearing. Before I award Mrs O'Neill her decree absolute, have you anything more to say? This is your last chance."

By the tone of the judge's remarks, Sutherland knew that he was on his last chance and he was treading very dangerous ground for when the judge's gavel, which was already in his hand, hit the bench, it was all over.

Had Mark left it too late to introduce this new evidence? Were his chances slipping away? Would Fagan win after all? What would Duffy say? How would Gabriella feel? These were the questions racing through Gavin's mind as he sat nervously on the edge of his seat.

CHAPTER 52

Gabriella and Duffy sat outside the courtroom in complete silence. The mosaic floor of the corridor echoed their every move and footsteps could be heard from around corners long before people came into view.

Gabriella fumbled in her handbag and found her lipstick but realising that she had applied some only a few minutes ago let it drop into her purse again. She fumbled once more and found her make-up compact and, looking at her face in the circular mirror, applied a few dabs of powder that wasn't really necessary.

Duffy was looking down at his feet and undoing his shoe laces; he then pulled the strings tightly together and diligently tied them again in what he considered a better bow.

He looked at the large painting opposite him. It was of George Washington standing in his characteristic pose in a black velvet suit with outstretched arm. He had seen this painting many times in the past but he had not studied it closely and never realised that Washington had such pronounced features. Apart from this, the face looking back at him depicted sterling qualities.

As he reflected on the painting, he thought it most unusual that Washington was carrying a sword when he wasn't in uniform and wondered how that could be. These thoughts had never struck him before and then, out of boredom, he started to scrutinise the large gold frame. He realised that this meant nothing at all to him and his eyes once again shifted from right to left searching for various new distractions. Gabriella and Duffy were trying to fully occupy themselves to counteract the worries that filled their minds concerning what was happening behind closed doors.

Although the voices from inside could not be heard distinctly from where they were sitting, the courtroom seemed to get quieter and quieter and the ticking of the large clock on the wall beside the entrance desk at the end of the long corridor seemed to get louder and louder.

CHAPTER 53

Mark was on his feet immediately.

"Yes, your Honour, I do have something else to add."

"Then be quick about it, counsellor," snapped the judge.

"Your Honour, the transcripts and the contents of both letters are very meaningful, but I have to inform you that the sheets of headed notepaper are not identical. The letter headings are completely different. One bears the coat of arms of the Cardinal Archbishop's office in New York where Mr Fagan administered as a priest, and the other bears the coat of arms of the Foreign Office of the Vatican Secretariat. The crests are very similar in appearance and colour and that is the reason why Mr Fagan accidentally got them mixed up when he wrote to Father Slattery from New York. He unintentionally used the Vatican letter heading instead of the Cardinal Archbishop's letter heading.

"This happened again in court today, your Honour. Neither Mr Fagan nor Mr Thompson noticed the difference between the sheets of letter heading. This is very understandable as both coats of arms are similar in colour and there are no other distinguishing marks or printing on either sheet to say where they emanated, other than the crests."

"You mean to say the sheets of paper are different?" interrupted the judge.

"Yes, your Honour. My private investigator Mr Duffy noticed the differences in the headed notepaper when he visited Father Slattery in his retirement home in Ireland. He brought these four letter headings back with him, and I now offer them as *exhibit B*."

Thompson was now scrutinising the letter headings and his mouth was slightly open. He couldn't understand how he had missed such an important detail.

"We have checked and have been informed that all authentic Vatican headed notepaper is printed on special velum paper that is only manufactured in Italy. Further inspections have revealed that the Vatican letter heading with the crossed keys which originated from the Cardinal Archbishop's Office in New York Office is printed on bonded notepaper, which is manufactured in the State of Wisconsin, USA. To summarise, your Honour, the Vatican headed notepaper in front of you is a forgery. The original was probably smuggled out and copies made from it."

There were a few coughs and gasps from around the court when this was announced.

"Your Honour, these sheets of headed notepaper in front of you are enough to incriminate the witness and it clearly indicates that Mr Fagan is not telling us the entire truth. There is now a serious question mark over his entire testimony."

The courtroom went completely quiet. The judge pensively scratched his chin with his forefinger and thumb. Fagan did not move a muscle and now Mark held up the small key with the *exhibit A* tag attached to it and asked Fagan directly,

"Have you ever seen this key before?"

"Answer the question, Mr Fagan," instructed the judge, who was now infuriated.

This was exactly the reaction that Mark had skilfully planned as without the letter headings he would not have been able to successfully introduce the key as conclusive evidence. He had Fagan where he wanted him.

"No, I have never seen it before," came the confused reply.

"Your Honour, permission to approach the witness and treat him as hostile."

"Permission granted, Mr Sutherland," answered the judge, who was clearly agitated as he pulled his black robes tighter around him.

"I ask you one more time, Mr Fagan," enquired Mark. "Do you know the secrets behind this key?"

Fagan couldn't understand how the key could have come into Sutherland's possession and he remained silent. He must have thought that Sutherland was using a strategy to get him to confess as he couldn't believe there would be a way that anyone could have located the box that this key opened. If he completely denied knowledge of the key the case could still fall apart. Fagan's only action was to run his fingers around the inside of his collar and, in one movement, he opened the top button of his shirt and loosened his tie. Perspiration was now breaking out on his forehead.

"No," he repeated. "I have never seen it before."

Fagan was playing a bluff.

"Your Honour, if I may continue."

"Please do, Mr Sutherland,"

Mark took a deep breath.

"According to Mr Duffy's investigations, I know where you lost this key, Mr Fagan, and so do you. You realised that you lost it while staying at the Papal Legation when you were last in Rome, but you were not unduly worried because you also knew that the lady in charge would either throw it away or place it in the Vatican Archives. In due course you would apply for a duplicate key from the bank and no one would be the wiser. Either way, Mr Fagan, the possibilities of it ever being found again were extremely remote, or the likelihood of it ever connecting you to a deposit box in Bridgeport seemed completely impossible. I have to state that had it not been for other items found in your belongings while you were in the Vatican Legation, we might not be standing here today at all. I am very pleased to say that you totally underestimated us, Mr Fagan.

"Your Honour," continued Sutherland, now looking at the judge. "This is the key of a safety deposit box which is held in the Brunswick Banking Company in Bridgeport, Connecticut in the name of Anthony Fagan. This box contains sixty-five annulment documents which are all signed and sealed by Cardinal Babatisto. Even though they look authentic, they are all forgeries. The box also contains ninety-five sheets of Vatican headed notepaper, similar to the one shown to the court today and marked *exhibit B*. I wish to state that all these documents are forgeries.

"By his own admission, your Honour, Mr Fagan is well acquainted with Cardinal Babatisto who has absolutely no authority to act or sign any documents on behalf of the Vatican Secretariat. He also is a scoundrel in priest's clothing.

"My enquiries have revealed that Mr Fagan has been selling forged annulments for $55,000 each to willing Catholics who thought that they were getting the genuine article. In the eyes of the Catholic Church, these annulment documents are worthless and useless pieces of paper. On the other hand, there was $450,000 in used fifties in the box and I can confirm that all these bills are genuine. Unfortunately there is no proof of where this money came from. Possibly it was diverted from an illegal source to assist in the profiteering of these illegal operations, or perhaps it was the proceeds from the unlawful sales of the forged annulments, or perhaps it was money that was mysteriously diverted from the *Mafia*. Mr Fagan will more than likely have to answer these and other questions in another type of court of law in due course.

"I would go so far as to say that when Mr Fagan was a Monsignor, he was not only a senior representative of the Roman Catholic Church but he was also a *sleeper cell* and a *courier* for the Mafia. His cover was excellent and he could be awakened at any time. This man's position was contrived by none other than his grandfather, Don Luigi Fagione, and personally nurtured by Cardinal Babatisto. Yesterday we were informed by the CIA that both of them are quite influential people and have frequently been seen together with members of the Italian *Cosa Nostra*. Unfortunately Mr Fagan got himself involved with a married woman, which has led him to his present dilemma."

Mark was still on his feet and there was nothing that could stop his flow.

"Your Honour, I now wish to refer to the divorce and request that in view of these new revelations, Mr Fagan must be treated as a totally disgraced witness who manipulated Mrs O'Neill in such a way as to keep her husband away from his family, and from his home. Mr O'Neill was only acting on medical advice when he resided in Manhattan and, as he stated on the stand, always regarded the house in Tarrytown to be his real home.

"It is a fact that the marriage did break down and that breakdown may have been irrevocable, but it is also a fact that the financial situation could have been resolved in a much more harmonious manner. Mr Fagan did not want this to happen and, with his skilful manoeuvrings, Mrs O'Neill acquired the house as part of her settlement deal. This is what Mr Fagan wanted as his eventual plan was to get everything signed into his sole name so that he could operate his dishonest businesses from a legitimate address. He was not in the slightest bit interested in Mrs O'Neill's welfare. All he wanted was a respectable front."

Mark concluded: "This fraud has all the hallmarks of a Mafioso operation."

The judge was stunned and amazed at what he had heard, and took a drink of water before asking Fagan if he had anything to say. Fagan neither moved nor uttered a single word.

"Mr Fagan," roared the judge. "I am accepting your silence as an affirmation of your guilt and I am totally discrediting you as a witness in this case. By the power invested in me as Appellant Judge of this hearing, I hereby overturn the verdict of Judge Rosemount, on the grounds that your evidence was entirely unsafe, and you completely misled that Honourable gentleman just as you tried to mislead me today. I now award these proceedings including all property rights to Mr Gavin O'Neill. I am not finished with you yet, Mr Fagan, and I will make my closing statements tomorrow morning at 10.00am sharp. In the meantime, do not leave the State of New York. Better still, do not leave the city of New York.

"I now have to advise you that I am handing this case directly to the District Attorney's Office for criminal investigation. Instead of playing golf today, which I was looking forward to very much, I have to spend the afternoon arranging an interview with a Superior High Court Judge, so that a proper decision can be reached. If I had the authority, Mr Fagan, I would lock you up myself without bail. You are an absolute disgrace. This case is now adjourned."

Fagan remained inside the court talking to Ken Thompson for a few minutes but when Gavin walked out into the hallway he didn't have to say a word as the expression on his face said it all.

CHAPTER 54

"Thank you so much, Mark," said Gavin. "You really played a blinder in there today. I don't know what we would have done without you."

"Not at all," came the response. "Thanks to Brendan's shrewd thinking back in Ireland, we were able to blow their illicit conspiracy wide open. Little did poor Father Slattery realise when he suggested that a young up and coming Monsignor should instruct your ex-wife in marriage guidance that he would be recommending the grandson of a very powerful Mafia leader. It's really stranger than fiction."

With that Gavin and Gabriella walked down the steps of the courthouse in the direction of a taxi stand, and hailed a passing cab. Sutherland remained talking to Duffy for a few minutes and then also left.

Duffy stood alone on the steps of the courthouse looking slightly agitated. Something still wasn't right. Once or twice he took off his hat and scratched his head. He looked at his watch and decided that it was probably hunger that was bothering him and it was time for lunch. He walked into a small diner that he often frequented when he was in that neighbourhood, and ordered coffee and a hamburger.

He was just about half way through his hamburger when his gaze fixed upon an imaginary object directly in front of him. As if he had had a premonition, he drank the remains of his coffee, left the rest of his burger, put a five dollar bill on the table, replaced his hat, and walked very briskly out into the street.

CHAPTER 55

At Chamber Street station Gavin and Gabriella were fortunate to get an *express A* train uptown as far as 42nd Street. Then they changed to a local train. The entire journey to 72nd Street took less than twenty minutes. They entered their building and as they stepped out of the lift on to the third floor they heard the phone ringing from inside their apartment. They ran down the corridor, opened the door and answered it immediately.

"Hello, is that Mr O'Neill?" a voice enquired.

"Yes, yes it is," replied Gavin.

"This is Doctor Henderson from St Catherine's Hospital. I just want to let you know that your wife Geraldine is very seriously ill, and is asking for you. She is drifting in and out of consciousness at the moment. She is in room 553."

"OK, doctor," answered Gavin. "Thanks for ringing. I appreciate your call."

"Not at all," came the reply and they hung up.

He explained the circumstances to Gabriella who agreed that he should go to the hospital to see Geraldine, but remembering Mark Sutherland's words of wisdom she also decided that she would go with him. As the mid-afternoon traffic was now quite congested around Columbus Circle, they decided to have a quick snack before leaving. They returned to 72nd Street subway station where they boarded a *local B train* downtown towards Houston.

CHAPTER 56

It took Duffy about fifteen minutes to get back to the courthouse and he was astounded to see that Fagan was still standing at the bottom of the steps. This, of course, was the person that he was looking for but he had anticipated some serious leg work to pick up his trail. All this seemed too easy. He just couldn't believe his luck.

"What the fuck is this guy still doing here?" he thought to himself. "This guy sure gives me the creeps."

Duffy stayed well out of sight. He was very suspicious of Fagan's behaviour as most people awaiting a judge's summary decision leave court very quietly and slip nervously into a waiting car or taxi. Fagan was still standing at the bottom of the steps with a look of determination on his face that one would not expect from a person who had been disgraced in a major divorce trial.

From the time Duffy left the courthouse to the time he got back was no more than twenty minutes, but that was enough time to lose an army in New York City. Duffy was still puzzled as to why Fagan had been so easy to find, but now that he had found him he wasn't going to lose him.

Suddenly, Fagan turned on his heel and began walking determinedly in the direction of Warren Street. It took him almost fifteen minutes to walk the three blocks to a parking lot where his car was located. He paid the parking fee and confidently walked to his car. By coincidence, due to the proximity of the courts, Duffy had parked his car in the same car park. He also paid the attendant but approached his car very carefully in a roundabout fashion so as not to draw attention to himself. Once seated inside he noticed that Fagan's car had started to move out into Lower Manhattan.

Fagan turned right into Church Street, closely followed by Duffy, who deliberately left one car's length distance between them. They drove in tandem for approximately twenty minutes and eventually Fagan turned right into Canal Street and almost immediately left into Mercer. Duffy followed closely at a safe distance, not losing sight of him for a single second.

Traffic was starting to get heavy on Mercer and when they came to a major junction at Houston Fagan drove through the intersection on the amber light. Unfortunately Duffy caught the red and had to stop on Mercer, but kept his eyes firmly fixed on the rear of Fagan's car. To his surprise Fagan turned right after the intersection into the new multi-storey car park that is operated by St Catherine's and situated just across the street from the hospital.

He couldn't understand why Fagan was leaving one car park and going into another, and he drummed his fingers on the steering wheel as he sat impatiently waiting for the light to change. While he was waiting, he noticed a large black Plymouth Saloon coming from Houston. It passed in front of him and entered the multi-storey car park a few seconds after Fagan's car. He thought nothing more about this and when the lights eventually turned green, Duffy eased his car forward and drove into the car park at the same entrance. The journey uptown had taken approximately forty-five minutes.

Fagan had now reached a vantage point on the seventh floor directly overlooking St. Catherine's Hospital and, getting out of the car, he took a sniper's rifle from under the rear seat. Positioning himself across the bonnet of his car and, looking through the telescopic sights, he adjusted the lens until he could clearly see the door handle of room 553. He was waiting for Gavin to open Geraldine's hospital door, which would then position him fully in his cross wire sights. A few seconds later, a single shot rang out.

Duffy heard the shot but was not clear where it had come from. It definitely came from within the multi-storey car park. He pressed his accelerator pedal to the floorboards. He did not know what had happened but knew that whatever it was it involved Fagan. He kept driving up the ramps as fast as he could until he reached the seventh floor.

CHAPTER 57

A young nurse ran up the long corridor of St Ignatius's ward in a very agitated state and said, "Excuse me, sir, the lady who was in that room died about twenty minutes ago and I am not sure if her body has been moved to the morgue or not. I would appreciate it if you did not go in. Thank you very much, sir."

Gavin realised that the nurse didn't know who he was, and he courteously thanked her. Then, looking at Gabriella, he shrugged his shoulders and gently squeezed her hand. She reciprocated his affection, and they slowly walked together along the corridor to the Reception area of St Catherine's. They walked in complete silence, unaware of the drama that was being played out in the building opposite.

He had known that Geraldine's condition was terminal and there was nothing anyone could do, and in a way this was the bittersweet news he had been expecting. It was inevitable. Unfortunately there's never a good time to receive such news, and he would have to tell his daughters as soon as possible.

The news was bitter in so much as his children had lost their mother, but also sweet as now he could be with Gabriella without complications. On the way to the subway, they discussed what had just happened and both of them agreed that he should attend the funeral when the final arrangements were announced. Gavin knew that he had been given a second chance at finding happiness and wasn't prepared to gamble with this blessing so, putting his arm around Gabriella, he said,

"Sweetheart, I bet you never thought you would be proposed to outside a subway station", and looking sincerely into her eyes he asked, "Gabriella, will you please marry me?"

"Of course I will, darling" she replied. "I have loved you since the first minute I saw you."

They exchanged a kiss there and then at the entrance to the station. They were completely in love and oblivious to the commuters hurrying past.

Gavin had not known how to accept the remark that Doctor Murphy had made to him when they spoke at his father's funeral but he could still hear the words ringing in his mind, that *there would be happier days ahead,* and now for the first time he felt that this had become a positive reality.

CHAPTER 58

When Duffy arrived on the seventh level of the high rise parking lot, he saw Fagan's car parked at the open end overlooking the street. As he didn't know what had happened, he got out of his car very carefully. He had his snub nosed revolver in his hand. When he got close enough, he observed that Fagan was slouched over the bonnet of his car, shot through the back of the head with a single shot from a high velocity weapon. This was the shot that Duffy had heard when he was driving up the ramps inside the building.

There was no doubt about it. Fagan was dead. This had to be the work of a professional hit man. Still clasped in Fagan's hands was the telescopic sniper's rifle with the attached tripod. A cold shiver ran down Duffy's spine when on further inspection he observed that there was a bullet in the breech. The gun was primed for firing. He decided not to touch anything.

He looked over the parapet and was amazed when he saw the black Plymouth that he had followed into the car park exiting at street level and slowly disappearing into the busy traffic on Mercer. There was nothing he could do.

"It must have been *The Mob* in that black saloon," he thought to himself. "It couldn't have been anyone else as no one else knew anything about this bloody business. Christ, they whacked the bastard with a fucking torpedo!"

From his car radio he called Chief O'Malley on the police frequency, and informed him about the homicide. He emphasised that it was definitely a contract killing, as it had all the hallmarks of a Mafia execution. He deduced that the New York brotherhood of La Cosa Nostra had acted swiftly after some crooked official within the court system had conveyed to them the results of the appellant hearing.

When *the Mob* heard the intricate details they at last had the positive proof they needed to finger Fagan for milking Mafia funds. Fagan was behaving like a loose cannon. The Order was given that he had to be eliminated immediately as too many important people within the *North American Brotherhood* would be placed at risk if he were taken to a criminal court. Within minutes their ruthless instructions were put into action.

Duffy exchanged another few words with the Chief, and it was decided to send some uniformed officers up to the crime scene, together with a coroner's ambulance. Duffy told him that he would wait until a member of the NYPD arrived, and then he would drive downtown and make his full report.

CHAPTER 59

It was about 4.30pm when Gavin and Gabriella got back to the apartment. They were sitting on the large sofa sipping coffee and going over the court case and Geraldine's death when the phone rang. Gabriella leaned over and answered it.

"'Allo," she said in her beautiful Spanish accented pronunciation. Then looking at Gavin she continued, "It's for you, pet, it's Mark Sutherland."

Gavin took the phone. "Hello, Mark, is everything all right? You did a fantastic job today."

"Thanks, Gavin," came the reply, "and I have wonderful news for both of you. The Archbishop's Office has just been in touch with me and they are offering you an out-of-court settlement if you decide not to proceed against them in a Civil Court. They consider that you might have a case so they want to make you an offer to offset any stress and pain that you have suffered in recent times. If you refuse the offer and if you decide to go to court they will be able to say that a proposal had been made and you turned it down and this would auger very much against you. They were quick enough to point out that this offer is made without any admission of guilt or liability on their part. They are just regarding it as a legal transaction.

"The Catholic Church does not usually make offers unless they are running scared so I think we should rattle their cage a bit. Of course, they haven't mentioned a figure yet so, whatever it is, I told them we would start discussions early next week."

"You're pulling my leg, Mark!" gasped an astonished Gavin.

"No, I'm not, and after what you have been through, it's only what you deserve. News sure travels fast in the City of New York."

It took Gavin three attempts to replace the receiver correctly. He was taken aback and astonished with such news, and he made sure that Gabriella was sitting down before he told her everything that Mark had said.

They looked at each other quietly for a few minutes savouring the news and feeling that the nightmare was at an end. Gabriella took Gavin's hand into hers, caressed it affectionately and tenderly whispered to him,

"Darling Gavin, it's been a long journey since Oakwood College and thank God it's finally over. Let's go and get the girls."

EPILOGUE

It was early evening when Duffy arrived at the Police House. He poured himself a cup of coffee as he knew it would take him a while to explain everything to O'Malley.

"Do you know something, Chief? Gavin is a very lucky man to be alive today. With the aid of that tripod the telescopic sight was lined up on the door handle of his ex-wife's hospital room. He was nearly a goner. Fagan was just waiting that extra second for Gavin to move fully into his sights and then – pop – a perfect shot. Thank God the Mafia hit man got there just in the nick of time.

"And do you know something else, Chief? That bastard Fagan must have known that his number was up with *the Mob* and he was determined to take Gavin with him. I am being cynical of course, but when all's said and done the Mafia saved the State a lot of money today. I never trusted that good-for-nothing in the first place, and now I know why he was still hanging around the courthouse when I returned from the diner.

"That puzzled me for a while, but that was the time he needed to set Gavin up. He must have made the phoney call pretending he was ringing from the hospital. Good God, now that I think about it, he had the entire scenario planned well in advance. I'm really angry about this now. He was some fucking bastard."

"I know, Brendan," the Chief responded, in his New York Irish twang. "I had no idea that a scam of this magnitude was going on under my nose. Not only that but also in my bloody precinct. Now the Mayor will be crawling all over me, but you can rest assured I will do all in my power to investigate this matter fully. There will be no cover ups, and no hidey holes for anyone. Without doubt there are some crooked cops involved, just as there are some crooked court officials, and also some crooked clergy, but I guarantee you they will all be flushed out. The first thing I am going to do is to get the names and addresses of all those clerics that were sitting outside the doors of the court during the first divorce hearing. That's as good a place as anywhere to start, for when I see smoke I always look for fire. This is not over yet."

The word *smoke* reminded Duffy of the shocking thoughts he had had in the event of the election of a new Pope, when he thought that Fagan was on his way up the ladder of hierarchy within the Catholic Church. Thankfully, Pope Paul VI had made yet another remarkable recovery, and was continuing to enjoy moderately good health. He thanked the Lord that those thoughts had only been fleeting and did not come to pass.

When Duffy had finished relating the events of the last few days, the Police Chief stood up and, shaking his head from side to side, walked from behind his desk. O'Malley knew that without Duffy's intervention and good detective work, this crime may never have come to light. He was fully aware that when two very powerful organisations such as the Mafia and the Catholic Church start working hand in glove to set up a fraud or deception, it is almost impossible to infiltrate their inner circle. He then asked Duffy to dictate his report to the young desk officer before leaving the Police Station.

"Thanks, Brendan," he said. "You have been a big help and may I say that I have never seen you in better shape."

"Thanks, Chief, it's wonderful what good food and a few early nights can achieve. Unfortunately," continued Duffy, "Fagan has taken a few names and faces with him permanently to the grave, but I have a couple that I can give you. Regrettably, I doubt if you will ever get any convictions."

"Fake annulments," reflected O'Malley to himself. "Worthless pieces of paper for rich Catholics. A brand new type of conspiracy. It's no wonder the Church is now being criticised by so many. It's definitely going down the tubes. It will never be the same again."

Raising his head, he looked at Duffy again.

"Sorry, Brendan, I drifted away for a few seconds. What did you say?"

"I have a few names for you," repeated Duffy. "But I reckon that Cardinal Babatisto, who signed all the incriminating documents, has already been safely shifted to the sanctity of the Vatican."

O'Malley nodded and shrugged his shoulders again.

"The other person involved is a Don Luigi Alberto Fagione from Sicily," continued Duffy, "but I am fairly positive that he is practically untouchable in that part of the world as well."

"This is a desperate state of affairs," commented the Police Chief, "and sadly there is nothing more we can do. There's far too much corruption in the Catholic Church and what's more it's becoming blatant."

O'Malley stated that he would pass the files to Interpol in case the Italian authorities decided to investigate the matter at a future date. The two men stood up and shook hands again. They had done all they could do and now the matter would shortly be in the hands of the FBI and the CIA.

"As I said, whatever you're doing, Brendan, keep doing it, for you're looking great. And thanks for everything; it's been like old times again."

"Thanks for the compliments Chief," replied Duffy who, completely unaware of Mark Sutherland's phone call planned to look in on Gavin and Gabriella the following morning. He was going to get the surprise of his life when they told him about the offer of compensation that the Catholic Church was preparing to make to them.

The Chief thanked him again and as Duffy reached the door he turned and, looking back at his old pal one more time, lifted his hat in his usual courteous manner and smiling broadly said,

"Chief, it's been my pleasure. And if you want me for anything else in the near future, the only place that you are likely to find me is in Killarney."

THE END

Lightning Source UK Ltd.
Milton Keynes UK
21 January 2010

148927UK00002B/6/P